I was lucky in so many ways.

I told myself this every morning when we opened our eyes, every night before we went to sleep.

I am lucky. So lucky.

I was alive. I was, in some ways, free. In a country where hybrids were forbidden and locked away, Addie and I had escaped. And I—

I could move and speak again. Me, who had known since childhood that I was the recessive soul, destined to fade away. But I never disappeared completely.

We had been lucky.

Perhaps, if we stayed lucky, we would be allowed to live just as we were: Eva and Addie, Addie and Eva.

Two girls inside of one.

THE HYBRID CHRONICLES

What's Left of Me

Once We Were

Echoes of Us

KAT ZHANG

ONCE WE WERE

THE SECOND BOOK IN THE HYBRID CHRONICLES

HARPER
An Imprint of HarperCollins*Publishers*

ONCE WE WERE: THE HYBRID CHRONICLES, BOOK TWO

www.epicreads.com

Library of Congress Cataloging-in-Publication Data
Zhang, Kat, date.
Once we were : the second book in the Hybrid chronicles / Kat Zhang. — First edition.
p. cm.
Summary: "In the sequel to What's Left of Me, fifteen-year-old Addie and Eva struggle to share their body as they are drawn deeper into the fight for hybrid freedom from the government's oppression"— Provided by publisher.
ISBN 978-0-06-211491-4
[1. Sisters—Fiction. 2. Identity—Fiction. 3. Government, Resistance to—Fiction. 4. Science fiction.]
PZ7.Z454Onc 2013 2013032811
[Fic] CIP
AC

Typography by Torborg Davern
14 15 16 17 18 CG/RRDH 10 9 8 7 6 5 4 3 2 1
❖
First paperback edition, 2014

For Dechan, who may not be my sister in blood, but is in soul

PROLOGUE

We share a heart, Addie and I. We own the same pair of hands. Inhabit the same limbs. That hot June day, freshly escaped from Nornand Clinic, we stood and saw the ocean for the first time through shared eyes. The wind batted our hair against our cheeks. The sand stuck to our salt-soaked skin, turning our pale legs tan.

We experienced that day as we'd experienced the past fifteen years of our lives. As Addie and Eva, Eva and Addie. Two souls sharing one body. Hybrid.

But the thing is, sharing hands doesn't mean sharing goals. Sharing eyes doesn't mean sharing visions. And sharing a heart doesn't mean sharing the things we love.

Here are some of the things I loved.

The cold shock of the ocean when I stood waist-deep in the water, jumping at the crest of each oncoming wave. The sound of Kitty's laughter when I tickled her. The breathless joy of Hally's dancing. The way Ryan smiled when I turned to look at him and he was already looking at me.

Addie liked these things, too. But she didn't cherish them

the way I did—*desperately.* Because I never should have had them. Millions of recessive souls never reached age five, let alone fifteen. That was the way of the world—or so Addie and I had been taught. Two souls born to each body. One marked by genetics to disappear.

I was lucky in so many ways.

I told myself this every morning when we opened our eyes, every night before we went to sleep.

I am lucky. So lucky.

I was alive. I was, in some ways, free. In a country where hybrids were forbidden and locked away, Addie and I had escaped. And I—

I could move and speak again. Me, who had known since childhood that I was the recessive soul, destined to fade away. That my parents would mourn quietly, quickly, then move on. That they would tell themselves this was the way of the world, the way things had always been, and who were they to question the workings of nature?

Children were supposed to shed recessive souls, leaving them behind like they would one day discard their baby teeth. Just another step on the journey to adulthood.

The alternative, never settling—retaining both souls—meant staying trapped in the chaos of a perpetual childhood, never gaining the steady, rational mind of an adult who could be trusted to control her own body. How could a hybrid ever fit into society? How would she marry? Would she be able to work, with two souls pulling and yearning in two different directions? To be hybrid was to be forever unstable, forever torn.

I was twelve, two years past the government-mandated deadline, when I succumbed to the curse lettered in my genes. But I was lucky, even then. I lost control of my body, leaving Addie to command our limbs, but I never disappeared completely.

It was better than dying.

Are you all right, Addie? Mom asked, those first few weeks after I was declared gone. She spoke the words like they pinched her lips on the way out, like she didn't want to acknowledge the fact that Addie might not be okay, even then. Addie should have been normal.

I'm fine, Addie said, even when I screamed and screamed in her head, even when she was holding me as she smiled for our parents, telling me she was sorry, begging me to be as *okay* as she supposedly was.

Hally and Ryan Mullan were the ones who released me from the prison of my own bones. Where would I be if Hally hadn't convinced Addie to go home with her that afternoon? Still paralyzed. Still alone. Not entirely, because I would always have Addie, but—alone, in every other sense of the word.

<We'd be home> Addie said once, when I whispered the question to her. The words floated between our linked minds, where no one else could hear us. *<Mr. Conivent wouldn't have taken us to Nornand. We wouldn't be here.>*

Here in Anchoit, this shining city by the western sea,

smelling the salt the waves tossed into the air.

It had been my turn, then, to say *I'm sorry.* Because Addie was right. If Hally hadn't—if *I* hadn't convinced Addie to go to the Mullans' house, to take the medication, to take that first step away from normality, we would still be home. We wouldn't be out of danger—as hybrids, we could never truly relax—but we would be a little safer. We'd be going to school and watching movies and laughing at our little brother when he clowned around the kitchen.

<Don't apologize, Eva. That's not what I meant. I—> She'd hesitated, staring at the ceiling of this strange new apartment. Our new hideaway. *<I never could have done it. Let you live like that. Not when I knew there was another way. And we're out of Nornand. We're going to be okay.>*

Not like the other children who'd walked through those hospital halls. Like Jaime Cortae, who'd lost his other soul to a scalpel.

Addie and I had been lucky.

Perhaps, if we stayed lucky, we would never again have to see Mr. Conivent with his pressed, white button-up shirts. We would never again feel Jenson's cold grip on our wrist—never come under the jurisdiction of his review board.

We would be allowed to live just as we were: Eva and Addie, Addie and Eva. Two girls inside of one.

ONE

It was stuffy in the phone booth, even with the door propped partway open. Our desire for privacy couldn't override the sickness that gripped us in the small, enclosed space. Squished cigarette butts littered the ground, their smoky smell lingering in the early-morning air.

<*We shouldn't do this*> I said.

We weren't even supposed to be outside. We'd snuck out of the apartment before Emalia and Kitty woke up, and we had to make it back before then as well. No one knew we were here, not even Ryan or Hally.

Addie pressed the phone receiver against our ear. The dial tone mocked us.

<*The government will be expecting something like this*> I said. <*Peter said they'd bug our house. They'll trace the call. And we're not far enough away from the apartment. We can't put the others in danger.*>

Our free hand slipped into our pocket and closed around our chip. Ryan had given it to us right before we arrived at

Nornand, and it had connected us to him during our time at the clinic. Habit made us rub it between our fingers like a good-luck charm.

Addie's voice was soft. <*He's eleven today.*>

Lyle was eleven. Our little brother.

The night Mr. Conivent confiscated Addie and me, Lyle had been at the hospital, doing one of his thrice-weekly rounds of dialysis. Unlike our parents, he'd had no say in letting us go. We never got to tell him good-bye.

It would only be one call. A few coins in the slot. Ten numbers. So quick. So simple.

Hi, Lyle, I imagined saying. I pictured his flop of yellow hair, his skinny arms and legs, his crooked-toothed grin.

Hi, Lyle—

Then what? *Happy birthday. Happy eleventh birthday.*

The last time I'd wished Lyle *happy birthday*—actually spoken those words aloud—he'd been turning seven. After that, I'd lost the strength to do more than watch as Addie spoke for me. I'd hovered in a body I couldn't control, a ghost in a family that didn't know I still existed.

What did one say after four years like that?

Thinking about what I'd tell Mom was even worse.

Hi. It's Eva. I was there the whole time. I was there all those years, and you never knew.

Hi. It's Eva. I'm okay—I think I'm safe. Are you okay? Are you safe?

Hi. It's Eva. I wish I were home.

Hi. It's Eva. I love you.

I could see Mom so clearly it hurt: the panes of her face, her laugh lines, and the deeper lines on her brow not etched by laughter. I could see her in her waitressing uniform: black slacks and a white blouse, stark against her corn-silk hair. Addie and I had always wanted hair like hers, so smooth and straight it glided through our fingers. Instead, we had Dad's curls, lazy and halfhearted. *Princess hair,* he'd called it when Addie and I were small enough to sit in his lap, breathing in the smell of his aftershave, begging for stories that ended in *Happily Ever After.*

I wanted, so badly, to know how our family was. So much could have happened in the nearly two months since Addie and I had last slept in our own bed, last woken up staring at our own ceiling.

Had Lyle gotten the kidney transplant we'd been promised, or was he still chained to his dialysis appointments? Did our parents even know what had happened to Addie and me? What if they thought we were still at the clinic, being *cured* of our hybridity?

Was that better or worse than them knowing the truth? A month and a half ago, Addie and I had broken out of Nornand Clinic of Psychiatric Health. We should have brought all the other patients with us. But we'd failed. In the end, we'd left with just Ryan and Devon, Hally and Lissa, Kitty and Nina. And Jaime, of course. Jaime Cortae.

Now we were hiding outside the system entirely, sheltered

by Peter and his underground network of hybrids. We were the fugitives we'd heard about in government class. The criminals whose arrest—and they were always arrested in the end—blared across the news.

Would Mom and Dad want to know that?

What would they do if they did? Come charging across the continent to take us home? Protect us, like they hadn't protected us before? Tell us they were sorry, they'd made a terrible mistake in ever letting us go?

Maybe they would just turn us in again.

No.

I couldn't bear to think they might.

They're going to help you get well, Addie, Dad had said when he called us at Nornand. *Mom and I only want the best for you.*

Peter had warned us how the government might bug our phone lines. Maybe Dad had known someone might listen in on our call at Nornand, and he'd had to say whatever they wanted to hear. Maybe he hadn't meant those words.

Because that wasn't what he'd whispered as Addie and I climbed into Mr. Conivent's car.

If you're there, Eva, he'd said. *If you're really there . . . I love you, too. Always.*

Always.

<Addie> I said.

The knife of her longing cut us both. *<Just a few words.>*

<We can't> I said. *<Addie, we can't.>*

No matter how much we ached to.

When Addie didn't release the phone, I slipped into control and did it for us. Addie didn't protest. I stepped out onto the sidewalk, the city greeting us with a slap of wind. A passing car coughed dark exhaust into the air.

<You think . . . > Addie hesitated. *<You think he's okay? Lyle.>*

<Yeah. I think so.>

What else could I say?

I waited at a crosswalk with a small crowd of early-morning commuters, each sunk in their own thoughts. No one paid Addie and me any attention. Anchoit was the biggest, busiest city we'd ever seen, let alone lived in. The buildings loomed over the streets, contraptions of metal and concrete. Every once in a while, one was softened by a facade of worn red brick.

Peter had chosen Anchoit for its size. For the anonymity of its quiet alleyways and busy thoroughfares. Cars, people, thoughts—everything moved quickly here. It was a far cry from old, languid Bessimir City, or the all-but-stagnant Lupside, where Addie and I had lived before.

It seemed like more happened in a night in Anchoit than in a year in Lupside. Not that Addie or I would know. Since Peter had brought us here from Nornand, I could count on one hand the number of times we'd been allowed out in the city. Peter and Emalia weren't taking any chances.

In Anchoit, it might have been easier to hide what Addie

and I were—hybrids, fugitives, less-than-normal. But it didn't change the facts. I dreamed of roaming the neon streets after dark. Of playing games and buying junk at the boardwalk. Of splashing through the waves again.

<*Police officer*> Addie said quietly.

Our legs froze. It took three thundering heartbeats before I calmed down enough to move again. I crossed the street so we didn't have to pass the policeman directly.

Chances were, his presence had absolutely nothing to do with us.

But Addie and I were hybrid.

Whatever the chance, however small, we couldn't take it.

TWO

Emalia's apartment building was silent but for the buzzing of overhead lights, which flickered on and off like struggling fireflies. A trash bag slouched, stinking, in the corner.

Peter had housed us Nornand refugees together in his apartment as long as he could. But he spent as much time traveling as he did living in Anchoit, and eventually, we'd been separated. Kitty and Nina lived with us at Emalia's. The Mullan siblings were only a few floors up, with Henri, but it wasn't the same.

Even worse, Dr. Lyanne had taken Jaime away to a little house on the fringes of the city. None of us had seen him in three weeks.

The apartment was still dim when I slipped back inside, the living room half-lit by hazy morning sunlight. Emalia and her twin soul, Sophie, kept their home achingly neat, softly decorated. In a weird way, Peter's apartment—since Peter was so frequently absent—had seemed like *our* place, *our* home. Here, Addie and I felt like intruders in a sanctuary of muted sweaters and woven placemats.

<So> Addie said. We sank onto the couch and stared at Emalia's potted plant. Every leaf looked meticulously arranged. Even her plants were orderly.

<So, what?> I let our eyes slide half-closed. We'd hardly slept last night, wanting to make sure we were up in time to sneak out. With our adrenaline gone, the lack of sleep dragged at our limbs.

Addie sighed. *<So, what do we do now? What do we do today?>*

<Same as we do every other day, I guess.>

Kitty and Nina spent most of their time curled up in front of the TV, watching whatever was on: Saturday-morning cartoons, daytime soap operas, afternoon news reports, even late-night talk shows when they couldn't sleep. Hally and Lissa stared out the windows, listening to the music thumping from car radios.

Ryan filled his days with making stuff. Trinkets, mostly, pieced together using tools he borrowed from Henri or Emalia. Emalia was no longer surprised to come home to a salt-and-pepper shaker that rotated between the two at a press of a button, or some other vaguely useful invention.

And Addie—Addie had started drawing again. She sketched Kitty on the sofa, capturing the soft snub of her nose, the wide, brown eyes. She caught the glint of light on Hally's glasses, spent an hour perfecting the way Hally's curls fell, some in lazy almost-ringlets, others barely more than a dark wave.

It was nice to have Addie drawing again. But after so many days, we were all going stir-crazy.

"Oh!" came a voice behind us. It was Emalia, draped in a pink cardigan and a cream-colored blouse. She looked as soft and pastel as the dawn. Her smile was flustered. "I didn't know you'd gotten up . . ."

She didn't ask, but the question hung between us: *Addie? Or Eva?*

"Addie," Addie said when I took too long to answer. By then, of course, it was. She climbed to our feet and surreptitiously stepped on the back of our heels, kicking our shoes under the couch. Addie had a thoughtless ease with our body I still didn't.

"You're up early," Emalia said. "Something wrong?"

"No." Addie shrugged. "I just woke up and couldn't fall asleep again."

Emalia crossed to the kitchen, which was separated from the living room by only a stretch of counter. "It's these city noises. They take a while to get used to. When I first moved here, I couldn't get a good night's sleep for weeks." She gestured questioningly toward the coffee machine, but Addie shook our head.

Emalia had a bit of a caffeine addiction, but maybe that was to be expected with everything she had to do: hold down her regular job, take care of us, and complete her work for the Underground. She was the one who had forged our new documents, printing birth certificates for people who'd never been born, casting our faces onto lives we'd never lived.

I associated her now with the heavy, bittersweet smell of coffee. Even the first time we'd seen Emalia, her hair had reminded us of steam—cappuccino-colored steam curling against her pale cheeks, reaching just under her chin.

"You're up early, too," Addie said.

"I'm headed to the airport today. Peter's flight arrives in a few hours."

"No one told us Peter was back." The words came out sharper than I'd expected. Sharper, perhaps, than Addie had intended.

Emalia's hands stilled. "Well, it—it was a bit unanticipated. Something's come up, so he caught an earlier flight. I'm sorry. I didn't realize you'd want to know."

"I do," Addie said, too quickly. "But it's okay. I mean—"

"Okay, in the future I'll—" Emalia said.

The two of them looked at each other awkwardly.

"Kitty showed me your new drawing yesterday." The thin, golden bracelets on Emalia's wrists clinked as she reached for the cereal box. "It was lovely. You're such a fantastic artist, Addie."

Addie pinned a smile to our lips. "Thanks."

Emalia was always complimenting us like this. *Your hair looks so pretty in a bun*, she'd say, or *You've got such lovely eyes.* Each of Addie's sketches, even the doodles she drew for Kitty's amusement, got a verbal round of applause.

In return, we tried to compliment Emalia, too. It wasn't

hard or anything. She wore delicate, pale-gold sandals and faded pink blouses. She always found the most interesting places to order food from, coming home with white Styrofoam boxes from all over the city. But our conversations with Emalia never got beyond that. We spoke in a language of comments on the weather, polite greetings, and slight smiles, all underlaid with a sense of Not Quite Knowing What to Do.

Emalia had only fostered one other escaped hybrid before, a twelve-year-old girl who stayed three weeks before Peter found her a more permanent family down south. Emalia herself was in her midtwenties. She and Sophie had managed to remain hidden all these years, escaping institutionalization. They and Peter had connected mostly by chance.

Maybe that was why Emalia acted as if she didn't know how to handle us. As if, poked too hard, we might break.

Addie leaned against the counter. "When's the meeting going to be?"

"With Peter? Tomorrow night. Why?"

"I want to go."

Emalia tipped some cereal into a bowl, her smile hesitant. "It's going to be at Peter's apartment, Addie. Like usual."

"That's barely a five-minute walk."

"You aren't supposed to be—"

"It'll be nighttime. No one would see us." Addie fixed the woman with our stare. "Emalia, I need to talk with him. I want to know what's going on."

Nornand's hybrid wing had shut down, but its patients had

been shipped elsewhere instead of being set free. Peter had promised we'd work to rescue them. But if anything had been done, Addie and I hadn't been told.

"I'll tell you whatever you want to know," Emalia said, "and I'm sure Peter will drop by here at some point."

"It's a five-minute walk," Addie repeated. "A five-minute walk in the *dark*."

The coffee machine beeped. Emalia hurried toward it. "I'll ask Peter when I see him. How about that? I'll tell him you want very badly to go, and we'll see what he says."

<She's only trying to shut us up> I said, and I knew Addie agreed.

Aloud, though, she just murmured, "Okay."

"Okay." Emalia smiled and nodded at the pot of coffee. The smell, usually heady and comforting, now made us feel slightly sick. "You sure you don't want just a little bit? It's nice to have something hot when the morning's chilly."

Addie shook her head and turned away.

It was chilly outside. We weren't going to be outside.

THREE

Addie and I were back in bed, curled against a pillow, when Emalia left for the airport. We hovered between wakefulness and dreams, the corners of the world worn soft.

The knock at the front door split us from sleep. Addie startled upright, automatically checking on Kitty and Nina. They were still asleep, huddled beneath their blanket so far we could just barely see their eyes.

The knock came again. I caught the glint of red light on the nightstand, where Addie had tossed our chip before collapsing into bed. It glowed steadily now, an indication its twin was near.

<*It's just Ryan*> I whispered.

We had to be calm. We couldn't keep jumping like this, fearing every knock at the door was someone coming to snatch us away.

I didn't have to ask Addie to ease control to me. I took charge of our limbs as she let them go, hurrying into the living room and opening the front door.

The morning sunlight caught Ryan's skin, giving it a glow like burnished gold. His dark curls stuck up in ways that laughed at gravity. He reached toward us, like he might touch our arm, brush his fingers against our skin. He didn't. His hand dropped back to his side. "I wasn't sure if you would be awake this early."

"We couldn't sleep," I said.

"It's summer break." A wryness twisted Ryan's smile. "We should be sleeping in."

I drew him to the sofa. He'd brought a small paper bag with him—probably containing yet another invention—and he set it on the floor beside his feet.

"Well, we did skip all our finals," I said.

Addie's amusement colored the space between us. It relaxed me a little. Being with Ryan—talking with Ryan—I always kept one finger on the pulse of Addie's mood.

Ryan laughed. "That's what keeps you up at night?"

"You're the one who should be worried," I said, mock solemn. "You're going to be a senior next semester. You should be applying to colleges soon."

His smile slipped, and I winced. Ryan and Devon *ought* to be applying to colleges soon. But it would be enough of a miracle just to get us into a classroom in the fall. Even if Peter and the others decided that it was safe to let us out of the building by then, there were more things to be faked: immunization records, transcripts . . .

Besides, where would they go? There was a college

downtown, but that was about it. It would be too dangerous, surely, to send him away by himself.

"Guess I'll just have to repeat eleventh grade, then." Ryan's shrug was as lazy and exaggerated as his smile. He glanced at me sideways. "Be the same age as everyone else in the class for once."

Our shoulders relaxed. I laughed, leaning toward him. "Oh, the horror."

For a moment, it was just Ryan and me, looking at each other. A stillness. Twelve inches between us. Twelve inches of morning sunlight and Addie's growing unease and the sound of traffic from four floors down. It would have taken him a second to break that distance. It would have taken me less. But the twelve inches remained. A foot of distance, filled with all the reasons why we couldn't.

There came another knock.

"Hally?" I asked Ryan, frowning. Unlike their brothers, Hally and Lissa weren't morning people. It was nearing eight now, which meant they'd usually be asleep for another two or three hours at least.

Ryan stood, but motioned for me to stay seated. Before he could take a step toward the door, someone called out, "It's me, guys. Let me in?"

It wasn't Hally's voice, but it was familiar nonetheless. Ryan threw me a look that was half relief, half exasperation, then crossed to open the door. "Hey, what's up?"

Jackson strolled inside. Over time, I'd learned to

differentiate between Jackson and Vincent—Vince. I discovered the subtle traits that separated the two souls despite their ownership of the same lanky frame, the identical shaggy, brown hair and pale blue eyes. Vince was the one who made me blush. Who seemed to always be making fun of me—of everyone. Who was never out of jokes. Maybe that was why he and Jackson were forever smiling.

But this was Jackson. I was sure. It was the way he looked at Addie and me that made it clear—like he wasn't just *looking*, but studying. As if there would be a test later on Addie and Eva Tamsyn, and he was making sure he'd do well.

He'd visited Addie and me frequently since our escape, playing tour guide to our new life. It was through him that we'd learned about Emalia's past, and Peter's, and Henri's.

"Hey, Jackson," I said, and was rewarded with a grin.

Jackson and Vince were familiar and safe. The girl who entered next was a stranger.

She was just a little older than Jackson—perhaps nineteen—with dark eyes, thick, brown hair, and long, blunt bangs. A faded denim jacket sat bulkily on narrow shoulders, dwarfing her dancerlike frame. Jackson opened his mouth like he was going to introduce her, but she beat him to it.

"I'm Sabine." She stuck out her hand. Her smile softened some of the gesture's formality, but not all of it. Her grip was cool and firm, stronger than I'd expected from someone barely taller than we were.

It had been weeks since we'd met anyone new. I couldn't

help staring at her, studying everything from the missing gold button on her jacket to the scuffs on her turquoise ballet flats. Her nails were cut almost to the quick, but smooth, not like she'd bitten them.

<Stop it> Addie said. *<She knows you're staring.>*

I looked away, but too late. Sabine's eyes caught ours, and she smiled. Not disparagingly, though. Gently, like she understood.

"Josie and I have seen you around before," she said. "When you guys were still staying at Peter's place."

Josie and I. Josie and Sabine, then—the two souls who shared this body. I still wasn't used to the easy way hybrids here referred to themselves. Of course, they only did it in private, among other members of Underground, but it seemed like such a risk to even speak the names aloud.

"It's Eva and Addie, right?" Sabine said. "And Ryan and Devon?" She turned to him. "We were just up at your place, but no one answered the door. Jackson's been talking about these inventions you make. They sound amazing. Which was the one you were telling me about yesterday, Jackson? The clock—"

Ryan cut Sabine off with a harried smile. "I'm just messing around. It's something to do."

"I figured you guys were bored." She looked around the apartment, as if she could flip through the days we'd spent cooped up here as easily as I flipped through Addie's sketchbook. "Everyone goes through this when they first escape. It's like quarantine. But you guys are planning to stay, right?"

"Stay?" Ryan asked.

Sabine nodded. "In Anchoit, I mean. You're not going to let Peter ship you off somewhere?"

"No," I said quickly. I looked toward Ryan. "Not if it would mean getting separated."

"It probably would," Jackson said. "Peter and them, they've got connections with sympathetic families across a pretty wide net, but they're spread out. I doubt they'd be able to place you all in the same area. Especially since . . ." He looked at Ryan, then shrugged awkwardly. "Well, you know."

"Yeah," Ryan said. "I know."

Placing Ryan and Hally would mean finding a family that looked like them. They were only half-foreign, on their father's side—and their father wasn't even *really* foreign; he'd been born in the Americas—but it still came through in the olive complexion of their skin, the shape of their brows, the large, deep-set look of their eyes, the curve of their chins. At least one member of any foster family would have to look like them. A nonforeign family adopting a foreign child would draw more attention than it was worth.

"We're staying," I said.

<We can't live with Emalia forever> Addie said.

<It wouldn't be forever. Only—>

We had three more years before we were eighteen. Of course, couldn't Emalia forge us papers saying whatever she wanted? We could be eighteen in a few months, if need be. We could be eighteen right now.

"You guys can always come stay with us," Sabine said. I looked at her in surprise. We'd only just met, and she was offering us a place to live? "I share an apartment with a friend of ours. There isn't an extra room, but there's a couch someone can use, and we could fit mattresses if we rearranged some furniture."

"I'd offer my place, too," Jackson said, "but it's smaller. And between my roommate and me—"

"Between his roommate and him, they keep the place a complete dump," Sabine said, laughing.

Jackson spread his hands and shrugged. "We're busy people."

Jackson and Vince worked part-time jobs all around the city. To date, we'd heard him refer to waiting tables, walking dogs, manning food stands at the park, and working in grocery stores. He seemed to lose jobs as quickly as he gained them.

He had to keep working. No one else was supporting him. But watching him smile now, he looked like any other eighteen-year-old boy on summer vacation. Never mind that he and Vince no longer attended school. They didn't see the point. Neither, I supposed, did they have the time.

The phone rang before I could thank Sabine for her offer. Emalia had instructed us to take calls. Most of the time, it was just a telemarketer. The chance of someone recognizing our voice was small—smaller than the chance of Emalia or Peter needing to get in contact.

I smiled apologetically at the others as I answered the phone. "Hello?"

"Hey." A boy's voice, gruff and urgent. "Are you Eva? Addie? One of them?"

Our eyes flew to Ryan, who was halfway across the room before I managed to say, "What? Sorry, who is this?"

<*Eva—*> Addie said, but couldn't finish her sentence. Even my name had been little more than a tremor.

Who is it? Ryan mouthed. Behind him, Sabine and Jackson had gone still, both staring at us.

Our heart pounded. Should I hang up?

No. No, that was stupid.

"It's Christoph," the boy said. "Is Sabine there? Can you put her on?"

Slowly, I took the phone from our ear and covered the speaker. Our voice was halting. I forced it steadier. "Do you know someone named Christoph?"

Sabine sighed and nodded. I found myself relaxing slightly as I handed her the phone. "Hey, Christoph. Next time, you could try not scaring everyone to death, you know?" She paused as he said something. Her exasperation melted away. "Which station? Okay, thanks." She closed her eyes. Just for a second. Then she took a sharp breath, opened them again, and hung up. "Mind if we turn on the television?"

I shook our head. At her touch, the TV flickered on with its usual grainy quality.

On the screen was Jenson.

FOUR

Our muscles, bones, organs liquified.

Jenson.

Jenson of the review board. Jenson of the dark suits and creased pants and never-ruffled voice.

Jenson, who had chosen Hally and Lissa for surgery. Whose cool, steel voice frightened us more than Mr. Conivent's silk. A man who didn't need Mr. Conivent's slick smiles or ready excuses. Who had watched us like he owned us.

He looked just as I remembered. Dark hair. Light eyes. Suit jacket. Not young and not old, and brutal in the way a panther was brutal—claws retracted inside soft paws. He stood before a podium, his expression crafted from a block of marble. A band of text ran across the bottom of the screen: *Mark Jenson, Director of the Administration for Hybrid Affairs for Sector Two. Nationwide address.*

Director for all of Sector Two? The Americas were divided into states, which were grouped into four sectors: two in the northern continent, and two in the southern. The president presided over us all, but lesser government heads watched over each sector. I'd known Jenson was part of the review board that had come to examine Nornand—I'd seen the importance the clinic had put on his visit—but I hadn't realized just how powerful he was.

"Our country was formed as a haven for the single-souled," Jenson said. "Since the first rise of civilization, the hybrids have thought themselves better—smarter, more able. For thousands of years, our ancestors were subjugated to slave labor and then near–slave labor, to monstrous and inhuman treatment. Finally, they took a stand. They fought for their right—our right—to be free of hybrid rule." He paused. "The Americas were truly a new world—colonized, perhaps, by hybrids, but built on the backs of the single-souled. We fought for and won this land during the Revolution. It is our haven in a world gone mad. And as such, it must be protected."

<*What is this?*> Addie said softly.

Our initial sickness hadn't faded, only soured and curdled.

"In past times, when the world was a more barbaric place, the hybrids were able to maintain their power through sheer brutality and superior numbers. But today, we can see them for what they truly are: mercurial in mood, unstable in action. That is, if they do not simply succumb to insanity. Who but the insane could so savagely treat their fellow human beings for thousands of years? Who but the unstable would continue to fight endless wars, until they'd all but driven themselves into the ground?"

Ryan had come to stand beside us, slipping his fingers through ours. We felt the heat of his arm through his sleeve. It wasn't until he gently squeezed back that I realized I was crushing his fingers.

Jenson stared out from the television screen. It felt like he was talking specifically to us. To me. "We've long closed our borders to the hybrids overseas. But unfortunately, that didn't solve the problem of the ones being born into our midst. For a long time, the institutions were our best solution to the hybrid condition. Institutionalization allowed hybrids to be secured and cared for away from those they might harm. It allowed them to be protected from themselves. But times are changing. As a country, we improve and move forward, discovering better ways to resolve our problems. And that is what I wish to introduce to you today—the next step in our answer to the hybrid issue: not containment, but a cure."

A cure.

A cure was what they'd been looking for at Nornand. Child after child had died on the operating table in search of a cure. Jaime Cortae—thirteen years old, funny, brilliant—had gone under the knife and lost a part of himself he would never get back. All because they'd been searching for a cure.

<Dr. Lyanne> Addie said. *<She said they'd given that up. She said that the review board—the government considered Nornand a complete failure. She said there would be—there would be backlash—>*

Surely, they hadn't changed their minds so quickly. Surely,

Dr. Lyanne had been right. But Dr. Lyanne's hand in our escape had been discovered soon after the breakout, and she'd had to flee. Since then, she'd been in hiding just as much as the rest of us.

What if she'd heard wrong? My voice was quiet. <*Maybe this is their way of responding. Instead of hiding it, keep doing it until they get it right.*> The last word was a twist in our gut. <*If they can find a way to fix hybrids, it won't matter if people learn the truth about Nornand. It won't matter if Nornand was a failure, because they could say it was just the first step. If they succeed, then Nornand was just a trial, and nobody will care.*>

If they succeed, then all those children who died were just collateral damage.

On-screen, Jenson explained that a cure for hybridity wasn't yet available for widespread use, but research was being conducted. They hoped to implement it in certain areas before beginning the program nationwide.

"Security levels will be increased across the country," he continued. "This will stay in effect for the immediate future as a preemptive measure against the possibility of hybrid backlash. Safety, as always, is our primary concern. In this case, there is a second reason."

Something hardened in Jenson's face. For a second, things became personal, not professional. Then it passed, and he was just a government official again, just a guy at a podium giving a speech someone else had probably written for him.

"We are searching," said Jenson into the microphone, "for a child."

There existed nothing, nothing in the world except for his words.

"A thirteen-year-old boy named Jaime Cortae was stolen from a hospital after being successfully treated for hybridity. Investigations have been launched, and it is believed that he was kidnapped by a small group of hybrid insurgents."

He was talking about our Jaime.

"Eva?" a small voice floated out behind us.

Kitty stood in the hallway, dressed in pajama pants and a soft blue T-shirt, her long hair plaited down her back. Outside of Nornand, Kitty and Nina never wore skirts. They almost never wore their hair down. They never wore blue. Their big, dark eyes were the same, their almost luminous skin, their matchstick limbs. But here in Emalia's apartment, a flush in their cheeks, they'd lost a bit of that fairy look.

Until she saw the screen, saw Jenson, and her face went white. "What's he saying?"

Just as she spoke, the video feed of Jenson cut away, replaced by a shot of a dark-haired couple.

Mr. and Mrs. Cortae, read the caption.

They stood outside, their hands twined together, looking themselves like lost children. The woman wore a long, heavy skirt, though it was summer. Her husband's eyes stayed fixed on the ground, but hers kept moving—around and around, in all directions, searching. Searching for what? For Jaime? For answers? For justice? Or for a way out? An escape route from the camera jutting into her private grief.

"He was healthy," she cried. "He was healthy, and they took him. They—"

Then she and her husband were gone. Jenson once again dominated the screen.

No. No, go back. Let her speak. Let us hear her. I needed to know what she had to say. What did she know about Jaime and her other, lost son? Was she fighting for him? Did she want him back, no matter what? Had she been coerced into giving up her child, like our parents? Did she regret it, every day?

"His family is, of course, devastated to have come so close to having a healthy child back home," Jenson said. "We are likewise highly concerned for Jaime's well-being and are working diligently to secure his safe return."

Was that really what Jaime's mother had meant by *healthy*? A boy with part of him unnecessarily stripped away? Or had she thought Jaime healthy before he ever left for Nornand?

<Kitty> Addie reminded me softly. *<She's scared, Eva.>*

I forced myself to focus back on Kitty's face. Her hands had rolled into white-knuckled fists at her sides.

Sabine stepped forward, shielding her from the screen. "Hi, I'm Sabine. Sorry to barge in while you were sleeping."

I grabbed the remote and lowered the volume, reducing Jenson's voice to a murmur. "It's just a speech, Kitty. Don't worry about it, okay? Why don't you go get dressed?"

Kitty studied our face, then nodded, her expression

unreadable. I never knew exactly how much to screen from Kitty and Nina. They were only months older than Lyle. Sometimes, they seemed younger. Sometimes, so much older.

"She seems sweet," Sabine said once we heard Kitty shut our bedroom door. "I'm glad you guys—" She hesitated. "I mean, just, it's always nice when they can rescue them young." She stared at the television again, her cheeks flushed but her eyes cold.

"You know Jenson," Ryan said to her. "Personally, I mean."

Now that Ryan brought it up, I could see it, too. Sabine didn't watch Jenson like he was a stranger, a hated figurehead. She watched him like we did. Someone who had felt his fingers press our skin against our bones.

"Personally?" Sabine's voice was a darkly amused trill. "I guess. He came personally to my house when I was eleven years old. He personally forced me into his car. Personally delivered me to his institution." Her smile was so bitter I could taste it on our tongue. "He's moved up in life since then. But we were personally acquainted once."

The phone rang. Numbly, I answered.

"It's Christoph again," the voice on the other end said. "Put Sabine back on."

I handed the phone over. Sabine walked a little ways away, her back to us, the phone cord stretched out behind her. "Yeah, I'm watching. Christoph, calm down; I'll be right there." The phone clanged back into its cradle. Sabine was already moving for the door. "I've got to go. Christoph's going to explode if I don't find him."

"Are you going to the meeting tomorrow night?" I called after her.

"It's not going to be tomorrow night anymore." Jackson hurried after Sabine, speaking over his shoulder. "Peter should be back home in less than an hour. Meeting will probably be late tonight, once everyone's off work."

"I—" I began to say, just as Sabine asked, "You guys are going to be there, right?"

"Emalia's against it." I shrugged, shaking our head. "She's worried we'll—I don't know—get snatched off the street or something."

Sabine nodded. "I'll talk to Peter, see what I can do."

We said our good-byes, and then Sabine and Jackson were gone. The television played some commercial about toaster pastries. I put it on mute.

I sank onto the couch. After a moment, Ryan joined me.

"Jaime will be all right." He took our shoulder, tried to guide us gently against the backrest. "He's with Dr. Lyanne."

Dr. Lyanne, who was also in hiding. Who had been wrong about the government's views on Nornand. But what was the point of saying all that aloud? It wouldn't help.

"Yeah," I said. "Yeah, he'll be fine. We'll all be fine."

<You sound about as convincing as he did> Addie said. I didn't bother responding. Our gaze drifted away from Ryan and to the small paper bag he'd set by the couch. I'd forgotten all about it.

“Did you make something?” I asked.

“Yeah. Here.” He handed me the bag. Whatever it was, it was heavy for its size. “It’s for you.”

“It’s not another salt-and-pepper shaker, is it?”

He smiled faintly. “Not exactly.”

The paper bag crinkled as I opened it. I drew out a small metal bird, just the right size to fit in our cupped hands. Its spread wings framed the round face of a clock, its eyes staring upward, head arched back, as if looking to the sky.

Ryan tapped a fingertip against the clockface. “It plays music when the alarm goes off. Not great music or anything, because I got the recording from—well, anyway . . .” His fingers slid down the metal’s cool, smooth ridges until they touched my hands. “You said you didn’t like the one Emalia gave you. Since it sounds like—since it’s so loud.”

Since it sounded like a siren.

“Thanks.” My eyes traced the overlap of our fingers, up his arm, catching against the way his shirt creased down from his shoulder, across his chest, up to the hard edge of his chin, his mouth, his nose, his eyes. “Thanks,” I said again, but softer, because he was leaning toward me. My eyes closed.

His lips brushed against my cheek.

I held utterly still, and so did he. As if sudden movement would break something. As if tasting his mouth against mine—as if being less than so, *so* careful—

Would cause something to shatter.

I didn’t want to be careful. I didn’t want to have to stay so *still*, or try *so hard* to keep always that breath of distance. That last-minute shift of his mouth from mine.

I didn't want to think about Addie. Or Devon.

Just for a second.

Just for a moment.

Just for this *one moment*—

But I had to. My body did not belong solely to me. That was the way it was, no matter how utterly unfair it sometimes felt.

"It's going to be okay, Eva," Ryan said, and the words skirted over the edge of my jaw.

He leaned back, and there was air in the world again. Our eyes held. Then his gaze slipped to the little golden bird between us, half-hidden beneath our fingers.

His hands squeezed mine.

Ours.

FIVE

A month ago, on the beach, Jackson told Addie and me how hybrids coped with their situation—or at least how they coped with part of it. Some things we didn't talk about. He didn't teach me how to suppress the nightmares of Nornand's white walls, didn't let me know if it was okay that sometimes I felt so furious with my mom and dad for what they'd allowed to happen to us.

But Jackson explained how hybrids could achieve a semblance of independence when their bodies could never truly be theirs. They forced themselves to disappear, one soul slipping into unconsciousness.

I'd done it once, by accident, when Addie and I were thirteen, but never since then. It had been an unspoken promise between Addie and me that I'd never leave her again. But we were fifteen now, and though leaving Addie *forever* was unthinkable, a few minutes or a few hours was something else entirely. The possibility of freedom taunted me.

<*What if you don't come back?*> Addie said every time

I brought up the possibility of *going under*, as Jackson called it.

<Jackson said—>

<Jackson could be wrong.>

A week ago, I'd finally drawn up the courage to ask Sophie: *If I make myself disappear, is it possible I won't come back?*

She laughed as if I'd asked if we might stick our head out the window and be struck by lightning.

"Of course you'd come back, Eva. Haven't you ever done it before?"

"But how do you control how long you're gone? What if you're gone for days? For weeks?"

She'd smiled. "Then you'll have to let me know, because that would be a world record."

"So it's never happened."

The urgency in our voice must have reached her; her expression gentled. "The longest I've ever heard of anyone being out is half a day, Eva. If you've never done it before, it *can* be hard to control how long you're gone. You might only manage a few minutes, or it could be a couple hours. But you get the hang of it. You learn to control it."

"How?"

"It's—it's hard to explain. It's something you learn through doing, more than anything. Just keep trying. You and Addie will figure it out."

But Addie and I had figured out nothing, because Addie refused to try.

<It's normal, isn't it?> I said. *<It's what hybrids do.*

That's what Jackson told us, what Sophie told us. Devon and Ryan—they're trying it now.>

<Since when have you cared about normal?>

Addie was right. It had always been Addie who yearned for normality. She'd had the luxury of thinking about it. Growing up, there had been no version of normality that could coexist with my survival.

Now there was. And I wanted it, more than anything.

Still, it was Addie's choice as much as mine, and I could feel how torn she was. But I could also feel the ghost of Ryan's lips against our jaw, and the phantom twist in our gut every time he got too close—the pain that wasn't mine.

I couldn't stay like this forever.

Maybe it was Emalia who convinced Peter to let us attend the meeting. But something in me felt it was Sabine who pulled through for us in the end. Jenson's speech had set everyone on edge, even Emalia. Ryan shot us an exasperated look behind Emalia's back as she fluttered around, giving us instructions: *don't talk, keep walking, attract as little attention as possible.* By the time we left the building, it was dark out, the streets lit only by sallow streetlamps and the occasional headlights. From what Jackson had told us, this was the part of the city tourists didn't visit. No one lived here but the people who had to, the ones who couldn't afford better housing. Or, I supposed, the ones like us, in hiding.

Usually, only a select few were called to Peter's meetings,

or chose to attend. But tonight, there must have been at least thirty people. It was overwhelming to look around, see these faces, and know that almost all of them were hybrid, like us. Living in secret, like us. Carrying on relatively normal lives in a country that wanted them dead.

They looked like anyone else. There was a middle-aged man who might have been a banker. A young woman in sweats like she'd come here straight from the gym. An older lady who reminded me a little of our fifth-grade teacher. I caught Hally's eyes flickering from person to person, too, drinking in this crowd. Even Kitty had been allowed to come—if only so she wouldn't be left alone. But not everyone was here. Two, at least, were missing: Dr. Lyanne and Jaime.

<There's Sabine and Jackson> Addie said. They stood in the dining room along with two others: a strawberry-blond boy about Jackson's age with a constellation of freckles, and a girl with platinum-blond hair but dark eyebrows. Sabine caught our eyes and smiled. Addie smiled back. Other than Kitty, we were the youngest in the room.

Peter stood, and conversations dwindled. Physically, he was intimidating—tall, broad-shouldered, and sturdy, but with a face that could be kind. It was at his most austere, though, that I best saw his resemblance to his sister, Dr. Lyanne. They had the same strong brows, the same sharp eyes.

He resembled her now, as he said, "I'm sure by now you've all heard about Mark Jenson's address this morning." He took a long, slow breath. "But not all of you have heard about the Hahns institution, and that's where I'll start."

The room sat silent as Peter explained. He'd been keeping tabs on an institution in the mountains of Hahns County, up in the north, since before the Nornand breakout. The conditions were frigid during the winter, the building old, the children ill dressed and uncared for. In other words, they died like flies when the snow came in.

Plans for rescue developed slowly. The mountain terrain complicated things, so it was decided that any attempt would have to be conducted in summer, when conditions were fairest. A woman, Diane, had been seeded as a caretaker—institutions weren't staffed by nurses and doctors, like Nornand, but caretakers—and Peter had flown up to meet with her.

Everything fell apart when Diane's cover was blown. Desperate, she stole away six children in her car as she made her escape.

She didn't make it far.

She and two children died when their car went over the side of the winding mountain road. The remaining four kids extracted themselves from the wreckage and fled before the officials arrived.

Ten hours later, they stumbled into a small town still wearing their institution uniforms, filthy and bleeding and exhausted. The eldest of them was twelve, the youngest ten—just past the government-mandated deadline.

The police were called, the children whisked away. But not before their story of terror and pain spread, twisted in eager, gossiping mouths.

Peter laughed low, humorlessly. "It was an ugly thing for

the townspeople, I'm sure, on a Sunday morning."

Easy to not think about other people's suffering, when it was hidden away. Harder to stomach when it collapsed on your front porch.

At Nornand, we'd all worn blue.

What color did they wear at Hahns?

"But it'll never get beyond that." Sabine's voice was quiet, but clear. "The media will never be allowed to pick up the story."

Peter shook his head. "It was unlikely to begin with. It's impossible now, with the announcement Jenson made this morning. Which was probably the point."

Addie frowned, but I understood. By saying they were making headway in a hybrid cure, they could quash the Hahns story. And by saying something about possible hybrid retaliation, they now had an excuse to dial up security without having to admit to the recent breakouts.

"Diane was a cautious woman," Peter said. "But someone found out enough to be suspicious. We don't know if they'll connect the dots between this incident and the Nornand breakout—or if they have anything that might tie her back to us. So everybody, be alert. Be cautious. We'll have to lie low for a while."

"What about that new institution at Powatt?" It was Sabine again. She fingered one of the golden buttons on her jacket as she spoke, running her thumb along the smooth edge.

Peter turned toward her. "What about it?"

"Powatt's barely an hour and a half from here. We're not

concerned they're starting to build institutions within easy driving distance of major cities?"

"Say what you mean to say, Sabine," Peter said.

Sabine began to reply, but the redheaded boy cut her off. "She means: Don't you think it's a problem that it's okay now to stick institutions near a bunch of people? Everyone *knows* about them, but once upon a time, they still had enough of a conscience to not want a hundred dying children in their backyard. Now nobody cares?"

His voice was familiar—rough and heated and laced with anger. It had to be Christoph, the boy who'd called this morning.

"The country's getting more and more apathetic, Peter," Christoph said. "And the government's getting bolder. Soon, they're not even going to worry about covering up stuff like the Hahns institution. They'll be able to round up hybrid kids in the street and put bullets in their heads—"

"Christoph," Peter said just as Jackson nudged the other boy's shoulder with his own. Christoph quieted, but didn't control the mutinous look on his face. "We're gathering more information about the Powatt institution. Once we know what we need to know, we'll address it as it needs to be addressed."

I had a sudden, gut-wrenching thought. *<Is this how they talked about Nornand?>*

How long had Peter "gathered information" before he decided to launch a rescue plan? The first time we'd spoken with Jackson, when he'd pulled us into that storage closet at Nornand, he'd told us to *keep hope* because a rescue was coming, but it needed more time. We'd told him we didn't have more time, that Hally and Lissa were due for the operation table.

If Jackson hadn't spoken to us that day, the rescue might have happened days or even weeks later. Hally and Lissa might be dead.

Addie's disquiet weighed heavy against me. *<Do you think they could have acted earlier, but didn't?>* She hesitated. *<Do you think they could have saved Jaime?>*

There was no way to know.

The rest of the meeting passed in a blur. By the time I managed to refocus on something other than my own tumbling thoughts, the room had broken up into more private conversations. I didn't notice Sabine heading toward us until she'd almost reached our side.

"Hi again," she said to us and Devon. There was a casual warmth to her voice, as if we'd met more than once. "I'm glad you ended up making it."

"Yeah." Addie didn't bother making our voice sound anything but dull.

The look in Sabine's eyes said she understood. Hally broke the awkward silence that followed by smiling and introducing herself. As the two of them chatted, I snuck another glance at Peter. He was still seated at the dining table, deep in a conversation with Henri and Emalia.

<We can't say anything about the other Nornand kids now, can we?> I said.

How could I demand Peter rush into a rescue after what had happened at Hahns?

Still, I couldn't help my impatience. Every day we didn't act was another day those kids had to suffer. We'd survived Nornand. We knew what it was like.

Peter didn't notice our furtive looks, but Henri, sitting across from him, met our eyes. He smiled and nodded in acknowledgment.

Jackson had told us Henri's story early on. Ryan and Hally only looked foreign, but Henri truly *was* foreign. He hadn't been born here—hadn't grown up in the Americas, hadn't even learned English until he was in his twenties.

He and Peter had met nearly five years ago, when Peter made his first trip overseas. Then a fledgling journalist, Henri got to hear firsthand about a locked-down country, one that few had entered or left in decades, since the first few years of the Great Wars. The two kept a clandestine correspondence even after Peter's return to the Americas. And a few short months ago, Henri made the trip here himself.

I couldn't imagine the danger he'd put himself in, sneaking into a country that hated him, where the ebony-dark gleam of his skin and the strange lilt in his words could so easily give him away. The latter was the real problem. There were people who looked like Henri in the Americas—many more, in fact, than there were people who looked like Ryan and Lissa. But no one spoke like Henri did. He couldn't open his mouth without ruining the ruse.

Henri wasn't even hybrid. And yet he'd come all the way across an ocean to try and help. Addie and I had seen the drafts of his articles, pages filled with strange sequences of letters, some with odd additions—extra marks where they didn't belong. *French,* Henri had explained, and read us a little, the syllables sliding and flowing into one another.

They'd spoken French once, in parts of the Americas, especially far to the north. But languages other than English had been officially stamped out before Addie and I were born.

"How often do Peter's plans fail like this?" Devon said abruptly. He was looking toward the dining table, too.

Hally sighed. "*Devon.*"

"Not often," Sabine said. "He's meticulous."

"Peter knows what he's doing." Hally looked to Sabine, as if for confirmation. "He's been at it for years."

"Almost five, now." Sabine smiled, just a little. "I was in the first group he ever rescued—me and Christoph."

"Long time," Devon said.

A long time to be free, and yet not really free.

Sabine and Devon observed each other like careful statues. Devon was a couple inches taller, but somehow Sabine made it seem like they were exactly eye to eye.

"Yeah," she said finally. And listening to that one word, I could hear the long, trembling echoes of every one of those years.

SIX

Addie and I were still awake that night, thinking about Hahns, and Nornand, and dying children, when the nightmares came for Kitty.

At first, it was just a restlessness in her limbs. An inability to keep still. Then she cried out—not a scream, but a whimper, as if even asleep she knew she had to hide.

I hurried from our bed. It was too dark to see much, but Kitty had curled up into a ball beneath her covers, her breathing erratic.

"Kitty?" I whispered. "Kitty, wake up." I gripped her shoulders as she rocketed upward. Her eyes snapped open. "*Shh . . . shh* . . . It's all right."

There were no tears. No screaming. Just two wide, brown eyes and five dull fingernails digging into our hand.

"It's okay," I said. "You're okay."

She pressed her face against our shoulder, a blunt, animal need for warmth and safety. I wrapped our arms around her. For a long time, neither of us said anything. Sometimes, the sight of Kitty in the bed next to ours—or just the feel of her in our arms—shocked me back in time to another shared bedroom. One where the beds were made of metal, not wood. Where the floor was cold and nurses came at intervals to check on us in the night.

Kitty spoke, her voice thick. "Eva, are Sallie and Val dead?"

"What?" The word dropped, a startled, black stone from our mouth.

Kitty's hand tightened around our wrist until it hurt. "Our old roommate at Nornand. Sallie and Val. The one we had before you and Addie. The one—the one they said had gone home. Like Jaime."

I shifted, trying to see her face, but Kitty resisted. Our shirt muffled her words. "You rescued Jaime. And Hally. You would've rescued Sallie and Val if they'd been down there, right?"

I couldn't speak. I could only think *Oh, God. Oh, God.*

Kitty and Nina having nightmares was nothing new. But neither had brought up their old roommate since leaving Nornand. Had the meeting earlier tonight sharpened old memories? Or had they been silently wondering all this time, too frightened to ask?

I'd forgotten that they didn't know Sallie and Val's fate. I hadn't stopped to imagine what it might be like for them, not knowing.

Still, I didn't want to answer.

Go back to sleep, I wanted to say.

It was only a dream, I wanted to say.

But sleep wouldn't solve anything, and this—this horror that had happened at Nornand—was not a dream.

How were we supposed to tell an eleven-year-old girl that her friend was dead?

That she had been, for all intents and purposes, murdered?

That no justice had been exacted?

But Kitty and Nina were waiting.

<Tell her> Addie whispered.

I crushed Kitty against us, not knowing if we were doing the right thing, if we were doing it the right way. "Yes, they are."

She didn't reply. Her hands tangled in our shirt.

<She was all right before> I said helplessly. *<Yesterday, she was laughing—>*

But she hadn't been all right, any more than we'd been all right, or Ryan, or Hally, or Jaime. We'd been out of Nornand for six weeks, and sometimes, I wasn't sure what *all right* really meant anymore.

Kitty and Nina weren't the only one with nightmares.

"You're safe," I whispered fiercely in Kitty's ear. "Nothing will happen to you. I promise."

I stayed with her for nearly an hour in the darkness, until she drifted back to sleep.

Henri had given us a world map three weeks ago, when Addie and I first arrived at Emalia's apartment. *Since you love it so much*, he'd said in his lilting, accented voice, and laughed when Addie fixed it above our bed with sticky tack. He'd brought the map from overseas, so it was like no map Addie and I had ever seen. We'd been fascinated since we first found it rolled up in a corner of his apartment.

Now, as dawn broke, sunlight seeped through the yellow curtains and crawled across the ceiling. Bit by bit, the map came into view. Our eyes took in the neatly labeled countries, each stained a different color. Russia, with its bulk, its eastern mountain ranges and great, thick, blue river veins. Australia, lonely in the southeast, a country and a continent. I thought of Australia most often. Despite the distance between us, there was a comforting familiarity to its loneliness.

The Americas were alone, too. Almost all the other countries of the world shared continents. A few were nearly the size of our northern half, but most were hardly a hundredth our size. How strange it must be to live in a country so small, surrounded so claustrophobically by other nations. The Americas dominated the entire western half of the map, two continents attached by a thread.

A familiar whirring and clicking came from Nina's side of the room, and I shifted to face her.

"Nina Holynd." I kept my tone light even as I examined her, searching her expression for signs of the pain she and Kitty had crumpled beneath last night. Nina had always been better than Kitty at hiding pain. The mornings after the girls had a particularly bad dream, it was almost always Nina who took control. Who got out of bed smiling like the nightmares had never happened. "You have *got* to find somebody else to film."

"There's nobody else to film." Nina directed her video camera right at our face, giggling. I groaned and pulled our covers over our head. "You move a lot in your sleep, you know that?"

"No." The blankets muffled my words. "And I don't need cinematographic proof, thank you very much."

Nina's camcorder really belonged to Emalia, who had accidentally broken it years back. Nina had unearthed it in a cabinet, and Ryan had fixed it. Since then, Addie and I woke far too often to a camera lens hovering above our bed, filming the apparently fascinating movie of *Addie & Eva Asleep*.

The video camera was enormous and heavy, but that didn't seem to dissuade Nina. She and Kitty had gone through two Super 8 film cartridges already, keeping them in our dresser drawer in hopes Emalia might go through with her promise to develop them. I didn't have the heart to tell her that Emalia would probably wait months before deeming it safe enough—if she ever did.

"*Eee-va.*" Nina drew out my name on a two-toned pitch. "Come on. Get up." When I didn't move, she sighed. "Fine. I'll just look through Addie's sketchbook, then."

This jerked Addie into control. "Nina—"

Nina pulled the sketchbook from the nightstand drawer and flipped it open with stubborn glee. After years of hiding her drawings, Addie still disliked people looking through her sketches.

"Who's this?" The sketchbook had fallen open to a picture

of a young boy, light-haired and eager-eyed.

"Lyle." Addie slipped from our bed and crossed to Nina's. The younger girl leaned against us, like it was automatic.

"Why's he dressed like that?"

Our lips crooked in a smile. Addie had drawn him in a soldier's uniform right out of one of his spy-and-adventure novels. "Because he always wanted to have adventures. For a while, he was convinced he was going to be a soldier when he grew up. He taught himself Morse code and everything. By the time he moved on to the next thing, I'd practically memorized it, too."

"Do you still remember it?"

Addie nodded. Nodding was easier than speaking around the sudden lump in our throat. She picked up the pencil and reached for her sketchbook, drawing a line and a dot; then two dots; another line and dot; and finally a dot followed by a line.

"*N-I-N-A*," she said, and tapped the letters out with the pencil.

Nina stared down at the pattern, her own fingers moving slowly. "Can you teach us the whole alphabet?"

Addie grinned wryly. "Sure. Numbers, too."

Nina tapped out her name again, a little faster. "What's *Kitty*?"

Addie wrote and tapped it for her. Funny how we remembered it even better than I thought we would. Mom and Dad had learned a few words, too, but we were the ones Lyle tapped messages to after we went to bed, rapping on the wall between our rooms long after he was supposed to be asleep. He never stopped until Addie tapped something back.

Addie shut her sketchbook and slipped off the bed, pulling Nina after us. "Come on, have you eaten breakfast?"

"Nope. I was waiting for you. I'll make you pancakes, if you want."

"That would be great." Addie smiled as Nina grabbed her camcorder and headed for the kitchen.

We glanced, one last time, at the map stuck to the ceiling.

The world maps we'd studied in school had always come with the disclaimer that they were old, made before or shortly after the Great Wars began. *World War I* and *World War II*, as Henri called them.

The Great Wars had always smashed through our history classes like a giant's fist, leaving the rest of the world fragmented, unworthy of mapping. We'd been told country lines were muddled, contested to the point of being barely existent. They shifted constantly, as some desperate people attacked another and were assaulted in turn.

Lies. So much of it lies.

World War I and *World War II* seemed so neat in comparison.

Wars can destroy a country completely, Henri told us. *But they can also shape it, push it forward. Some of the world was destroyed. Some was shaped. And some was pushed forward.*

What do they have that we don't? I'd asked. *Flying cars?*

Henri laughed. *No, no flying cars. But faster cars. And cell phones. Internet.*

We'd never heard of them. He told us about tiny, cordless phones everyone carried around in their pockets, so widespread that pay phones were all but extinct. He tried to describe some sort of information network that connected computers, allowing one to instantaneously send data to another. He kept running into words he didn't know how to translate, and the entire concept baffled Addie and me, who could count the number of times we'd even sat down in front of a computer.

He told us mankind had been to the moon.

I laughed. *You're kidding.*

But he wasn't.

He said it had only happened once, a few decades ago, but after the end of the Second World War. It was a show of power by one of the countries that had emerged least scathed from the years of combat. The project had proven too financially costly to attempt again, though there were other countries still eager to try.

There were also satellites floating out there in the blackness, orbiting our planet. Henri showed us one of his devices, a *satphone* that seemed more miniature computer than phone. Using these satellites, the phone allowed him to both send information and make calls to his headquarters overseas.

There were satellites beaming information around in outer space. There had been men on the moon. I had never known the world beyond the Americas' borders, but there were people out there who'd experienced life beyond our very *planet*.

How terribly insignificant we must all seem from the moon. Our battles. Our wars.

Addie sighed and pulled our blankets straight, tucking in the edges. The map was a comforting reminder of the rest of the world. One that included countries where hybrids like us weren't vilified, weren't feared or hated or locked away.

But sometimes, those bright, colorful countries seemed to mock us with their distance.

The phone shrilled, and Addie hurried into the living room to answer it. "Hello?"

"Hey," a voice said. "This is Sabine. Did I wake you up?"

"I was awake," Addie said. Nina watched us with obvious curiosity, arms cradling a mixing bowl.

"Good. I would've called later, but I'm about to leave for work. Do you want to meet up with me and a couple friends tonight?"

Addie frowned in confusion. "Sorry?"

"I wanted to introduce you to some people." Sabine's voice dropped a little. "You can sneak out, right? We can meet you right at the end of your block. There's a fast-food place that's open until two a.m. Can you be there at one thirty? There'll be five of us; six if you get Ryan to come."

Would Ryan go? He hadn't been the warmest to Sabine and Jackson yesterday. But I thought about all the weeks of boredom crushing down on him, hour after hour, and I said *<He'd go.>*

<Are we going to go?>

Six weeks of barely stepping foot outside the building, and now we were thinking about sneaking out twice in as many days, not to mention the Emalia-sanctioned trip last night.

<Yes> I said.

<What if we get caught?>

<We won't get caught. It's not like Emalia checks on us in the middle of the night.>

<I don't mean by Emalia. Jenson said security was going to go up> Addie reminded me.

<It's summer break. A group of us, out at night—why should that be suspicious?>

Still, Addie hesitated.

<Addie, we have to go. Do you want to tell her we can't go because we're afraid we might be caught?>

<It's a legitimate concern.>

But when Sabine asked, "You still there? Can you guys come?" Addie sighed and said, "Yeah. We can."

<What about Hally and Lissa?> I said.

"Great," Sabine said before Addie could bring them up. "I'll see you and Ryan at one thirty, then. I've got to run."

"Who was that?" Nina asked as soon as Addie hung up. She stood barefoot in the kitchen, on the other side of the counter.

"Just Sabine." Addie swung around to the kitchen doorway. "It was nothing. Come on, weren't you going to make pancakes?"

Nina frowned. For a moment, I thought she might press

harder. But then her expression cleared, though her eyes didn't leave ours. "Yeah. I can't find the baking soda."

"Did you check in the top cabinet?" Addie walked past her to look.

I tried not to think about the deliberate way Nina's frown had disappeared. As if she'd forced it away, along with her curiosity. As if, even at eleven, Nina had learned that her life would always be full of other people's secrets, and some were dangerous, and sometimes it was better not to know.

Maybe that was good, since there wasn't anything that could be done, anyway. Should Addie and I have lied about Sallie and Val? Or at least told Kitty we didn't know?

I was so terrified of doing something wrong. I wanted, so badly, for Kitty and Nina to have a life where they didn't need to worry about these sorts of things at all.

SEVEN

Ryan and Hally came downstairs a little after noon, just in time to help Kitty and me polish off that morning's leftover pancake batter. Hally fooled around with Kitty in the living room, laughing and striking poses while Kitty filmed her on the old camcorder. I kept them both in the corner of our vision as I told Ryan about Sabine's phone call.

"You said you'd go?" Ryan kept his voice to a murmur. "What about Hally and Lissa?"

"She didn't mention them." The pancake batter glopped onto the oiled pan. I prodded at it with our spoon, spreading it out. "They could come, I'm sure. Maybe she just forgot to invite them."

Addie's skepticism was tangible. *<She didn't forget.>*

"She said she wanted to show us around town?"

"Yeah. And have us meet her other friends."

Ryan's gaze stayed on our face, but I felt his focus stray. Whatever conversation he and Devon were having, it distracted him.

I'd learned a lot about Ryan since our escape from Nornand—that he was a morning person, that he didn't have much of a sweet tooth. That he and his sisters used to play at being soldiers when they were little and lived in the country, fighting wars that sometimes his sisters won because he and Devon let them and sometimes because the girls were really very vicious when things got down to it.

But I hadn't learned what he was like around other people—people who weren't me or Kitty or his sister or adults. There hadn't been much room to make friends at Nornand, and we'd never hung out at school. Was he curious about Sabine and her friends the way I was?

"You wouldn't have that much trouble sneaking out," I said. Ryan and Devon slept in the living room, where Henri had a foldout couch. Hally and Lissa had appropriated the spare bedroom. "I don't think—"

"I'm going, Eva."

I looked up at him. "Yeah?"

"Yeah," he said. "You're going, so I'm going. I never said I wasn't."

"Okay." I smiled. I slipped my hand over his, and he leaned toward me like it was the most natural thing in the world.

He was going to kiss me. I could sense it. I could almost feel it already—his mouth against mine. But I couldn't let it happen. Not with Addie squirming beside me.

I caught the moment Ryan hesitated. Saw him hold himself back, rein himself in.

"Eva," he said.

"Hm?" My voice was barely more than a breath.

He grinned and looked away. "Your pancake's burning." The heat suddenly shooting through our body had nothing to do with the stove. I rushed to scrape the pancake from the pan. "You know, I thought you were lying when you said Kitty was a better cook than you are, but—"

I shoved at him, laughing. "Shut up! You were distracting me. We were having a very distracting conversation."

The pancake was blackened, but salvageable. I kept a hawk's eye on it, but couldn't help the ridiculous smile that spread over our face. It would be all right. Being with Ryan like this—being with him but unable to really be with him—was crazily awkward, borderline insane. But it was what it was. It was my life, and I understood it. He understood it. We could laugh about it. We could still be happy, and that was what mattered, wasn't it?

"What are you two doing in there?" Hally called from the living room.

"Slaving away to feed you," Ryan shot back. He gave her a dark look that quickly melted when he couldn't bite back a laugh.

"Well, somebody's got to do it, brother dearest." Hally and Kitty were bent over the camcorder, fiddling with its controls. "Emalia's not actually going to develop this film, is she?"

Kitty pulled the video recorder from her hands and pressed the record button before turning the lens in our direction.

"She promised she would."

"Dear God," Hally said. She winked at me. "Well, there go my plans for political office."

I burst out laughing again. Addie unwound a bit, then even more as my happiness infected her. Guilt suddenly pressed cold hands against our heart. Sabine hadn't asked for Hally or Lissa to show up tonight.

<She'll come with us next time> I said. *<We'll mention her, and they'll invite her along.>*

<How do you know there's going to be a next time?>

I didn't, of course. But as I turned back to the stove, I realized I already hoped there would be.

Anchoit's streets were not completely empty, even at nearly two a.m. Still, they were quiet as Ryan and Addie slipped from our apartment building into the warm summer night.

There would be more people downtown, where places stayed open late. I imagined music flowing out from low-lit bars, people laughing and stumbling from party to party. Emalia's neighborhood was more known for pickpockets and the occasional gang fight than dance clubs.

"Is that it?" Ryan said as we approached a fast-food joint. It gleamed yellow and red in the darkness.

Addie hesitated. "I think so."

We peeked through the windows. The tiny restaurant looked deserted but for the cashier lounging behind the counter and a band of four people squished around a cheap plastic table. The blond girl had her back to us, as did the red-haired boy sitting next to her, but Sabine and Jackson faced us. The latter noticed us first, lighting up with a smile.

"There you are," Sabine called out as Addie came inside. Jackson pulled out an empty chair. It scraped against the linoleum floor.

Ryan took the seat on our left, beside Sabine. Or maybe it was Josie, the other soul sharing her body. We didn't know either of them well enough to tell.

"Sabine," the girl said, as if reading my mind. She smiled, then gestured to the redheaded boy. "You've already spoken with Christoph. And that one there—" *That one* rolled her eyes. Her bleached-blond hair curved to frame her face. Her eyebrows, which had been left dark, stood out in sharp contrast. "That's Cordelia."

"And Jackson," Jackson said before Sabine could continue. He smiled his match-strike smile. "Hopefully you haven't forgotten *that*."

Sabine grinned. "You are so forgettable."

"We make him reintroduce himself every Thursday," Cordelia said, but softened her words with an arm hooked around Jackson's neck. She pulled him toward her, laughing.

Addie smiled and snuck a look toward Ryan. But the boy on our left wasn't Ryan anymore. Devon looked around the table with the air of someone studying a complicated puzzle.

<Think these are their real names?> Addie said.

I hadn't even considered the possibility that they weren't.

<Jackson, Sabine, and Christoph are using their real names, anyway> I said. *<That's what they use in private, too.>*

<Unless they're so used to pretending to be someone else, they just use a fake name all the time.>

I didn't like to think about that. Sabine had been rescued just under five years ago. In five years, Addie and I would be twenty. Would we still be in hiding? Would we have slipped into the skin of someone else's life so fully their name slipped off our tongue like our own?

"I'm—" Addie started to say, then hesitated. We couldn't drop either of our names in public, even if there was no one around to hear but the guy reading behind the counter. We had the identity Emalia had forged for us. But it stuck in our throat. We didn't want to introduce ourself with somebody else's name.

"It's all right." Sabine smiled. "We know who you are."

They might know our names, but how could they know if Addie was in control right now or me? How could they know if the boy next to us was Devon or Ryan?

"Jackson said you guys have gone down to the beach already?" Cordelia asked as she let go of Jackson. He rolled his eyes at her and ran his hand through his shaggy hair, trying to get it to lie down flat again.

Addie shrugged. "Only once."

"But not at night?"

"No."

Cordelia threw out her arms, as if trying to capture and express the sight of the ocean after dark. "It's beautiful. We should go right now."

"It's a little far to walk," Sabine said. She caught Cordelia's drink as it almost tipped off the table. "And a little late to take a bus."

Cordelia laughed. "Okay, okay. The voice of reason reigns. We'll go straight to the shop, then."

"The shop?" Addie asked.

"Sabine and I recently opened a photography shop a few streets down," Cordelia said. "We hang out there sometimes."

<*They own a photography shop?*> Addie said.

I wouldn't have guessed either Cordelia or Sabine was over twenty, if that. But such was the magic of a forged identity. Perhaps they'd convinced Emalia to fudge a date or two, give them years they'd never actually lived.

"Did you guys want to order something before we left?" Sabine asked as the others picked up their things, clearing the table. "They've got—" I caught the moment she realized neither Devon nor I had any money. How could we? "Here." She took Addie gently by the arm and led us toward the counter. "You've got to try their milkshakes."

"It's all right," Addie protested. "I don't—"

The man behind the counter straightened as we approached, setting aside his book.

"No arguing, okay?" Sabine smiled. "I'm sorry I never properly welcomed you guys to Anchoit when you first arrived. Two milkshakes, please," she said to the cashier. Then to Addie, "What flavors? Do you know what your boyfriend likes?"

Addie went cold next to me. "He's not my boyfriend." Our voice was barely above a whisper, but the cashier heard, anyway. He tried to look as if he hadn't.

Sabine wore embarrassment like an ill-fitting coat. "Sorry," she said with forced lightness, and I could feel Addie trying to look blasé about it, too. We couldn't attract attention.

"Chocolate," Addie said. "Both of us. Please."

The cashier nodded and called the order to whoever was in the kitchen.

"Sorry about that," Sabine murmured again while the man was out of earshot. "I shouldn't have assumed."

"It's all right," Addie said. It wasn't. Not really. I could tell.

Neither of them spoke again until after the cashier came back with the milkshakes. Sabine paid, brushing aside Addie's thanks.

"Just let me know if you ever need anything, okay?" she said as we headed for the exit. The others had already gone outside, laughing in the darkness. Devon stood a little apart from the rest.

The milkshake was rich and sweet and cold. Addie shivered as we stepped outdoors, but smiled. "I will."

Devon accepted his drink without comment, though he nodded at Sabine in what passed for his version of thanks. Jackson slipped between the two of us as we headed down the street. "Did you guys have any trouble getting here?"

"No." It was the first thing Devon had said all night. "Do you all live in the area?"

<My God> Addie said. *<Is Devon making small talk?>*

I laughed. I didn't tell her this wasn't Devon making small talk at all. This was Devon investigating, questioning, studying. There was a light in his eyes that I recognized; Ryan had worn that same look when he took apart Emalia's camcorder to figure out what was broken.

I never knew what to make of my feelings toward Devon, or what sort of feelings he might have toward me. Sometimes, his presence grated. His wall-like silences and unreadable eyes seemed like such wastes when I could be having Ryan's smiles, his surprised laughter, his quiet jokes.

But other times, I was overcome by a fierce sort of affection for Devon. It wasn't at all what I felt for Ryan. But it wasn't like anything I'd ever felt for anyone else, either.

"Sabine and Cordelia share an apartment about fifteen minutes away," Jackson said. "Christoph and I live a little farther."

Christoph looked over at the sound of his name. Sabine and Cordelia had left the rest of us behind a little, and they turned now to wait for us to catch up. I saw the moment Sabine's face changed, her easy smile pulling tight, her eyes focusing on something—*someone*—over our shoulder. A beam of light struck us from behind.

"Hey! You lot—wait a minute."

Addie jerked around. A police officer in full uniform directed a flashlight at us.

Our heart rate rocketed. Heat flared through our body, setting our blood alight like it was gasoline.

Devon, I thought.

Devon, who stood beside us, as immobile as we were. Devon, who, even more than us, should not be seen by anyone. He was doing nothing wrong, breaking no laws, causing no trouble. It was not actually illegal to be foreign, much less look foreign, and a police officer ought to know that better than the average person. But still.

Someone took hold of our shoulder. Jackson.

"Something wrong?" he asked the officer. His voice was light. He took a few steps toward the man, pushing us along though everything in me screamed that we should be going in the opposite direction.

The officer lowered the flashlight beam so it wasn't blinding us. The stars in our vision didn't fade.

He frowned at Addie and me. "Bit late for you to be running around, isn't it?"

Our lips couldn't form a reply. Jackson's hand tightened on our shoulder, but he laughed. "She's fine; she's with us."

"You know about the curfew?"

"That doesn't start until Monday," Cordelia said. Without my noticing, she and Sabine had joined us. She grinned. "We're running wild while we still can."

The officer ran his eyes over her short, platinum hair, her red lips. "Well, don't run too wild. It's two in the morning. Be careful."

“We were headed back anyway.” Sabine tilted her head at the milkshake in our hands. “Just came out for some food.”

<*Smile*> I hissed, and Addie obeyed.

We snuck a look at Devon, who wore a look of magnificent boredom. Our smile softened into something a bit more natural.

“It’s my birthday,” Addie said. Our voice came out quiet, almost shy. We sounded more like Kitty than ourself, which only made us more flustered. Heat crept up our neck, bloomed on our cheeks.

To their credit, no one looked surprised.

“All right,” the officer said finally. “Have a good night, then.”

We all stood quietly until the man was out of sight. Then Cordelia broke down into giggles. Jackson tried to shush her, but her laughter was making him laugh, too. Only Christoph looked as serious as Devon did. Sabine hustled everyone forward.

EIGHT

"That was a brilliant play by all involved," Cordelia said as we hurried through the streets.

"That was a close call," Jackson corrected, but there wasn't any real warning in his tone, only an amused sort of exhilaration.

"Not really." Cordelia skipped ahead of us, then turned to face Addie and me, walking backward. She grinned. "He was just worried we were corrupting your sweet fifteen-year-old mind. Gang initiation, maybe."

"It's not really your birthday, is it?" Sabine asked. Addie shook our head. "Good going, then. Nearly fooled me."

"It's my birthday," Cordelia said in a surprisingly good imitation of our voice—only higher and breathier. Addie blushed, and Cordelia laughed. "You sounded like an angel, my darling. Nobody in a thousand years would ever suspect you of anything."

The photography shop was marked by nothing more than a plain door and a wooden sign declaring *Still Life* in elegant, black script. A long display window stretched along the wall, but I only got a glimpse of picture frames and black-and-white photos before Cordelia moved to unlock the door.

A bell jingled as we entered. Photographs crowded the small shop's limited wall space. Inside one silver frame, a little boy pressed his face against a set of slender, white stair railings. An enormous, broad-shouldered man with an equally enormous pumpkin-colored cat sat within the frame beside it.

Cordelia led us to a storage room at the back of the store, everyone crowding inside among the array of empty frames and dusty cardboard boxes. The ceiling here was surprisingly high. Even Jackson, tall as he was, needed a stool to get a good grip on the string hanging from a hatch door.

"The string used to be longer," he explained. "It snapped about half a year back, so we have to use the stool."

"Tie another string," Devon said.

Jackson smiled as he pulled the trapdoor creakily open. "But the stool is more interesting. A longer string would also make the door more noticeable." He stepped off the stool, still pulling on the door. A series of steps unfolded, groaning and creaking. "And this," he said, yanking the steps so they clicked into place, "is a secret."

Automatically, Addie took a step backward.

Once, when Addie and I were little and still lived in the city, our family was invited to a party thrown by one of Mom's old friends. They'd moved to the suburbs, had a big house and a pool and a barbecue. It had been summer. Hot. The adults milled about outside, our parents busy as they mingled and looked after Lyle and Nathaniel, who'd been only two.

I don't remember how many people were present. To seven-year-old me, it had seemed like a hundred or more. There were at least ten kids. That much I remember. We played hide-and-seek. A girl in a yellow dress was *It*.

I'd told Addie to follow the others into the house. Two boys had headed for the attic, one pausing halfway up the stairs to beckon us up with them. Addie had hesitated, but I'd said *Go*.

Because he'd beckoned. Because he'd picked us to go with him, and I'd been hopeful.

It had been sweltering inside the attic. A dead sort of heat, the kind that sucks all the air from a room. There had been an ornate, old-fashioned trunk. There had been more than one, probably. And I vaguely remembered boxes, too. But more than anything, I remembered the biggest trunk, because that boy, he'd said, *No one will look in there*.

So Addie and I crawled inside, curled up to fit in the darkness.

He'd lowered the heavy lid, his friend watching behind him.

He locked it so quietly we didn't hear.

"Go on," Jackson said, gesturing up the stairs. "You guys first. Guest courtesies and all."

Having a panic attack here, in front of everyone, would be devastating.

<It'll be fine.> I'd said as much back at Nornand, when we'd been forced to climb into a torturously small machine for testing. I'd been lying then. But an attic we could handle, especially if it had windows and wasn't too cramped. We just had to relax.

Addie pressed our lips together and moved forward. The stairs—more ladder than stairs, really—shuddered and creaked with each step.

We emerged in that familiar attic warmth. The ceiling here was a dark, bare wood, sloped until it almost touched the equally bare wooden floors. Someone had pounded a series of heavy-duty nails all around the room, then tangled a string of fairy lights around them. The end of their cord lay near the top of the stairs, and Addie bent to plug it in.

The entire attic lit up with a soft glow. Two lumpy, faded couches slumped at angles to each other. The dark green one leaked yellow stuffing. At first I wondered how on earth anyone had managed to get them up here. Then I noticed the screws where the couch frames could be taken apart. A tall lamp stood in the corner, opposite a small window that looked out onto the street. We couldn't see clearly through the curtain.

One by one, everyone climbed up to join us. Cordelia turned on the lamp, which brightened the attic further. It wasn't as bad as I'd feared. There was only one room, but it was large enough to fit many more than our six bodies. The heat-heavy air was cloying, but bearable.

"So," Sabine said once we'd all settled down. She sat cross-legged on the green couch, looking more dancerlike than ever in a pair of dark gray leggings and a faded T-shirt. Her gaze fell on Devon, then Addie and me. "One of you, go first. Tell us about yourself."

Of course, Devon said nothing. Addie cradled our milk-shake in our hands. "We're both from Lupside. I—"

"Lupside?" Cordelia was half sitting, half curled against Sabine, her smile lazy but her eyes sharp. "Didn't you live there for a while, Christoph?"

Christoph nodded. "For two years, back in elementary school."

Before Addie and I moved there, then. We'd have still been living in our old apartment, just starting to realize how utterly strange it was—how truly awful—that we hadn't settled.

"Did you ever go to the history museum?" Addie asked.

Christoph had a sweet face when he wasn't scowling. He looked younger, with his slight frame and pale freckles. He had stopped twitching around so much, like a bomb that might go off any minute.

"Every year. Do they still have that god-awful poster? That supposedly authentic one from nineteen-whatever with the twisted-looking hybrids on them?" He screwed up his face and raised his hands like claws, making Cordelia laugh.

I remembered that poster. Christoph's impression of it wasn't terribly exaggerated. The entire museum was dedicated to the struggle between the hybrids and the non-hybrids. It covered everything from the servitude forced upon the single-souled when they were first shipped to the Americas, to the great Revolution that had followed, and the years of fighting on American soil at the start of the Great Wars.

Addie told the others about the flood and fire damage that had ruined portions of the museum during our last visit. She hesitated, then explained how everything had been blamed on a hybrid man. Described the mob that had gathered around his arrest, crushing and trampling and screaming like spectators at a blood fight.

"I've always wanted to visit the East Coast," Cordelia said. "See the water there, you know?"

Sabine rolled her eyes, but indulgently. "I'm sure the ocean looks the same."

"No, I don't think so," Cordelia said. "Does it, Addie?"

"I don't know," Addie admitted. "Lupside isn't on the coast, and I never went."

"Someday, I'll go. Once I've got enough money to fly." She looked to Jackson. "Maybe I'll get Peter to send me. He flew you over to Nornand, after all."

"He flew me to Nornand to *work*," Jackson said.

Cordelia shrugged languorously. "Yes, well, I'm sure there are institutions on the East Coast. One day, however I get there, I'll go."

"Don't you want to see the . . . I don't know, the Indian Ocean instead?" Jackson asked. "Or the Adriatic?" He smiled at Cordelia's raised eyebrow. "Adriatic Sea. I saw it on one of

Henri's maps. It's in Europe. I liked the name."

Cordelia shrugged. "As if I'll ever get to leave the country."

There was a storm cloud over Devon's face that he didn't bother to hide. I could guess what was running through his mind.

<They're being awfully flippant about the whole thing> Addie said.

I remembered Jackson pulling us into the janitor's closet at Nornand, babbling about Peter and secret plans. Telling us to *keep hope*. We'd been shocked and irritated by his smiles then, his almost lackadaisical air. But he hadn't been flippant. Not truly.

I thought about the meeting we'd attended last night. The room silent with grief after Peter explained what had happened at Hahns. Christoph's barely contained anger, and how Jackson had tried to keep him in check.

Sabine and Christoph had been in Anchoit for half a decade. What about Cordelia and Jackson?

<Maybe after years and years, this is how you deal with it all> I said quietly. *<By pretending to be indifferent.>*

"When's Peter's next meeting?" Christoph sat the farthest from the standing lamp, and the fairy lights softened his features.

Sabine shrugged. "He's talking with some people one-on-one. I don't think he'll be having a general meeting anytime soon, though. Not unless something big happens."

Christoph snorted and looked up at the ceiling. "Something

big has already happened."

"And we had a meeting when it did," Sabine said. "We'll have another when—"

Christoph's voice turned rough. "When the earth slows, and the seas rise, and Peter finishes making his plans and remaking his plans and—"

"And remaking those plans," Sabine finished for him. She smiled, and he didn't quite smile back, but he quieted. Sabine's gaze flickered to Addie and me, then to Devon. "It isn't that we don't appreciate everything Peter's done. We do. We're here because his plans worked. But no one can deny that Peter's slow. Meticulous, yes. Careful, yes. And that's all good, but slow. He believes in taking his time, and sometimes—"

"Sometimes there isn't any time," Addie said.

Sabine nodded.

"That institution you mentioned at the meeting," Devon said slowly. "Powatt. How long has it been open?"

There was a hiccup of silence. Sabine shifted in her seat. "It hasn't opened yet. They're still setting things up, I think. Powatt's going to be one of the institutions spearheading the new hybrid-cure initiative. They're going to be testing some kind of—some kind of new machine that's supposed to make the surgeries more precise."

The word *surgeries* flashed us back to Nornand's basement. To the feeling of cold metal, to Jaime's voice babbling through the door, and sallow-lit hallways.

"There's this guy," Sabine said, "Hogan Nalles—he's

lower-level government. He'll be downtown next Friday at Lankster Square, going on about how proud we should be, and all that. A pep rally of sorts. Stage and balloons and a couple hundred people, most likely."

"A big, screaming crowd," Christoph said. "Cheering on the systematic, government-supported *lobotomization* of children."

Sabine grinned wryly. "I don't think lobotomization is quite the same thing. And if we don't do anything . . . if we just sit here and let Powatt open in a couple months, are we really that much better than they are?"

"Say what you mean to say, Sabine," Cordelia intoned in what was obviously supposed to be a mockery of Peter's voice. She giggled quietly into Sabine's shoulder, and the other girl wrapped an obliging arm around her.

When Sabine spoke, though, her voice was utterly serious. "We're going to stop Powatt from ever opening."

As if it were really that simple. As if by Sabine declaring it, we could make it so.

"How?" Devon said.

"I don't have a complete plan yet. I'd need more information. But I know how to get that information, and that's a start." Sabine watched Devon as she spoke, but if she was trying to read him, he gave her nothing to see. "I worked under Nalles for a few months last year, before Cordelia and I opened the shop. Pushing papers, making appointments. Things like that." Her lips twitched up at the corners. "Don't let Peter know. He's got strict rules about getting involved with government. Anyway, Nalles has access to information. He'll know the details of the Powatt plans—exactly when they'll open, when they're going to install the machinery, when the children arrive. Maybe even who the kids are."

The chances were slim to none, I knew, but I couldn't help imagining the possibility of a familiar face ending up at Powatt. What if Eli and Cal went under the knife? The doctors at Nornand had already tried so many experimental medications on them, attempting again and again to eradicate the less *desirable* soul of an eight-year-old boy. We'd seen the harmful side effects. No one had seemed to worry then. Nothing would keep them from trying surgery.

"Lankster Square is a block from the Metro Council Hall, where Nalles works. He'll have everything on his computer, and I know where his office is. I stole my old work pass, too. It'll get us past preliminary security."

"By us you mean you and me," Devon said.

Sabine considered him carefully. "I've heard you're good with computers."

Devon nodded. He was frowning, but it was concentration, not worry, that put the crease between his brows.

"You could break into his account?" Sabine asked. "Quickly?"

Devon had broken into our school system's files. That much I knew. He'd seen how late Addie and I had settled; it had been one of many signs that convinced him and Hally to reveal their secret to us.

"Maybe," he said. "Probably."

"Would you?" Sabine asked. Anyone sneaking into a government building and hacking into their computer system was taking a ridiculously enormous risk. For Devon and Ryan, it was ten times worse.

"Wait," Addie interrupted before Devon could answer. "You want him to just waltz in and break into this guy's computer right in the middle of the workday?"

"That's where the rally comes in." Sabine didn't miss a beat. "If we do this on the day of the speech, Nalles and most of his support staff will be at Lankster Square. And if we happened to cause some sort of disturbance at the rally . . . enough to distract everyone at Metro Council—"

"Like dropping a grenade right in the middle of the square?" Christoph mimed a throwing motion, and Jackson laughed, supplying the explosion sound through his teeth.

Sabine gave them a censuring look, but didn't entirely suppress her smile. "A disturbance that doesn't include death and flying limbs."

Christoph leaned back against the couch. "I wouldn't say no to some flying limbs."

"He's not serious," Jackson told us quickly.

"I'm completely serious," Christoph said.

Sabine ignored them both. "All we'd need is something no one will be able to look away from. Something that will draw attention—and security—to the Square and away from Metro Council. On the other hand, it wouldn't hurt to have it be something that'll serve as a reminder."

"A reminder of what?" Addie asked.

"Of how these institutions and this *cure* have left a body count thousands high. Tens of thousands. More." Sabine looked like a sculpture in the attic's soft lighting. I hadn't thought her a particularly beautiful girl before, but there was something striking about her now, as she spoke. "I was thinking fireworks, like on Memorial Day. This could be our own kind of memorial. A reminder."

A way of paying respects.

By now, the tenor of the attic had transformed. Sabine had changed it with a sentence. An idea. A hope.

"Addie can draw," Jackson said suddenly. Addie looked at him in surprise, and he rushed to elaborate. "If we want it to be like a reminder, we could make posters, you know? Include the names and faces of some of the children who have died."

"Good idea." Sabine's bangs, cut bluntly above her eyebrows, only brought more attention to the unwavering nature of her stare. I found myself both slightly unnerved and utterly unable to look away—as if I were being sized up and couldn't, *couldn't*, be found wanting. "We'd have to find deserted places to set off the fireworks, of course. There are a couple buildings in the area where you can get access to the roof. We could toss the posters down from there; rain them on the crowd. We'd have to figure out the specifics, but no one would get hurt."

What are the chances we get caught? I wanted to ask, but Addie was still in control, and Addie's emotions were too tangled now to let her speak.

"Flyers and fireworks," Christoph said, like he was musing over the idea and found it sort of funny.

Sabine nodded. She looked toward Devon. "But in the end, it all hinges on whether you're able to get that information from Nalles's computer."

Devon was quiet. His expression stayed utterly impassive, his body still. Then he said, "I can do that."

Sabine's shoulders relaxed, just a little. She looked around the room at the rest of us. "So? What do you say?"

"*I'm* in," Cordelia said.

Jackson wore that match-strike smile of his. "Same."

Despite his earlier exasperation, Christoph was quick to nod, too.

<Addie?> I said.

She hesitated. *<I don't know.>*

<It would send a message> I said tentatively. *<It would tell everyone that the hybrids in this country aren't just going to let them treat us however they want. And—and it could mean Powatt never opens.>*

I was so tired of just sitting around. I was tired of being cooped up in our apartment building, going up the stairs and down the stairs but getting nowhere.

<Addie—>

<I don't know, Eva.> Her voice sharpened. I felt her confusion rising, her frustration at her own inability to decide. *<You choose. You've always wanted to choose, haven't you?>*

She ripped away from our body's reins. Control fell to me like a great weight, nearly suffocating in its pressure.

She was right. I'd dreamed so long about being in control. Now that I could be, I had to start making my own decisions, not relying on Addie. Not relying on anyone.

I exhaled and spoke quickly. Before I could think too much about it. Before I could talk myself out of it.

"I'm ready to start doing something."

NINE

Despite her claims otherwise, Sabine had obviously already given this part of her plan a lot of thought. The attic transformed from clubhouse to situation room as she briefed us on everything. In exactly ten days, Hogan Nalles would give a speech in Lankster Square downtown. Nearby traffic would be rerouted. There would be security, obviously, but the specifics were still unknown. The speech was planned to last about twenty minutes, the entire event roughly an hour.

"There are six of us," Sabine said, gesturing as she spoke. "Devon and I will be in the building. Preferably, I'd like to have at least one person at the rally—at the scene or looking right at it—and reporting to us on walkie-talkie. We'd want to know exactly what's going on. That leaves three of you to set off firecrackers."

<If Hally helped . . . > I started to say, then cut myself off. Would it be better to leave Hally and Lissa out of this? Maybe they wouldn't want to be involved. But I didn't want to keep secrets from them, either. It would be better, wouldn't it,

to let them decide themselves if they wanted to help or not?

"If Hally joined us," I said, "then we could do four."

Devon looked at us sharply, but said nothing.

Sabine hesitated. "You think she'd be up for it?"

"Maybe," Devon said before I could answer. The word held such an air of finality that no one touched the subject again.

"What we're doing," I said carefully, "won't it just make security even tighter at the Hall?"

Sabine shook her head. "Everyone important will be at the rally. Even if they get vigilant in the Hall, they'll be looking for possible violence or a demonstration or something. Trust me. It'll be fine. I know my way around the building."

It was almost four a.m. by the time we left the photography shop. Over the course of the night, Addie spoke with both Josie and Sabine, Jackson and Vince. Cordelia mentioned Katy, though if Katy actually took control at any point, no one noted it. But all night, no one said anything about the other boy looking through Christoph's eyes. I wondered when we'd get to meet him. I found myself looking forward to it.

Devon gave us a quiet *good night* when we returned to our apartment, then headed upstairs. I eased Emalia's door open as softly as I could.

The apartment was as still and silent as when we'd left hours before. I crossed the darkened living room, crept through the hall, and slipped into our bedroom. Kitty was a slumbering shadow tucked into her sheets. We exchanged our clothes for pajamas and slid into bed, our cheek pressed against the cold pillow.

Only then did the implications of what I'd agreed to hit me. Hard. I took a deep breath, and Addie must have sensed my sudden trepidation. She reached for me. Held me steady.

Did I choose right? I almost asked, but didn't. In the end, I didn't need to. Addie told me, without saying a word, that whatever I chose, we were in it together.

We fell asleep whispering about plans for the future. We hadn't had any, before.

Addie and I slept in the next morning, waking only when a knock came at the front door. We went to answer it in our secondhand pajamas, our hair a sleep-tangled mess of half curls. She yawned and looked through the peephole, probably expecting Hally or Ryan, like I was.

<God, we look a mess> Addie said when we recognized Jackson.

I wasn't a slob, but Addie had always been the one who liked our clothes pressed, our hair neat, who made sure our room was tidy. She could be forgetful, might misplace things from time to time, but Addie had always wanted things orderly.

<Tell Kitty to get the door while we change> I suggested.

<Then he'd think we were making a fuss about it. It would—> She sighed. *<Never mind. It's not a big deal.>*

She fumbled with the lock with one hand and tried to

tame our hair with the other, then quickly lowered our hand as she opened the door.

"Hey," she said.

Jackson studied us a moment. *Stop it,* I wanted to tell him. *Can't you see you're making Addie more embarrassed?* But he didn't look away, just smiled. "Late morning?"

Addie waved him inside. I could feel her *want* to say something, but no words came to our lips. We flushed. Jackson glanced around the room. "Where are Kitty and Emalia?"

"Kitty's in our room," Addie said. "Emalia's at Peter's."

"Ah," Jackson said.

"A*h*, what?"

He laughed and plunked down in one of the dining chairs. "Nothing. It's good that she's out. I came to see how you were. You know, after last night."

Addie lowered us into a chair as well. "We didn't change our minds, if that's what you mean."

"I don't remember getting an answer from you, actually," Jackson said. "Eva said she was ready to start doing something. But what about you?"

"I didn't know we had to speak separately."

Jackson's pale blue eyes never left ours, even for a second. They lent everything he said—despite the artlessness in his movements and the jaunt in his grin—a certain intensity. "I like to hear what you have to say."

Addie was quiet, picking at our pajama pants.

<Addie?>

"I'm in," she said.

Jackson leaned toward us, and Addie didn't back away. I felt the tension in our muscles, the strain it took to keep our position. He was pushing on too close—too close for Addie to take. "Good. What about Devon's sister? Hally? Do you think she's going to be okay with this?"

Addie nodded.

"Did you guys know each other a long time before Nornand?" Jackson asked. "You, Devon, and Hally?"

"Not a very long time," Addie said. She shrugged. "A month or so."

I waited for her to explain how she wasn't even there for most of it, or how Devon wasn't exactly the easiest person to get to know under any circumstances, for any length of time. But she didn't.

"Who's the other boy sharing Christoph's body?" she said instead. Jackson stiffened, but Addie pressed onward. "I'm trying to get to know everyone so I can tell who's who and when, but I don't even know his name, and—"

"It's always Christoph," Jackson said.

Addie paused. "Sorry?"

"It's always Christoph," Jackson repeated. His voice went toneless. "You don't need to figure anything out."

The words pierced our skin, injected ice water into our veins. We flashed cold, then hot. "You mean—but Jaime—"

But Jaime's the only one who survived that sort of surgery.

Jackson's eyes widened with realization. "No, that's not

what I meant. It's not like that. His name is Mason. But none of us have ever spoken with him or seen him take control. Sabine says . . . Sabine says that by the time she got to know Christoph at their institution, Mason had already gone silent. Anyway—" He hesitated. "Look, we all react to hell differently. Mason—maybe he still speaks to Christoph, but he gave up communicating with anyone else."

Addie swallowed. Nodded.

"Anyway." Jackson seemed to be trying to smile. "You're doing well."

"What do you mean?"

"Post-Nornand." His smile was genuine now. "I don't know what you were like before going in, but back in the hospital, you seemed—well, I don't know. Different. Different than now."

Addie surprised me with a quiet laugh. She rarely laughed in front of people unless she was completely comfortable. "You know, I hated you, when I first saw you. I'd just arrived at Nornand. You had a package for Mr. Conivent or something, and you kept staring at me, and I—"

I remembered, too. I'd thought Jackson's eyes looked like a doll's, so light blue they were almost clear.

"I thought you figured I was some kind of circus freak," Addie said. She laughed again, louder this time. "Turns out we're the same kind of freak."

Jackson grinned, raising an imaginary glass. "To freaks, then."

TEN

Jackson stayed a little longer to chat, but he was supposed to meet with Christoph for lunch. He left with a smile and a *You're sure you don't want to come?* It was tempting. Leaving the apartment so many times these past two days hadn't dampened our yearning for fresh air. If anything, it had made it worse. But Emalia was with Peter, not at work. She might return home any moment, and we couldn't be found missing. So Jackson left alone.

Addie was quiet long after he'd gone, moving slowly as we showered and got dressed. The steam from the hot water made us sleepy again, cloudy-headed.

We'd just left the bathroom when Addie said *<I want to try it, Eva. Going under.>*

Shock rippled through me. *<Now?>*

<Yes.>

I tried to quash my excitement—or at least hide it from Addie. I didn't dare ask what had finally changed her mind. Maybe meeting with Sabine and the others had affected her like it had affected me. Maybe she was finally ready to move on, to pursue a new kind of normal.

<Are you sure?>

Addie pushed our pillow against the headboard and leaned against it. Our damp hair clung to our neck. A breath shuddered through our lungs.

<I'm sure.> But her voice was quiet, hesitant. Frightened, I realized, and I almost said: *No, no, don't do it, Addie. Don't do it if you're frightened.* The last thing I wanted was for Addie to be frightened. Our teeth rasped against our bottom lip. When she spoke again, her words were stronger. *<Do you remember how you did it? When we were thirteen?>*

When we were thirteen? I'd been so angry then—I hadn't even known what I was doing. I'd just wanted to be anywhere but where I was. Lyle's sickness had started that year. Addie and I had fought, and in that moment, everything had been too much to bear. I'd willed myself to feel nothing at all, to disconnect from the world and dissolve like morning mist in sunlight.

Addie let me take control of our body as I tried my best to explain. Our chest quivered with my attempt at steady breathing.

It probably won't even happen, I thought, trying to calm myself.

Which was fine. Addie had agreed to try, and that was the important thing. We wouldn't achieve anything this go-around, but Addie had agreed to try, so there would be other chances, and sooner or later, she'd—

There was a feeling like a balloon popping inside us.

Then Addie was gone.

I did not shout her name.

That was the reaction I'd come to expect, and the one I'd steeled myself against: the urge to cry out. Then the urge to reach for her, to clamber toward that abyss where Addie should have been and stare over its edge, scrabbling for her in the darkness.

I was propelled back to all those after-school sessions at the Mullans' house, learning to move again as Addie floated in a Refcon-induced sleep. Refcon was a drug that suppressed the stronger soul. Hally had stolen some from her mother's hospital, and Addie drank it to give me a chance to regain my strength.

But this was different. Addie was gone by her own volition, without the aid of drugs, of *medication*, of any kind.

The first blink was followed by the first breath. Then the second. The third.

Addie was gone, and I was still here, sitting on the bed.

Alone.

The word echoed through the empty chambers of my mind.

Nobody but I knew.

I curled our fingers into a fist, harder and harder until our nails bit a painful line across the center of our palm. Then

I studied the stair-step pattern of red crescent moons etched into our skin.

The silence in the room—in our head—was enormous. It seemed at once a great, untouchable emptiness and some stifling, half-living thing that might, at any moment, break down the door hiding me from the rest of the world.

I stood. Our legs held. Of course they held. I'd been walking fine for weeks. But the steps I took now seemed no less momentous.

I took fourteen steps, just weaving around the room.

Emalia's spare bedroom wasn't large, and furniture ate up most of the floor space. In addition to the two beds, there were two matching nightstands—with two mismatching lamps—and a medium-sized dresser we shared with Kitty. Atop the dresser was the prettiest thing in the room, a large, rectangular mirror with an ornate wooden frame.

I stood before it. The shadowy girl in the glass stared back at me. The same girl who'd stared back at me my entire life. I reached up, touching my face.

Was it my face now, when Addie wasn't here?

The girl in the mirror frowned.

I returned to the bed, suddenly finding it difficult to breathe. The world seemed too big, and yet too small.

This was what being alone felt like.

This was how Mom, Dad, Lyle—all the other girls at school, our teachers, the people on the street—this was how they spent every second of their lives. This was the silence and loneliness in their heads, the echo of their thoughts.

It had felt different when I was immobile. I'd still been partially trapped, then. But now . . . I could do anything. I could do anything, and no one but me would ever have to know.

A little more than five minutes later, Addie was back.

I held her, tight, as she reemerged to the waking world.

<*What was it like?*> I asked.

Addie stared blankly at the television screen. Kitty had called us out to watch a movie, and we'd joined her, but neither Addie nor I could concentrate.

<*Like dreaming*> Addie said. <*But deeper. I can't explain it. It's . . . it's a bit like being under Refcon, but without the lingering effects.*> Refcon had always taken a few minutes to wear off, even after Addie woke, leaving her woozy and unsteady on our feet.

Back in Lupside, Addie had asked Hally about other potential side effects. There hadn't been anything very serious, which meant it beat the other drugs Addie and I had taken as a kid, all in attempts to get us to settle.

Still, Hally had whispered an apology one afternoon. *For not telling you*, she said. *I just—I still wasn't sure if you would do it. And I thought, if Eva just got one chance to know what it could be like to be free, she . . .*

Addie had just looked away, and nodded. They hadn't been friends then. They hadn't had reason to be.

Funny, how things changed.

Addie absentmindedly touched Kitty's hair. A key rattled in the lock, and our fingers stilled.

"Hey," Sophie said cheerfully, throwing open the front door. "Have you girls eaten yet?"

"Not yet." Kitty smiled and seemed to lose all interest in the movie. "Can you bring us something from that last place?"

"Which place is that?" Sophie hung up her purse and slid out of her heels, laying them neatly on the shoe rack. "There's a meeting in a few minutes, so I can't go too far."

"There's a meeting with Peter?" Addie jumped up and followed Sophie into the kitchen. It was Saturday, so Sophie couldn't mean anything for work. "Why now?"

Sophie shrugged and pulled a box of crackers from the cabinet. "Rebecca had something to do later, and—"

"Dr. Lyanne's coming?" Addie said. "Is she bringing Jaime?"

"I don't think so." Sophie's eyes scrutinized us. Again that look like she was afraid we might break. Emalia wore it more often, but Sophie wasn't immune to over-worrying about us. "I wouldn't think she'd want to bring him into the city, now that—well, you know."

"Is she at Peter's apartment already?"

"Actually, we're meeting at Henri's."

Addie didn't bother hiding our relief. If the meeting had been at Peter's, we'd have to fight Sophie about leaving the building, and I was almost positive she wouldn't have yielded. "When's it start?"

"In about ten minutes," Sophie said, but rushed to add, "Addie, it's not a general meeting. You're—"

"I just want to talk to her." We were already halfway to the hall.

"Wait and go up with me," Sophie called after us. "She might not even be there yet."

"She'll be there," Addie said. "She likes to be early."

Sophie smiled weakly. For a moment, the worry faded from her face, replaced by some emotion I couldn't name. "You talk like you know her well."

I thought about Dr. Lyanne watching Jaime pass in the gurney. Her soothing him in the darkness. Telling us the code to the basement doors. Showing up in the Ward holding Kitty's hand. Out with us on the fire escape at Peter's apartment, watching the cars below.

"Well enough," Addie said.

Addie was almost right. Dr. Lyanne wasn't at Henri's apartment yet, but we'd only gone up a flight of stairs when we heard the rapid click of heels echoing below us. It was ridiculous to say we recognized Dr. Lyanne by the sound of her footsteps, but instinct made us pause in the stairwell.

Little by little, she came into view. Her ash-brown hair was longer now than it had been at Nornand. It might have been the humidity in Anchoit, but her hair seemed a little less straight, as well. She wore it coiled over her shoulder, strands floating around her face.

She'd grown thinner. The delicate planes of her face were sharper, her limbs birdlike. We'd learned that she was a couple years younger than Peter, so she could have only been twenty-eight or twenty-nine at most, but she looked so much older as she came up those stairs.

Dr. Lyanne had played a hand in helping us escape from Nornand—had tried, in fact, to rescue all the kids there. For that, she'd given up nearly everything. Emalia managed to rustle up enough falsified documents to get her a job at a clinic, but I got the impression that it was basic work, something Dr. Lyanne was immensely overqualified for.

Maybe she enjoyed it, though.

Maybe she didn't. Maybe she regretted everything.

"Hi," Addie murmured.

Dr. Lyanne's head whipped up. For a moment, she didn't reply, just studied us as we'd studied her. Had we changed, too, in the past weeks? Or was she comparing us to an even earlier version of ourself? The girl who had arrived at Nornand in a shiny, black car, dressed in a school uniform and her parents' last hugs and the tattered remnants of her naïvety?

"Hi," Dr. Lyanne said. She closed the remaining distance between us. "Where are you going?"

Dr. Lyanne was not a comfortable-looking woman. She was all angles. She hardly ever smiled. She and Emalia had never gotten along, though Dr. Lyanne had stayed with her for a little while before finding her own place. Still, there was something *I* found comfortable about her. Maybe it was what Addie had told Emalia—we knew Rebecca Lyanne. We'd seen her when she sat shattered apart at Nornand, when her world lay in pieces and she had to choose how to put it back together. We'd watched her make the decision that brought her here, liaised with a hybrid resistance led by her brother.

There's a connection that's made when someone sees you at your lowest. But connection or not, Dr. Lyanne had told us the government would bury Nornand, and Jenson had done anything but bury it in his speech.

Our voice was a whisper. "You were wrong. About Nornand."

The warning in Dr. Lyanne's eyes read loud and clear. She moved past us. "We're not talking about this in the stairwell."

"You said they were going to bury it," Addie hissed, following on her heels. "You said they thought it was a complete failure!"

"I got it wrong. It happens."

"It *happens*?"

Upstairs, someone slammed a door, and we both flinched. Shouting drifted down, angry voices lifted in some unknown argument. Dr. Lyanne gave us a pointed look.

"Is he safe?" Addie didn't need to specify who. This, finally, stopped Dr. Lyanne's ascent. For a moment, the stairwell was silent again.

She looked down at us over her shoulder. "As safe as I can make him."

Did we trust her? She'd failed before. She'd let Jaime down. She might again.

It would be too cruel to point this out. But perhaps cruelty could be excused in a situation like this? Perhaps when something was so crucial, it was okay to be ruthless. The government would stop at nothing to get Jaime back. There had never been another person like him: a hybrid surgically stripped of his second soul. A thirteen-year-old boy who'd had doctors slice into his brain and rearrange it to their own liking.

But in the end, we weren't that heartless.

"Is he all right?" Addie said.

In the weeks between our escape from Nornand and his moving away, Jaime had gotten better in some ways and worse in others. On good days, he'd watched television with Kitty, helped us make sandwiches, and laughed like laughter was a language itself—one he hadn't lost. On bad days, he'd grown so frustrated with his inability to say what he wanted to that he'd flown apart in rages. On the worst days, he acted like the rest of us weren't even there. He wouldn't look at us, wouldn't try to speak, wouldn't even move.

He'll get better, Addie and I used to tell each other. *Today's just a bad day, and it wasn't as bad as the last bad day. Tomorrow will be better.*

We hadn't even wanted to consider the alternative . . . that Jaime might get worse. That whatever those doctors at Nornand had done, the full extent of the damage hadn't yet made itself known, and Jaime would continue deteriorating.

"He misses you and the others," Dr. Lyanne said. "But yes, he's doing well, overall."

I wished we could hear a response from Jaime's own lips.

So much had been stolen from him already. I didn't want anyone to forget that he was a person, that he was more than the victim of a horrific surgery, more than the first survivor of the supposed cure. More than a liability and a thing to be protected.

For years, I'd been reduced to the Recessive Soul, the worst half of the Girls Who Just Won't Settle. I knew what it was like to exist only as a label. And I knew what it was like to be voiceless.

Addie and Dr. Lyanne started up the stairs again. We'd almost reached Henri's door when Addie asked one last question. "This meeting—you'd tell us, wouldn't you, if they're trying to hide anything?"

Dr. Lyanne frowned. "Who's *they?*"

"Peter," Addie said.

"Why would Peter hide anything from you?"

It wasn't that we thought Peter *maliciously* kept things from us. It was more that he only told us what he thought we needed to know, and as far as Peter was concerned, we didn't need to know much. He hadn't said anything about Nalles's speech at Lankster Square, and he was sure to know about something like that.

What else had Peter withheld from us?

Dr. Lyanne sighed. "Peter isn't hiding anything. There are things that are best discussed by as few people as possible, or—"

"Like what?"

"—or everyone will butt in with an opinion, and nothing will ever get decided."

"How do you know if you've heard all the important opinions unless you hear them all?" Addie demanded. "Peter doesn't tell us everything. I know he doesn't. Maybe he can't. Okay. I understand. But anything—anything really important. Anything big that affects us or Jai—that affects us—you'd let us know, right?"

Dr. Lyanne looked at us for a moment, her hazel eyes steady on ours. Then she bent down a little so we were the same height. She said, quietly, "We're discussing plans to keep you kids safe. We're talking a little about the Powatt institution. That's all. No secrets, Addie." She pulled away. "All right?"

Addie hesitated, but she nodded.

ELEVEN

Somehow, without Addie and I really discussing it, it fell to me to tell Hally and Lissa about Sabine's plan. We didn't have to wait long for an opportunity. Soon after Emalia left for Henri's apartment, Ryan and Hally came downstairs.

"We were kicked out," Hally said, raising her eyebrows.

I was too busy sneaking glances at Ryan to immediately reply. He must have read the message in our eyes, because he gave a small nod.

"We've got something to tell you, Hally," I said, and she laughed like she thought it might be some happy secret. As if we still had things like happy secrets.

"Well, what is it?" Hally said once I'd shut the bedroom door behind us. Her smile turned a little more hesitant but at least it was still there. If it had been Lissa in control, the smile would have disappeared completely.

I looked to Ryan, and he looked to me, so I took a deep breath and explained everything.

Hally wasn't happy about it. Kitty was in the living room, so she couldn't make a fuss, but the look on her face said enough.

"Are you in?" Ryan asked. The television helped mask our voices, and he spoke just loudly enough to be understood.

Hally opened her mouth, then shut it again. She shook her head, forming each word slowly. "You're really considering this?"

"Yes," Ryan said.

"Because just what we need right now," Hally snapped, "is for one of us—or *all* of us—to get caught again."

I said nothing. The Mullan siblings didn't fight often, at least not with any kind of real heat, but being cooped up with the same group of people for more than a month will grind anyone's nerves. Addie and I quickly learned to stay out of things.

But I couldn't help wondering: Two months ago, would Hally have hesitated about this plan? She'd been the incautious one, the one who'd persuaded her brothers to reach out to Addie. Was this part of what Nornand had stolen from her? Her zeal? Her wholehearted enthusiasm? Her lack of fear?

"Hally," Ryan said quietly. "What are the chances, *really*, of someone recognizing one of us in the streets? We're a thousand miles from Nornand, even farther from Lupside. Do you really think, out of every city, they're going to figure out we're in this one?"

Hally glared at him. "They might if you start causing chaos at government-sponsored events. We're not six anymore, Ryan. These aren't war games in the backyard. The others—they're sending *you* where it's most dangerous. If anything happens . . .

if you get trapped in that building . . ."

"Remember why we used to play those games?" Ryan asked. Hally looked away, then back to meet her brother's eyes. For a moment, they were caught in some shared memory. "We wanted to be able to do something someday. Change something." His voice held a quiet intensity, a lightning storm wrapped in a blanket. "Back at Nornand, when they took you . . . when they said they were going to cut your head open—I couldn't do anything, Hally. I couldn't do anything then, but I can now, and I will. I have to."

The television filled in our silence. Addie's held breath was my held breath.

"Okay," Hally whispered finally. "Okay."

Once again, we snuck out after dark. The others met us on the street, then led us to the photography shop. I made sure to memorize the route this time, reading the street names as we passed.

Everyone quickly folded Hally and Lissa into the group, and Hally, true to form, managed a grin for everyone in return. But I caught the lapses in her smiles. The moments of apprehension, even fear.

"First things first," Josie said once we were all situated in the attic. The fairy lights caught the gleam in her hair.

Just as I'd tried to map our route, I tried to map the differences between Sabine and Josie. Josie moved differently. Quicker. Sharper. If Sabine glided like a dancer, Josie duck and wove like a bird. Sabine's smiles were a slow warmth, steady embers. Josie's were flashes in a pan. She and Vince got along well, I could tell.

"If we're going to do this," Josie said, "we can't keep meeting in the middle of the night. Curfew means no one's on the streets after midnight without a special permit. With everything else we'll be up to, it's not worth the risk. Do you think you'd be able to make it if we met in the evenings? Or late afternoon, anyway."

Ryan nodded. "Henri's already used to Hally and me spending a lot of time at Emalia's. He never comes to check. And Emalia's at work all day."

"What about Kitty and Nina?" I said.

He hesitated. "You could tell them. Say you need to go out, meet a few people. Make them promise not to say anything to Emalia. They'd listen to you, Eva."

<They probably would> Addie said.

<Not probably.> I was positive that if Addie and I asked Kitty and Nina to keep something secret, they would. They trusted us that much.

Did this count as a breach of that trust? I wasn't sure.

As we found out the following week, convincing Kitty to keep mum about our leaving the apartment was almost too easy. She was quiet as I explained how Addie and I, along with Ryan and Hally, planned to meet up with Sabine and her friends. How we were trying to make plans, trying to help, but it had to be a secret. Okay?

She nodded. "Okay." Anxiety must have clouded our face, because she smiled a little and said, "I get it, Eva. It's fine.

You're trying to help people like Sallie and Val."

"Yes," I whispered.

Soon we were going to the attic nearly every afternoon. It wasn't a long walk, but Addie and I never breathed easily during it. It got even worse once the posters went up for the speech at Lankster Square. We passed two just getting from our apartment to the photography shop—both bright yellow and blue, with a bold, black font.

Addie ducked our head every time we had to pass one. When I was in control, I wanted to avert our eyes, too, but I couldn't. The posters drew my attention like a car crash. But most people's eyes glazed right over them. Only a few stopped to read.

One day, one man—young, twenties—walked by, hands in his pockets. As he passed the poster, he reached out and tore it down.

I was so startled I stopped in my tracks. The man looked around. Our eyes met. He looked uncomfortable a minute, then tilted his chin up with something like defiance and disappeared around a corner, the poster now lying crumpled in a ball by the gutter. I never saw him again.

The next day, another poster had gone up in the exact same spot.

But I remembered the young man. And the defiance.

And I thought, maybe—maybe Anchoit wasn't all bad. Perhaps some of the people might, with a little push—a little encouragement—understand our point of view. Right now, our main goal was to stop the Powatt institution from ever opening. But we couldn't stop there, could we? One day, all the institutions needed to close. If change was going to happen in the Americas, it might begin somewhere like Anchoit. It might begin with a spark.

Cloistered up in the attic, we learned how to build homemade firecrackers. Although some Anchoit stores sold handheld sparklers and things like that, fireworks were banned. But it didn't matter, because as it turned out, making firecrackers didn't require more than Ping-Pong balls, black powder, duct tape, and some fuse. Sabine and Jackson gathered everything. No one asked how.

Katy chattered away as she showed us how to pack the powder in the Ping-Pong balls, then wrap them with duct tape. I'd quickly learned to recognize Katy by her magpie-like distractibility. The difference between her and Cordelia was so obvious I couldn't believe none of their customers ever noticed how unalike the two girls acted, how uniquely they inhabited their shared body. Cordelia hummed with energy; Katy floated through the store, their pale hair trailing behind like spun sugar.

"My brothers used to make firecrackers out of gunpowder and paper tubes," she explained. "We lived on a farm in the middle of nowhere, and they liked to set them off when they got bored. Pissed off my parents like nothing else."

"Didn't one of your brothers almost blow his hand off one time?" Jackson said.

"I thought that was the end plan." Katy pointed her foot at

Christoph. "Wasn't he going on about flying limbs and all?"

"I think Christoph, like the rest of us, would prefer to keep all his limbs intact," Sabine said. But she smiled easily. Everyone did, even Hally, who had quickly warmed up to the group. How could she not? Hally, who had been so desperate for a friend, she'd risked everything just to reach out to Addie and me.

Up in that attic, lit by afternoon sun and fairy lights, we talked about time frames. About transportation. Who would be where and when, and what they'd be doing. We studied road maps of downtown, especially the area around Lankster Square. We talked through things that might go wrong: being stopped by security, a malfunctioning firecracker, a loss of contact with the others, being spotted. Sabine told us as much as she could about routine inside the Metro Council Hall.

But before and after and in the middle of all that, we heard stories about Jackson's various day jobs. We learned bits and pieces of Christoph's past. Cordelia and Katy impersonated their more ridiculous clients, making us giggle until we couldn't breathe, until our stomach hurt and our eyes blurred and the attic walls reverberated with our laughter.

When Addie and I weren't at the attic, we were learning more about our own abilities to go under. To remove ourselves temporarily from the world.

I disappeared for the second time in my life on a warm Sunday morning. I'd thought this would be easier for Addie. That my disappearing would be less frightening, surely, than her having to do it herself. But I felt her terror, so strong it was almost a physical thing tying me in place, so I knew it wasn't true.

<*Ready?*> I whispered, as much to myself as to Addie.

She nodded. She turned toward the mirror as if she wanted to catch the instant I faded away. As if it might show up in our reflection.

Slowly, I shrank into myself, folding myself smaller and smaller in the nebulas of our mind. What would ten-year-old me think if she knew what I was doing? She'd clutched on so fiercely. She'd just wanted to live. To have a chance.

I couldn't think about that now. I couldn't think about anything. I focused on untying myself, on letting go, like a boat's sail finally ripped free of its mast.

Addie hadn't closed our eyes, so I couldn't, either. But the girl in the mirror wasn't me. I murmured this mantra to myself as I loosened the threads binding me to our limbs, our fingers, our toes.

The girl in the mirror wasn't me.

Blond hair. Brown eyes. Freckles. The swoop of a collarbone, the curve of an arm.

The girl in the mirror wasn't me.

The world reduced to our breathing, then our heartbeat. Then even that disappeared.

Addie reached for me, as if on instinct. *Come back!* I thought I heard her cry, the instant before it happened.

Her voice.

Come back!

I plunged and was gone.

Nathaniel
At three
Five jam-sticky fingers
And a jam-sticky mouth
A grin. My name on his tongue
Eva, look.

The apartment where I grew up
The fort beneath the table
Flashlights after dark

The park, where I climbed the tree
And fell
The lake
Where we went camping
Before Lyle and Nathaniel were born
When it was just Addie
And me
And Dad
And Mom
Soft breathing in the tent
The warmth between their bodies
The *swish* of our fingernail against
the sleeping bag

Eva.

The scrape of our fingernail against a coverlet.

<Eva?>

I woke.

Before sight, before sound, before smell or speech or feeling—was Addie.

Then came the first thought, as the world inked itself back into existence around me:

<I'm back. I came back.>

We were still sitting on the bed, our knees drawn against our chest, our fingernails digging into the blue-and-white patterned coverlet.

Addie stared at the girl in the mirror, who stared back. I struggled to reorient myself. Everything felt at once too sharp, too real, and not real enough. I hurt with the memory of—of what?

I wasn't sure. There had been so many memories, memories mixed in with dreams—truth swirled together with lies and hopes and fantasy.

Nathaniel. I'd dreamed about Nathaniel. For a second, his face floated back to me, how he and Lyle had looked as a baby. Addie and I had been four years old when he was born. We'd stood on tiptoe to stare down at him in his cradle, his hair so light and fine it looked like he didn't have any hair at all.

<How long—>

<Twelve minutes.> Addie's voice was steady, but I felt the force of will it took to keep it that way.

Twelve minutes. Twelve minutes of my life excised. In a way, it was no different from sleeping at night or taking a nap during the day. But I wondered if I could think the same once I started going under for hours at a time.

<Did you—>

<I just stayed here.> Addie plucked at the coverlet. *<What did you dream about?>*

<Nathaniel.> The image of him was fading. He was just a blurry face now, a baby that could be any baby. *<I think. It—it's hard to remember.>*

<It always is> Addie murmured. *<Once you wake up.>*

<Are you okay?> I remembered my first time alone after Hally and Devon had drugged us. I remembered how Addie had been at thirteen, after *her* first time alone, her fear burning in the back of our throat.

Addie shifted, leaning back against the headboard. The wood was cool against our shoulders. *<Yeah. I'm okay.>*

I'd had a month to get accustomed to being the sole occupant of our body. But this was Addie's first taste of it in nearly three years.

Funny, how *I* was more experienced than Addie at something. Me. The recessive soul.

<*You're sure?*> I said.

<*I'm sure. I'll—I'll get used to it.*>

Despite her words, Addie had more trouble than I did, both with dealing with my disappearances and with going under herself. Sometimes, instead of properly fading away, she slipped in and out of consciousness, jerking to and from the space next to me with such a dizzying tug and pull that I felt seasick. Sometimes, we sat there for half an hour and nothing happened at all.

But when I least expected it, I'd feel that lurch that meant she'd gone. The sudden emptiness, like a part of the world had dropped away. And it would stay like that.

The third time it happened, I sat very still, as I had both times before. Again, I was hyperaware of everything. Every breath. The brush of our clothes on our skin. A wisp of hair against our cheek.

I wrinkled our nose. My nose, for the moment.

The last few practices had lowered my hopes for this one, and Addie's sudden success left me blindsided.

Suddenly, I had the uncontrollable itch to move. I couldn't sit here another second—I jumped to my feet. Paced the room. The bedroom door was shut, as usual. The faint noise of Nina's television program filtered in; she never turned it up very loud.

I stared at the door.

I crossed over, twisted the doorknob, and swung the door open. I'd never left our bedroom before—not alone in my skin.

Nina sat curled up on the couch, picking at the bowl of

chocolate candies Emalia left on the coffee table. A small pile of bright foil wrappers lay at her feet. She glanced up as I passed, giving me a quick smile. I smiled back. She turned back to her TV show. No questions. No comment. No suspicions.

No idea. She had no idea.

Why should she?

The thought made me a little sick with the wrongness of it. Here I was, without Addie, and no one *knew.* How could no one know? How could it not be stamped on my forehead? Shining from my eyes?

I had the sudden urge to eat one of Emalia's chocolates. See if it still tasted the same with Addie gone. Was sugar as sweet? Sweeter? But I made myself continue onward, toward the front door. With every step, a new feeling started to overwhelm the initial *wrongness*, the initial sickness in my stomach. A new, dizzy, giddy feeling—like being on the crest of a wave, staring at the fast-approaching shore. It swept me out into the hall, made me run up the stairs so fast I stumbled.

I pounded on Henri's door. It swung open. I didn't react fast enough. Ryan caught my wrist before I accidentally hit him in the chest.

"Eva?" he said.

I reached up and kissed him. Crushed my mouth to his. I pulled my wrist toward me and his hand with it. He threw out his other hand to steady himself on the doorframe. My heart pounded so hard I couldn't hear anything else. I forgot where we were, who we were. I forgot if my feet were on the ground. I felt nothing but his lips eager against mine and his fingers through my hair, against the nape of my neck. He released my wrist. Slid his hand up my arm, pushing at my sleeve. He pulled me closer, his back against the doorframe, supporting both of us.

I had to pause for breath, and in that beat of space, Ryan managed to say, "What about Addie?"

"Gone," I said. "Devon?"

He laughed softly in the back of his throat. "Gone."

So I kissed him again. Because I wanted to. And I could. The giddiness was back, stronger. I laughed, and Ryan eased away, looking down at me.

"What?" He was smiling.

But so many weeks of waiting, of wanting, of thinking and hoping and daydreaming were catching up to me. Then he was laughing, too, shaking his head, the edge of his hand pressing against his forehead. A woman coming down the hallway gave us a nonplussed look, which only set us off harder.

I loved this. Laughing. Smiling. Kissing Ryan.

In that moment, I believed if I could spend the rest of my life laughing, smiling, and kissing Ryan, things would be just fine.

Addie slipped back into consciousness just in time to feel me slide to the ground, laughing so hard I could barely breathe.

TWELVE

I was standing with Nina in the kitchen that night, both of us staring into the refrigerator, when the doorbell rang. Nina hung back as I checked the peephole.

<Peter?> Addie said. *<What's he doing here?>*

The man offered us a slight smile when I let him in, his feet not moving from the welcome mat. Summer nights in Anchoit could be windy and cold, but Emalia's apartment was always warm. Still, Peter didn't bother shrugging out of his jacket.

"Is Emalia around?" he asked.

"No." Nina lingered by the shoe rack, a barefoot little girl next to Emalia's rows of stiletto heels and jewel-toned flats. "We thought she'd be with you."

It had been a while since Addie and I had seen Peter alone like this, just a man in a room, not a man trying to lead a room. He wore a slightly ill-fitting shirt, his sleeves rolled up and his tie loose. He straightened it as he spoke.

"We have plans, but I was supposed to meet up with her

here first. She probably got held up at work."

I took another step back, hoping Peter would get the hint that he didn't need to stay standing by the door. He took a few steps off the welcome mat.

"What about you two? What're you doing for dinner?"

"We've got it handled," I said.

He nodded, his gaze drifting to one of Ryan's inventions on the dining table. He'd been like this when we stayed with him, too. Absent. Not always, of course. Peter could be very, very present in a room. He could fill it up to the brim, the way he did at meetings, drawing every eye to him, grabbing every ear with his words. But when there weren't people around to direct and sway, weren't problems to solve and plans to make, he withdrew into his mind.

We hadn't even learned his second name until Jackson told us: Warren. Warren and Peter Dagnand, because they had used a fake last name since they escaped from their own institutionalized hell so many years ago.

What Jackson hadn't told us was how to differentiate between Peter and Warren. Everyone always addressed him as Peter at the meetings, and he'd never corrected Addie or me when we called him Peter. In fact, I couldn't remember anyone ever saying *Warren* at all.

Maybe Warren was the quieter, more reserved man in front of me now, while Peter was the leader? There was no way to know for sure, not when I had so few clues to go on.

He and Dr. Lyanne had been born to wealth. I knew

that much. He hadn't been institutionalized until he was fourteen—not because he and Warren had managed to stay undiscovered, but because his family had thrown enough money at the problem to make it go away. Temporarily. But money and status can only do so much. The government reached out its long arm, snatching him from gilded halls and marble floors to a concrete room with bare, steel beds. Sometimes I wondered if his ease in command came from fourteen years of being the older child of a moneyed family. But maybe that had nothing to do with it. Maybe it was the experiences that came later that shaped the boy into the man.

"Do you want something to drink or anything?" I said awkwardly. Peter's expression softened into something like amusement, and I felt ourself flush. Of course he would think it strange for me to play host when he'd been coming to Emalia's apartment long before I ever arrived.

But he nodded. "Sure. Water's fine."

Nina's interest in Peter's appearance and our conversation had waned. She didn't follow the two of us into the kitchen, disappearing instead down the hall.

"Actually, I did want to talk with you and Addie about something." Peter leaned against the counter and smiled briefly when I handed him the glass of water.

<*Please let it be about Nornand*> Addie said.

Please let him say he'd found one of the children whose faces streamed through our dreams, whose expressions of deadened fear melted, waxlike, in our nightmares.

An eternity passed as Peter took a sip of water. Then, thankfully, he set the glass down. "Eva, Anchoit isn't the safest place to be at the moment. Not with the Powatt institution so close by. Security has gotten tighter, and there's going to be more attention focused on the city than ever. Especially with regard to anything hybrid-related."

Addie and I had noticed officers in the streets, and police cars on patrol. We'd heard Sabine talk about the damage the curfew was doing to some of the businesses downtown, and the unrest growing from that. Walking through our own neighborhood, we'd heard the complaints.

"It's time for you guys to find more permanent homes," Peter said. "Somewhere safer."

<*No*> Addie said, so forcibly the word resounded in my mind, echoing through every part of me. <*No, Eva.*>

More permanent homes meant scattering us across the country. We'd never see the others again. We might not even be allowed to contact one another.

"No," I said, too loudly.

Peter reached out as if he might touch our shoulder, but I jerked back. His hand dropped. "Eva, you and the others can't stay here." He was getting that Peter-in-charge air about him again, and our gut tied into knots.

"What about Sabine? And Jackson and Christoph and—and Cordelia and the others? *They're* here."

He sighed. "It's been years since they got out, Eva. They're less recognizable now. And they're . . . well, they're older than you are. You're fourteen."

"Fifteen," I said. "How old were you when you escaped?"

His eyes flickered from ours to the countertop. I thought I saw him bite back a smile.

"Sixteen." His voice was gentle, and for some reason that upset me more than if he'd matched my own irritation. "And you know what I did? I found a home where I kept myself safe for the next few years."

"Jackson's barely two years older than we are." I struggled to keep from shouting. Sound traveled freely from the kitchen to the living room, and down the hall. I didn't want Nina to hear. "And he was a lot younger when he first got here, wasn't he? They all were, I bet. I—"

"That was before," Peter said. "This is now. Eva, I can find you a family to take you in. Someone who's willing to say you're a niece or a stepdaughter or something. Someone you can stay with until you're old enough to be on your own. You can go back to school, go to university—"

"I can go to school *here*, can't I?" Our fingers squeezed the handle of the water pitcher. I needed somewhere to direct our frustration. "Isn't it the same? Either way, we're pretending!"

"It's more dangerous here," Peter said. "If things escalate in the city, so close to the institution, people will start getting paranoid. They'll start double-checking documentation. Instead of overlooking a discrepancy, a mistake in your papers, they'll get suspicious. They'll ask questions. Then one day, you get a knock at your door, and it's the police come to investigate."

He leaned down. Sought our eyes. "And it's not just yourself you're putting in danger, Eva. Emalia—Emalia enjoys having you and Kitty with her, but she has a very important job, you understand? If she were discovered, who would help us free more children? She can't take that risk, Eva."

"I don't have to go to school, then," I said. School, university—it all seemed so inconsequential now, anyway. What did it matter if I learned calculus, if the government could lock me up at any moment? Why did I need to study history, when our history books lied? "Addie and I can help you guys. We don't even have to live here with Emalia."

We could live with Sabine. She'd said we could. We wouldn't stay with her long-term. Just long enough to get some sort of job. Until we could afford our own place.

Peter sighed. "Eva—"

I cut him off. "I don't want to hide anymore. I've been hiding for almost my entire life, Peter."

I didn't want to lose any more people, either. Ryan. Devon. Lissa. Hally. Kitty. Nina. Jackson and Vince and all our new friends. I'd already lost my parents, my little brother. I couldn't stand being parted from anyone else.

Peter and I both looked up at the sound of a key turning in the lock. Peter met our eyes again. "I know," he said. "I understand how you feel, Eva. But you're going to have to trust me on this one. We'll talk about it again later. It's not something that will happen anytime soon. There are still a lot of things to consider."

Of course there were.

There always were.

Addie and I watched him cross to the dining area, wearing a new smile and touching Emalia's arm as she came in from the hall. Our head was suddenly aching.

<*We can't let it happen*> I said. <*Never. Never.*>

We weren't a child anymore, to be packed up and shuttled off on a whim.

<*It's not going to be an issue*> I told Addie—and myself—fiercely. <*It's not going to be an issue because Powatt's never going to open. Sabine's got a plan.*>

Addie wrapped around me, a ghostly, intangible hug. But I could feel her shaking, too.

THIRTEEN

The day of the speech arrived.

We left the apartment a little earlier than normal that afternoon, but otherwise, things started out no differently than usual. Kitty and Nina barely reacted to us leaving anymore, just nodded and went back to watching television on the couch, their head sunk against Emalia's pillows.

I got caught in the doorway for a moment, just staring at Nina. If something happened today . . . There were so many things that could go wrong. We'd gone over most of them with Sabine and the others, but there were probably so many more that we hadn't thought of.

Devon and Lissa met us in the hallway. No one spoke. Our tension-lined shoulders said everything.

Josie waited in her car, Cordelia sitting beside her in the front seat. Jackson and Christoph were taking the bus; they'd meet us near the square.

"Ready?" Josie said as we clambered inside. The car looked ancient, the silver paint scratched off in great gashes near the bottom of our door. The handle felt strangely loose in our hand. Inside, a faint musty smell hung over the cracked upholstery.

"Can I open the window?" I asked.

"Sure." She threw the car into reverse and eased out of her parking space. "Whatever you need."

Josie's car ran so low to the ground that every car driving alongside us was a giant, the buses moving mountains. I wasn't sure what time rush hour was in Anchoit, but the streets were plenty busy now. Every block crawled by.

Finally, we reached Ducine Boulevard, which ran parallel to Lankster. Addie and I had memorized the maps Josie showed us, but the maps had done nothing to prepare us for the throngs of people lining the sidewalks. Parking took an eternity to find. Finally, Josie squeezed into a space several blocks away.

"Is it always this crowded?" Devon asked, slamming his car door shut.

"Depends," Cordelia said, but her tone said *no, not usually.* These people were here to listen to the speech.

Christoph and Vince were at the bus stop, exactly where they were supposed to be. We kept our distance so we weren't one big clump of people moving through the crowd. But eyes met, and we gathered in a back alleyway about a block from the square.

Josie glanced at her wristwatch. "We've got twenty minutes until they introduce Nalles. Everyone know exactly what they're doing?" Her eyes lingered on each of our faces. Seeing who was truly ready and who wasn't? Who would get the job done, and who might fail?

We wouldn't fail.

I wouldn't fail.

I snuck a look at Devon. All of us were at risk today, but none more than him. No way he didn't realize that. But his eyes, while lacking their usual boredom, didn't betray a lick of fear or doubt.

Josie nodded at him. "All right. You and I should start heading over to Metro Council. The rest of you can wait around a little more, or go ahead and get set up. Just make sure you're not spotted. Remember, we meet up at Robenston once this is over."

Robenston Road was a good mile or two away. Far enough, we hoped, to escape the aftermath of our plans and regroup. Right now, I couldn't think that far into the future.

<They'll be all right> I said, more to myself than to Addie. I expected her to say, *We should really be worrying about if* we'll *be all right.* Instead, she was quiet. The worry knifing up our insides wasn't mine alone.

Christoph was the one staying close to the crowd, judging the situation on the ground. He'd wanted to be a detonator and had argued with Josie about it. He'd lost. Cordelia and Lissa were headed for alleyways a short distance from the square, each carrying a firework in their shoulder bags.

Vince and I were stationed closest to the actual stage, three stories up on two separate rooftops around the perimeter of Lankster Square. The Square sat in the middle of so many buildings; the reverberating echo of each firecracker would confuse anyone trying to figure out where the noise had come from. The posters Vince and I showered down would hopefully add to the chaos.

Addie and I were shaking. Our hands. Our legs. I'd tied up our hair in the car because it had been so stifling, but now it left us feeling exposed. I pulled the hair band free.

Devon and Josie slipped from the alley. Josie without looking back. Devon glanced at his sister, then at Addie and me. But so quick a glance that I could read nothing in it. I watched his retreating back, our stomach tight and sick. I wanted to be with him when he stole into the building. I wanted to be his lookout when he sat down at the computer. Devon and Ryan lost sight of the rest of the world when they concentrated. Someone needed to make sure they were safe. Sabine would be there, but I wished it were me. I didn't trust anyone else to do it.

But I couldn't follow them. I had my own job to finish.

The rest of us fiddled around in the alley a few minutes longer. But no one could stay still. Finally, with grim smiles all around, we split up and went our separate ways.

"You worried?" Vince whispered. It was just the two of us now, walking through the street. No one gave us a second glance: Not the crowd of girls in bright sundresses. Not the mother or her surly preteen boy. Not the old man with the newspaper or the young man with the sunglasses or anyone else.

"No," I lied.

These were the people who would bear witness to our message. They just didn't know it yet.

Eventually, even Vince left us. Our rooftop was farther from the square than his, and accessible only by a metal ladder that clanked with each step. Addie and I were halfway up when we heard a roaring cheer.

I stopped climbing. From this distance and height, we could only see a small portion of the crowd; buildings blocked the rest of the square. But we could hear the people, loud and clear. They sounded happy. They sounded like they were at a football game or a concert.

Cold sweat pasted our shirt to our back. We clung to the ladder and stared at that sliver of the crowd, picturing its entirety. How many people had shown up because they believed every word of Jenson's speech? Because they wanted nothing more than a cure, and they were so proud that the Powatt institution would aid in its perfection?

Below us thundered hundreds of people who hated us, and they didn't even know who we were.

<Keep climbing> Addie said.

I forced us upward and upward until we reached the edge of the roof. The wind had picked up, or maybe we just felt it more strongly here. We took one more moment to stare at Lankster Square and the colored shapes of the people below.

Then I grabbed the sheaf of papers from our bag. On his

rooftop, Vince would be doing the same. I didn't need to look at the posters; Addie and I had helped Cordelia design them. We had three sets, Vince another three. Six sets in total. Six distinct posters, each bearing the face of a single child. Three girls, three boys, brought to life through Addie's pencil.

Each was a hybrid someone in the group had been locked away with. One who death had stolen before Peter came knocking with another, more gentle freedom.

Three girls, three boys. Their names and ages were printed below their faces:

Kurt F. 14

Viola R. 12

Anna H. 15

Blaise R. 16

Kendall F. 10

Max K. 14

I'd thought about choosing Sallie and Val, Kitty's old roommate, to be one of the children depicted. Addie had even prepared a sketch of her, asking Kitty for the little girl's description. But in the end, we decided it would be too dangerous. There hadn't been many hybrid children at Nornand, and fewer still had escaped. Anyone tracing Sallie's picture and name might be able to guess who was involved.

The wind battered at our hair, made the posters whip about in our hands. The face on top belonged to Anna H. Anna H., fifteen, with short, dark hair and light eyes and a smile like she wanted to tear up the world. That was how Cordelia and Katy had described her for Addie, watching carefully as Addie drew sketch after sketch.

Close enough, Cordelia had said finally. *God, it's been so long. I wish I'd had a camera then, you know? If I had, I'd still remember exactly what she looked like.*

In a few moments, dozens of copies of Anna's face would fly scattering into the wind. Would rain down to the streets below.

I dug around our bag for the walkie-talkie, then lifted it to our ear, listening. It was still quiet. I set the firecracker in the middle of the roof. It was so small—smaller even than our closed fist. I flicked open our lighter, stared at the flickering flame.

"Ready," came Lissa's breathless voice through the walkie-talkie.

A pause.

"Ready," said Vince. Then Cordelia.

"Ready," I whispered into the walkie-talkie.

There came another cheer from the crowd—a wave of noise that was sandpaper against our ears.

I gripped the lighter. A blast of wind blew the flame so close to our skin I felt a scorch of heat.

The walkie-talkie crackled with static. Then Josie's voice funneled through. "Go."

Wind scratched at our eyes. I knelt down, lit the fuse, and ran to the edge of the roof. I released the sheaf of papers. Threw them into the air.

The firecracker exploded.

Then, from across the square, another explosion.

Then another. Another.

Echoes. Echoes. Echoes.

The crowd screamed again. A completely different kind of scream.

The sky filled with paper wings, the names of dead hybrids, the words stamped across their faces: *HOW MANY CHILDREN HAVE DIED FOR THIS CURE?*

FOURTEEN

I'd known the *boom* of the fireworks would reverberate. I'd underestimated just how much. How four explosions bouncing around the closed-in square seemed like dozens.

I'd heard fireworks before. Fourth of July. Hot summer nights. This sounded different. There was no sharp, warning whine before the explosion—the explosion wasn't a deep, rolling *boom*. The firecrackers went off in sharp, staccato *pop*s.

Bam. Bam. Bam. Bam.

Like gunfire.

Our knees gave out. I dove down, arms covering our head, before my mind even registered what I was doing. When I stood again, half-bent over, the crowd was in chaos. A rippling, screaming, terrified mass of people that made me freeze in horror where I stood.

<*Run*> Addie yelled.

We bolted for the ladder. Our hands slapped against the rungs. We climbed down, down, down—

The crowd was still screaming. People in the building below us shouted.

People in the building below us.

A man stuck his head out the window, turned, and stared right at us. We stared back. He was thirty or forty or somewhere in between. He had short hair and a blond beard. He had old acne scars and dry lips and wide, round eyes that would not, would not leave ours.

Something unintelligible slipped from his mouth, something that was shock and fear and anger slammed together.

He knew. I was utterly, utterly certain that he knew.

There was a feeling like being knocked sideways—but it wasn't real. It was only in my head, in our minds. It was Addie shoving herself into control, grabbing the reins to our limbs, yanking our hands free from the rungs so she could scramble to the ground.

We couldn't hear the crowd anymore, or maybe we could and just couldn't distinguish it from the yelling coming from much closer by. The alley below us was still empty of people, but the shouting surged closer. Louder.

Our feet touched the ground. Addie threw us away from the ladder and hurtled down the alley. We didn't know which way we were going. We just ran.

Police sirens shrilled through the air.

Footsteps pounded behind us. We put on a burst of speed, our head whipping around. It was Cordelia. Her eyes lit up when she saw us. She shouted, gesturing wildly, urging us onward. Where was Lissa? Where was Vince?

We reached the end of the alleyway. Slammed a hard right. Nearly smashed into a store window. Saw the poster pasted there.

A poster with Jaime's picture.

For one confused, breathless second, my addled mind thought, *But we didn't make posters of Jaime.*

Picture-Jaime wore Nornand's blue uniform, with its starched collar and short sleeves. His hair was thick and curly, no part of it shaved to bare his scalp. A picture taken presurgery.

Who had been in control when the camera snapped the photo? Jaime? Or the soul who'd been lost?

Not lost. Murdered. Carved bloodily from his body with a violent scalpel.

The words on the poster finally registered. This wasn't like one of Addie's posters at all. This demanded Jaime's return to government hands. Without thinking, we snatched the poster from the window. Stuffed it in our pocket.

A stream of fleeing people gulped us down. Cordelia grabbed our arm and yanked us deeper into the crowd. We tried to tell her *No, no, we can't. Please don't. We can't—* but we couldn't speak and she wasn't listening.

More police sirens. An elbow rammed into our face, pain exploding in our cheekbone. We jerked from Cordelia's grasp. The crowd separated us in seconds. She spun around, fighting the mob to reach our side again.

Our feet couldn't find the ground. Our vision faded at the edges. We were in the streets of Bessimir again, in danger of becoming nothing more than a smear on the asphalt. We were seven years old again, locked in a trunk with nothing but the darkness and heat and our dried tears for company.

We stumbled to the sidewalk. Police sirens blared in our ears. We turned just in time to see Cordelia darting across the road. She was probably furious at us. She was probably wondering what the hell was wrong with us, and why couldn't we just keep up and do what we were supposed to do.

A police car swerved around the corner—

—And hit her.

It hit her. It slammed on its brakes, but it hit Cordelia, and she rolled across the hood, collapsing to the concrete. For a moment, she lay still, her arm thrown across her face, her pale hair stark against the dark road. Then she struggled upright. She kept running, limping. Back in the direction she'd come.

An officer jumped out of the car. Shouted after her, but the torrent of people had already swallowed Cordelia whole. Then he turned. Cursed. He stared at us—*rightatusrightatus*.

Another few yards, and he might have hit us instead. But right now, we were just another terrified, horrified, petrified face. Not worth his focus. He jumped back in the car and yelled unintelligible noise into his radio.

We stumbled, tripped, hobbled our way to Robenston. Our memorized maps fractured in our mind. We struggled to make sense of the pieces, moving from street to street, avoiding eye contact, hiding when the police passed.

It was only firecrackers, I wanted to say.

Where was Cordelia? We saw the car hit her again and again.

<She got up> Addie said. *<She kept running, so she must be okay.>*

She must be.

Were Devon and Josie okay? Was Lissa? Vince? Christoph?

We'd lost our walkie-talkie in the chaos. There was no way to make contact.

We found a street sign that said *Robenston Rd.* Relief brought a tremor to our hands, a rush of heat through our body. We were supposed to meet at the bus stop. We weren't sure which direction that was, but we picked the one that would take us farther from the Square.

<There!> Addie said.

We saw Christoph's red hair first. We caught the freckles on his pale skin and his bright eyes that grew brighter when he saw us, too. Then Ryan was turning around; he was walking—running—walking toward us. I forced myself to keep from running, too. We couldn't attract attention.

His arms went around us. I pressed our forehead against his shoulder, blocking out the world. I said, "It's okay. I'm okay. Where's Josie? Where's Cordelia? She—"

"She's fine." Ryan's words were a whisper in our ear. "Josie and Lissa found her. They're driving back to their apartment. They're going to drop Lissa off. Where have you been?"

"I got lost." It was the only thing I could say about it. I looked up from Ryan's shoulder and saw Vince watching us. No, Jackson. "Did you get it?" I whispered to Ryan. "The information?" He nodded.

Christoph interrupted before either of us could say more. "We've got to go." His voice was curt, but his eyes raked over us, and he frowned at our cheek. It was still throbbing. I touched my cold fingers to the hot skin. "We've got to go, now, before Peter and them hear about this and someone discovers you're not where you're supposed to be."

We waited, but the bus didn't come. It took eons to flag down a taxi. Even longer to reach Emalia's apartment building. Here, everything was as we'd left it: calm, undisturbed.

"Come up with a story for that bruise," Jackson said as Ryan and I clambered out of the car. I promised I would. The taxi pulled away again.

Ryan and I ran up four flights of stairs. I scrambled to unlock Emalia's door. We burst inside to see Lissa already waiting, pacing the living room. Nina sat nervously on the couch behind her.

"Thank *God*," Lissa said, hurrying toward us. Then: "Your cheek—what happened?"

By the time Henri came downstairs, face grave, shoulders stiff, Addie and I had an answer. I'd had one of my moments—lost control of our feet for a minute and tripped into one of the chairs. Nearly poked an eye out. Bit of a klutz, aren't I? I can't—Henri, what's wrong? No, we haven't watched television since this morning. Lankster Square? What happened? Tell us.

Please tell us.

FIFTEEN

Henri stayed with us until Emalia came home. Then the two of them disappeared back to Henri's apartment with Peter, leaving us alone to watch the aftermath on the evening news.

I called Cordelia's apartment as soon as they were gone. Josie answered, her voice brisk and casual until she realized who was on the other end. Then she dropped her pretense. Cordelia was in a lot of pain, but nothing unbearable. She refused to go to the hospital. She'd fractured her ribs when she was younger, and they hadn't done much for her then.

"I've got her pretty drugged up on pain meds," Josie said, "but I think she's right. Even if she's fractured a rib, there isn't a lot that can be done for that."

"How do you know it's not something worse?" I said. "What if she's got internal bleeding?"

"Look, we can't afford a trip to the hospital right now," Josie said quietly. "We don't have the money for it, and we don't want to take the risk—however small—of someone putting two and two together. Cordelia's fine right now, I promise.

If anything comes up to suggest differently, anything at all, I'll take her to the hospital."

I hesitated. "No, if anything comes up, contact Dr. Lyanne."

"Okay," Josie said. "Right. Good thinking. And, Eva? I'm sorry it got so crazy out there today. I know you might not have been expecting that."

I looked over our shoulder, at Lissa curled tight on the couch, eyes glued to the television screen. At Nina white-knuckled beside her. Ryan was the only one who looked back at me.

"Thanks for keeping your head clear," Josie said.

I thought about the hazed walk to Robenston Road, the way I'd frozen on the ladder when I should have kept climbing, the way I'd broken down in the middle of the crowd, dizzied by the crush of bodies.

"Head clear," I said. "Yeah. I guess."

"I mean it," she said. "Some people fall apart when things get tough. Some people aren't strong enough to keep going."

I bit our lip. "Did you get what you needed?"

"Yeah," she said. "But ask Devon about it, all right? Some things . . . the phone isn't best. I've got to check on Jackson and Christoph. Look, you know we can't let Peter suspect anything, right?"

I told her I wouldn't. She promised to get back in touch soon. I sat down next to Ryan in the living room and squeezed his hand, nodding to tell him everything was all right. He gave me a brief, tight smile.

Nina hadn't inquired about where we'd been. Something in her eyes, in the quick, furtive looks she threw in our direction, told me she could guess. Something in the tight line of her mouth told me she didn't want to ask.

Peter didn't call a general meeting after the incident at Lankster Square. It was better, Sophie explained, if everyone went about their regular business and didn't do anything the slightest bit suspicious. Large gatherings, even if they were in the supposed privacy of Peter's apartment, might be noted.

The Mullan siblings, Addie, and I had our own gathering, secreted in our bedroom while Kitty watched TV. Devon was remarkably nonchalant as he explained how he and Sabine had snuck into the Metro Council building with out-of-date identification, altered to look like new. They'd found Hogan Nalles's office quickly enough.

"Sabine knows how to pick a lock," Devon said. He didn't sound impressed. Devon never sounded impressed. But he did sound a little less bored than usual, maybe.

"I'm not really surprised," Hally said.

Devon shrugged. "We should learn. If we'd known how to do it at Nornand . . ." He trailed off, his eyes meeting ours. "It's a good skill to have."

"For criminals, maybe," Hally said. Her brother didn't argue, but he didn't look entirely like he agreed, either.

News of the fireworks in Lankster Square had reached Metro Council Hall quickly. Devon and Sabine heard the commotion outside as Devon set to work on Nalles's computer, but no one thought to check his office, and they were able to sneak out without being detected.

"So you found it," Addie said. "The information Sabine wanted. The plans for Powatt." We were the only one seated on our bed, our legs tucked tightly beneath us. Hally and Devon sat on the ground, her leaning against the nightstand, him with his back against our bed frame. Devon nodded.

"And?" Hally said. Her arms were crossed, her hair spilling over her shoulders, hiding part of her face. Her usual brightness had sharpened to a hard point. I saw everything I needed to see in the unhappy slant of her mouth.

"I didn't have time to read it all." Devon shot her a look. "There was a timetable. They'll be delivering and installing the machinery in a few weeks. There will be groups of officials coming to scope out the place. Some kind of open house before the kids get there. Sabine saved it all to a disk."

Hally frowned. "She has a computer?"

"She uses one at the college downtown," Devon said. "Apparently, she's been sneaking on campus for years. Even sat in on a few of the bigger lectures. No one notices."

"Did you find names?" Addie asked. "Of the kids who're going to get sent there?"

Devon shook his head. I thought about the poster of Jaime we'd grabbed while fleeing from the Square. *JAIME CORTAE*, it read. *AGE: 13. HAIR: BROWN. EYES: BROWN. HEIGHT: 5'0". WEIGHT: 85 lbs.*

It reminded me of Jaime's patient file at Nornand. I'd folded the poster up and slid it underneath our mattress. We couldn't bear to get rid of it, but we could hardly bear to look at it, either.

Hearing Jenson announce a search for Jaime on national television was bad enough, but it was still just a man on a screen. There was a certain distance, a certain belief that one young boy was too small to be found in this enormous country, that danger still wheeled high and unseeing in the clouds. Stumbling upon the poster here was like seeing a flash of talons, feeling them nick our cheek.

"Well," Addie said, a word and a sigh. "Now what?"

No one responded to that, either. We looked at one another. Sitting in the pastel softness of our Emalia-decorated bedroom, it seemed insane that earlier today, we'd been tearing through the streets, terrified of being caught. Of getting thrown in jail or worse.

I remembered the terror of the crowd. I remembered the sound like gunshots ricocheting around the Square. I hadn't—hadn't realized. Hadn't thought. Each memory of the screaming, trampling crowd punched a hole on our gut, made us sick.

We'd done that. We'd made that happen. With just four little firecrackers and plans laughingly made in a hidden-away, fairy-light-strung attic, we'd terrified hundreds of people. The feeling of power was horrifying. Was this how change began? This feeling like standing on the edge of a cliff, wanting to fly but terrified of falling?

"Sabine supposedly has a plan," Devon said. He shrugged.

Hally stared at the wall. "I, for one, don't want anything to do with Sabine's plans anymore."

The TV stayed tuned to the local news for the rest of the night. A revolving group of anchors, reporters, eyewitnesses—and then police officers and, finally, government officials—chimed in.

We knew there existed the possibility of hybrid hostility, they said. *Precautions were put in place,* they said. *This afternoon's situation was quickly and effectively contained, with no casualties. Investigations to track down the perpetrators are fully under way.*

We will not allow this act of violence to affect the course we know to be right.

We will not back down.

Violence? *There was no violence,* I wanted to protest. It was just flyers and fireworks. That's all. But no one said the word *firecracker.* They called them *explosions.* They used the word *detonate.*

No one on the news mentioned anything about a security breach at Metro Council Hall. No one mentioned the posters we'd thrown from the rooftops, either. The six names.

Kurt F. 14

Viola R. 12

Anna H. 15

Blaise R. 16

Kendall F. 10

Max K. 14

But over the next few days, the names spread anyway. Emalia told us about it over quiet, tense dinners. The only thing that spread faster than fear was intrigue, and soon, everyone wanted to know the stories behind the drawings. Posters passed from hand to hand. One small, brave newspaper picked the story up. It was quickly quashed, but by then, it was too late.

For just a few days, the entire city was talking about Kurt, Viola, Anna, Blaise, Kendall, and Max. Six hybrid children who had died without anyone giving it a thought.

Our days slackened into their old routines, which basically consisted of doing nothing at all. Ryan and Devon sank back into their tinkering. Lissa and Hally drifted from couch to dining table to carpet, from books to magazines to idle card games with Kitty. They refused to talk about Lankster Square anymore. Their anger flared when anyone so much as tried to bring it up, so no one did.

"Does Peter know who did it?" Addie asked Sophie in a surge of courage one night. She waited for Sophie, instead of Emalia, because Sophie was calmer. Emalia tended to just flutter at us when we surprised her with a question. "The—whatever it was—at Lankster Square."

Sophie paused in the middle of clearing the table. Her stack of Styrofoam boxes tilted precariously, and Addie hurried to catch a fork slipping from the top. "No, he doesn't. Why?"

Addie fiddled with the plastic fork. "Everyone on the news

seems to think it was a hybrid who did it."

"Well, I'm sure we don't know all the hybrids in Anchoit," Sophie said. "And just because the news wants us to think it was a hybrid doesn't mean it actually was one."

"You think someone might have caused the commotion at the speech just so everyone could blame it on the hybrids?"

Sophie frowned, setting the Styrofoam boxes back onto the table and giving us her full attention. "It's possible. But what I meant was that someone—someone who isn't hybrid—might have done what they did because they're on our side. Henri helps us, right? And he isn't hybrid." Her head tilted slightly, her eyes seeking ours. It was a look unsettlingly similar to one our mom used to wear when she was concerned. It made our throat thicken.

Addie averted our gaze. "Here, I'll get it," she said quietly. She picked up the stack of white boxes and crossed into the kitchen.

Two weeks passed before Josie's visit. She never fell out of touch entirely—she called twice to let us know Cordelia and Katy were recovering well and to ask how we were—but after the frenzied days leading up to Lankster Square, it felt like a lifeline had been snipped. The apartment building seemed even smaller than it had before. Suffocating, like a padded room meant to keep us safe against our will.

Josie came early in the morning, so soon after Emalia left for work that I wondered if she'd been watching and waiting.

Kitty, who was still eating breakfast, could barely take her eyes off her. Josie flashed her a smile before joining Addie and me on the couch.

It was a relief to see her again, to hear more about what was happening in the outside world. After two weeks, the matter appeared mostly forgotten by the media. In Lupside, information about the museum flooding had circulated on the news for weeks.

Josie smiled wryly when I mentioned this. "Lupside's a small town, isn't it? Cities are different. And in the Bessimir case, they probably knew exactly who they were going to frame. They could afford to make a big deal about it—drag it on so the punch line comes so much stronger. Here, the government doesn't want to kick up *too* much of a fuss yet. Means they don't have any idea who did it."

<What if they just frame somebody?> Addie said, and I repeated her question aloud.

"They won't," Josie assured us. As she spoke, she took a pen from her pocket and began writing something on her palm. "If you frame somebody, and the real people responsible just do something else, it makes you look stupid."

"Well, that's good." I said. Our chest tightened. I'd known that Lankster Square was only step one of a larger plan. But not seeing Josie for so long had made me doubt a little, made me wonder if she'd been frightened off.

Apparently not.

Kitty was listening to everything we said, so we had to be

careful how we phrased things. Talking about the incident at Lankster Square was perfectly normal—expected, even. But we couldn't say anything to suggest we'd been there, let alone involved in any way.

Josie tilted her palm toward us. I stared at the small, neat black letters.

Meeting on Thursday. 5PM.

She smiled, waiting for my answer. I swallowed. I remembered the crush and squeeze of the crowd, the shouting lancing through our brain, the poster of Jaime taped to the shop window.

I thought about the last two weeks, cooped up in Emalia's apartment again, like little kids in a playpen, expected to be oblivious.

I thought about what Peter had said, how he wanted to send us away. He would try to do it, sooner or later. Sooner, if Powatt was allowed to open. And then what? Addie and I would be stuck with strangers in the middle of God knows where. Going to school. Doing homework. Pretending to be normal. To be like everyone else. Helpless to change anything.

It had taken Sabine and Josie five years to get to this point, to actually try to make a difference. I couldn't stand waiting another five years. I wanted things to change. Now.

I met Josie's eyes.

I didn't ask Addie for her opinion.

I just nodded.

SIXTEEN

Hally paced back and forth around her room, her gaze never leaving us. "You want to go *back*?"

I'd told her and Devon about Josie's visit. Devon, as usual, took the news without much reaction. I'd expected Hally to be resistant—she'd made it clear over the past couple weeks that she hadn't signed up for what had happened at Lankster Square. And I understood. I did. But her level of incredulity stung me.

Addie was no help. She'd stayed silent since I nodded at Josie, told her we would be at the attic for the next meeting. I couldn't read her.

I bit back the explanation I'd planned—about how maybe we'd gone about Lankster Square all wrong, but that didn't mean we should give up entirely. I still believed in Sabine's plans. And the fact remained that the Powatt institution couldn't be allowed to open.

"I need to go to see Cordelia," I said instead. It wasn't entirely a lie, but it tasted like a lie, felt slippery like a lie. "I was there when—I was there when she got hurt. It was my fault. I've got to go see her again."

"It wasn't your fault," Hally said immediately, but she didn't say anything else, just frowned and pressed her fist against her mouth. She looked toward Devon. Devon shrugged.

"Fine," she said finally. Her arms were crossed low over her body, not like she was angry, but like she was trying to protect herself. Lissa and Hally dressed differently now. I remembered the clothes that hung in their closet back home, the wild patterns and bright colors. Today, she wore a white blouse and black skirt, her long hair loosely braided back, her ears bare. It made her look stark. Severe.

"Will you come with us?" I said.

Hally's eyes stayed locked with ours. She shook her head.

I bit our lip. "Okay."

"I will," Devon said.

Addie and I were tense the entire walk to the photography store, recoiling when someone came too close, flinching when people shouted behind us. A passing police car, though nothing out of the ordinary, made our legs stiffen. I didn't know where to direct our eyes.

To my surprise, the sign on the storefront said *Open* when we arrived, and Cordelia was behind the counter. She flipped the *Open* sign to *Closed* after letting us in.

I found myself searching her for signs of injury. There was a small, mostly healed cut near her temple, but that was all I could see. Any other cuts or bruises had already healed or were hidden by her clothes. She'd tamed her pale-yellow hair into a short ponytail at the nape of her neck.

I tried to smile. "Sabine said you were feeling better, but I didn't realize you were working again."

Cordelia shrugged. She wasn't meeting our eyes, didn't reach for us or touch our arm like she usually did. Cordelia always seemed to crave human contact, but she kept her distance, now. "Got to keep the clients we have. Sadly enough, haven't found someone to pay me for lying around in bed yet."

<*We should apologize*> I said quietly. But I wasn't sure which words to use, how to phrase it.

I'm sorry I freaked out and you couldn't leave me behind? I'm sorry I should have warned you I hate crowds?

I'm sorry you could have been caught, or even died, and it was my fault.

"Don't worry about it," Cordelia said, as if she could read my mind. Now, finally, she met our gaze. "I'm feeling fine. Gone through worse."

"I'm sorry—" I started to say, but she cut me off with a faint smile.

"Really, Eva, it's fine. Had a nasty bruise for a while, and I think Sabine got some kind of sadistic pleasure out of drugging me out of my mind, but I'm right as rain now."

I almost thought we might be talking with Katy, who was usually less effusive. But Katy had a way of walking and talking like her head was just brushing against the clouds, and the girl who led Devon and us to the storage room was very much present and focused—just focused on something that wasn't us.

"There you are," Sabine said as we climbed up into the attic. She, at least, didn't look or act any differently than usual.

Her steadiness was comforting. Vince and Christoph were already there, reclined on the sofas.

Devon's eyes were strangely unfocused. He caught me watching him and shook from his trance. Not for the first time, I wondered what he and Ryan were talking about.

"What did you call us here for?" Devon's voice wasn't loud, but it silenced all the others. Eyes roamed the room, moving from one person to another. Eventually, we all turned to Sabine.

"Your sister didn't come," she said. The sentence seemed more observation than question, and Devon didn't reply. Sabine didn't appear to expect an answer, just nodded a little to herself.

<*They've left us out of something*> Addie said.

At first, I didn't know what she meant. Then I noticed the tension stifling the attic. The scrutiny everyone was directing at *us*. Only Devon still had his eyes on Sabine, a frown creasing his forehead.

This was building up to something. They were waiting for something. For Sabine to tell us and Devon what the rest of them already knew.

"I've looked over the information we got from Nalles's computer," Sabine said. She tucked a strand of hair behind her ear. "It's got everything about Powatt. Everything I needed to figure out what to do."

"And what's that?" Devon asked.

Vince's smile was a razor blade. "We're going to blow the damn thing up."

SEVENTEEN

Addie and I tried to speak at the same time. Nothing came out but a half-strangled sound in the back of our throat. Our next sound was almost a laugh—an unbelieving, rocks-grinding-against-rocks laugh.

"You're going to blow it up?" Devon said. "Then what?"

"Then it'll be gone," Christoph said.

"And after that?" Devon's words dripped cold disdain. "Everyone will suddenly come to their senses? Realize what a great thing we've done? They already hate us. They already think we're mentally unstable. You'd only give them more ammunition."

Christoph leaned forward. He'd flushed, his normally pale skin splotched with color. His hands gripped into fists at his sides. "It's not about making them *like* us. No one's ever going to give hybrids the chance to prove we're *likable*—"

"Wars and revolutions," said Vince, "are not won through being *liked*."

Wars and revolutions.

Was that what this was? A war? A revolution?

We shuddered. Wars did not belong here, at home. Wars belonged to history, or to those far-off nations beyond the ocean. And the only revolution we'd ever learned about was the one that had founded the Americas, when the non-hybrids had won their freedom from the hybrids over two hundred years ago. Wars and revolutions meant death and untold horrors. We'd been taught that much at school.

Addie shook our head. Up until that moment, we'd still been caught in the middle of our control, neither of us firmly at the reins. But with that movement, things shifted to her side. Our hand slipped down, worrying at the thin fabric of our skirt.

"Devon's right," Addie said. "All those people at Lankster Square—do you really think they're any more eager to help us than they were before?"

Devon glanced at us. He didn't seem thankful for Addie's support—or even surprised. Just that indecipherable look he sometimes wore, revealing nothing.

"Lankster Square," Sabine said quietly, "let the city know that not everyone here supports the cure. Getting rid of Powatt—it tells them that we're serious. That we're willing to fight. And even if it doesn't? Then at least it's an institution gone. It's surgical machinery gone."

No one spoke. Sabine was the one who broke the silence again, this time with a question. Her eyes were on Addie and me. "How many hybrids do you think there are? Here in the Americas, I mean."

"I . . . I don't know," Addie said.

"Me neither," Sabine said. "Peter doesn't know. Maybe the government doesn't even know—not with the percentage of hybrids in hiding. I think our numbers are small, but not as small as they'd have us believe. Say only one in five hundred people are hybrid. That's more than a *million* hybrids in the Americas, Addie. They make us feel isolated. And that's why a lot of people give up, you know? Because this isn't the sort of thing you can fight alone. It feels so big—the government feels so big and so powerful and all those parents, all those children—they can't talk to anyone about it. They don't know of anyone else going through it. So they give up because they feel too weak to do anything." Sabine didn't look at anyone as she spoke, her eyes focused instead on an empty spot on the sloping attic wall. As if it took all her concentration just to come up with what to say. "When you pick a fight, you have to keep going until you win or you can't fight anymore. We are *not* going to be another news story about how the hybrids were cowed."

Sabine's words expanded until they filled the entire attic, pressing against us, taking up all the air. I didn't think anyone could breathe, let alone fit any words of their own into the remaining space.

"Spending four years in one of those institutions," Sabine said quietly, "you get to dreaming about blowing them up. You fantasize about it."

Four years in an institution. Four more years since Peter had gotten her out. Eight years. In eight years, Addie and I would be twenty-three. Lyle would be nineteen. He'd be a freshman in college. Eight years was almost a decade. More than a tenth of a lifetime.

If things didn't change—if we didn't *force* things to change—then we might not see our little brother again until he was a grown man. If ever.

"But that's not why we need to do this," Sabine continued. "Because in the end, we'll never be able to blow up every single institution. Even if we could just keep going and going, they'd just keep building them. I want to give the other hybrids out there a reason to fight, Addie. I want them to know that the government's not the only power, that their neighbors aren't the only power. That we're a power, too."

Her eyes were as steady as ever. She didn't smile. But there wasn't a shred of antagonism in her voice or her expression. Just a calm, collected warmth. "But it's just an idea for the time being. As a group, we make decisions together. We take everyone's opinion into consideration."

She turned to Devon. "We would need your help again, anyway, to get things off the ground."

Devon didn't react in the least.

"So." Sabine looked around the room. When her eyes fell on Addie and me, they were gentle, but I felt the force behind them. "Let's take some time to consider things."

"Addie!"

Sabine and the others had already gone downstairs. Devon

turned along with Addie at the sound of Vince's voice, but Devon's eyes met ours, and whatever he saw there convinced him to keep going down the attic steps, leaving Addie and Vince alone in the attic.

"What, Jackson?" Addie stepped away from the trapdoor and leaned against the wall. A nail dug into our back.

<Jackson?> I said, but Addie ignored me.

She must have been right, though, because the boy didn't correct her. He ran his hand through his hair, pushing it out of his face. He seemed like he didn't know how to proceed. "What's wrong, Addie?"

What's wrong? He—Vince—had just dropped the fact that they were planning to blow up a government building, and now he was asking us what was wrong?

<Stop it, Eva> Addie said irritably. *<Calm down. I can't—I can't think.>* Our hand fluttered to our forehead, our fingertips rubbing circles against our temples.

Aloud, she said, "Look, Jackson . . . I've just got—I've got to think about things."

He approached us, gently tugging our hands from our face. His hands felt rougher than I'd expected, his palms callused. "Come on, what's there to think about?"

Addie laughed. "Blowing things up? Yeah, that takes a little considering, Jackson."

"Not just random *things*." His eyes were wide, earnest. His hands still grasped ours, left me feeling pinned against the wall. I waited for Addie to push him away, but she didn't.

"Addie, we're not planting explosives in playgrounds. It's an institution. A hybrid institution with nobody in it. And we're making sure nobody's ever *going* to be in it."

Addie stared past him, at the fairy lights on the far wall.

"Those people at Lankster Square . . ." she murmured. Too softly, maybe, because Jackson frowned in confusion. Addie bit our lip and raised our voice a little. "I know what you and the others want, Jackson. I do. And I want the same thing, but—"

"But what, Addie?" Jackson said. When Addie hesitated, he sighed and looked away. "Powatt isn't going to be anything like Lankster Square. The building's going to be deserted. No people. No crowds. Just a building full of empty beds, waiting for its prisoners. It's an *institution*, Addie—"

"I know." Our voice sharpened. "Eva and I were in one. We get it."

Jackson's smile held no warmth. "No, Addie, you kind of don't. Nornand wasn't an institution; it was a hospital. And it was terrible, I know. I'm not saying you spent a week at a five-star hotel. But Addie, you were there a week, and they fed you properly, and clothed you properly, and . . ." He hesitated, his grip on our hands loosening. "And there were windows."

Addie drew our hands tight against our sides, but his hands, entwined around ours, came with them. "There was also Jaime locked up in the basement and kids *dying* on those surgery tables—"

"Which is exactly what's going to happen in Powatt."

Jackson's voice was a half-hoarse whisper. "This new institution's twice as big as Nornand, Addie. And it's all for hybrids, every inch of it. How many kids do you think they'll be able to stuff inside? Can you picture them?"

Our breathing went ragged. Did my trapped feeling come from being cornered by Jackson? Or cornered by the images he threw into my mind?

"The ones who get picked for the surgeries will be the lucky ones, Addie. The others will just—" His voice cut off. He swallowed, his throat jumping. "Do you know how many kids die in hybrid holding tanks? That's what those are, those institutions. Holding tanks. They hold us until we die, and they do everything short of putting a bullet through our heads to speed up the process. They lock us up—stuff us into these rooms, as many as can fit. These places in the middle of nowhere. And there's nobody. Nobody but the kid dying in the bed next to yours of God knows what, and the caretakers who really don't give a damn."

Addie had been looking at Jackson's mouth as he spoke, or at his nose, or his chin or just to the left of his ear. But she met his eyes now.

"I went into an institution at twelve," said Jackson quietly. "And for three years, I never left the building."

He was quiet—quiet in a way Jackson was never quiet.

Keep hope, he'd said to us at Nornand. Had he kept hope for three years? How was that even possible?

Addie was gripping his hands now, not the other way

around. But it only lasted a moment. Then she disentangled our fingers from his and pushed his gently away. He stepped back, let us slide away.

"I've got to think about it, Jackson," Addie said softly. She waited, and he nodded once. She glanced over our shoulder as she walked down the stairs, like she couldn't take her gaze from this lanky boy with the pale eyes, couldn't take her thoughts from the child he'd once been, who'd lain in a tiny metal bed and dreamt of sunlight.

EIGHTEEN

We did think about it.

We thought about it at dinner while Nina and Emalia ate and laughed, blinking from our reverie only when Nina tapped us on the arm to ask, "Don't you like it?"

It took us a moment to realize she meant the food in our Styrofoam box. Some kind of fish. We'd barely touched it, but managed to nod and smile anyway. If either Nina or Emalia noticed anything off, they didn't mention it.

We thought about it while brushing our teeth. While in the shower. While we dressed for bed. After we clicked off our lamp. After we told Nina good night.

<We can't, Eva> Addie said. *<It's* crazy. *We should tell—>*

<Tell Peter?> Our hands were folded across our chest. A moment ago, they'd been at our sides. Before that, under our neck. We couldn't get comfortable. *<And then what?>*

<What do you mean, 'And then what'? And then he makes sure they never carry out this insanity and—>

<And they hate us forever> I said. *<Which won't even matter because in a couple months, Peter will have shipped us off to God knows where, and we'll be completely alone.>*

<We're not going to let that happen, Eva.>

I flipped onto our side and buried our face into the pillow. *<How? It's not like we can stay with Sabine if we back out of this plan.>*

<It wouldn't be backing out.> But I knew Addie felt, as I felt, that we were already inextricably linked to Sabine and the others. Saying no now would be backing out. *<If we do this, do you really think Peter will let us stay? The city is going to freak out, Eva. It's going to be a hundred times worse than what happened after Lankster Square.>*

My voice went sharper than I meant it to. *<Peter doesn't get to choose who people allow into their homes.>* Addie didn't respond, and I continued, more softly, *<If we do have to leave, in the end, don't you want to have actually done something before we go, Addie? Don't you think we should at least try to make a difference?>*

<Maybe> Addie said. She didn't say anything else.

I shifted again, turning to watch Nina's slumbering form in the other bed. She, at least, was sleeping peacefully tonight.

The next morning, Emalia was still brewing her coffee when I went in search of Ryan, taking the stairs two at a time. For years, I hadn't been able to communicate with anyone but

Addie. Ryan was one of the first people I spoke with after learning to talk again. He would listen until I tamed my jumbled thoughts into words.

I also needed to know *his* thoughts. Had Devon's words been his as well? Or had Devon's will simply overridden Ryan's? Maybe he just hadn't been sure. Maybe he'd needed time to think things over, too.

Henri, not Ryan, answered my knock. "They're still asleep," he said quietly once I'd stepped inside. Henri never spoke unless it was behind closed doors. His accent meant it was safer that way. He tilted his head toward the couch, where the boy I'd been looking for lay stretched out beneath a blanket, one arm curved by his head. His blanket trailed along the carpet.

The light above the dining table was on, but the rest of the apartment remained dim. Still, we could see the shape of his face, the curve of his mouth, the shadow cast by his eyelashes. Why was it always boys who got the ridiculously long eyelashes?

<Is it Ryan or Devon?> Addie asked.

<Ryan> I said without thinking. I never had to think about it anymore.

<How can you tell? You think one of them sleeps differently than the other?>

It sounded silly when she put it like that, but my conviction didn't waver. *<I don't know. I'm just sure it's Ryan. Aren't you?>*

<Yeah> she said after a moment. *<I am.>*

"Eva?" Henri smiled when I startled.

"Sorry," I said. I was already moving back toward the door. "I'll come back later."

"No, wait." Henri ran a hand against his dark, close-cropped hair, then motioned to the table. "Talk with me? We'll speak softly."

I hesitated, then nodded. When Addie and I had first met Henri, we'd been too nervous to talk with him. He'd come visit Peter, and we'd sneak looks at him from across the room, flushing when he caught us. Other than Peter, we'd never met anyone who'd traveled beyond American borders. And Henri hadn't just traveled. He'd lived his whole life overseas. He had the answers to so many questions we'd never dreamed we'd have the opportunity to ask. How did the hybrids live? Did any of them really go crazy, like the pamphlets at the hospitals claimed? What was it like, the hybrids and the single-souled mingling everywhere? Could people really be happy like that?

Henri had taken the time to tell us stories about his home, a small country in central Africa. He'd traced for us the journeys he'd taken to the Middle East and to Europe, where he now worked for a newspaper. He'd always loved to travel, he said. He'd always wanted to see the world, know its people. And with everywhere he'd gone, he'd come to learn that people are able to accept all kinds of *normal.*

The rest of Henri's apartment was spartan, but his table was always strewn with papers, haphazard legal pads, and manila folders that reminded me of the ones we'd seen at Nornand. The ones reducing us patients to photographs, test results, and hastily scribbled notes. To *progress* or *failure*. To experiments.

"Peter tells me the city has calmed down about what happened at Lankster Square," Henri said. "But they still don't know who did it."

I met his eyes. "Do you think they will? Find out, I mean?"

"I'm not sure," he said. He must have misread my concern, because he continued with, "You don't need to worry about it, Eva."

What had Josie said? That the government wouldn't just frame somebody, because getting it wrong would make them look stupid. It made sense. But never finding out would make them look stupid, too. Their only solution was to find the true perpetrators.

To find us.

They wouldn't find us. The possibility was too terrifying to think about.

"Overseas," I said, "they've found a way to get to the moon. Have they found a way to cure hybridity? One that doesn't end up killing the majority of its patients?"

Henri hesitated. He took a moment to think, carefully rolling down his shirtsleeves from his elbows. It was so early in the morning Ryan hadn't even woken yet, but Henri looked as put together as if he were heading out to a nice dinner. He always dressed like that; no matter that he hardly left the building. "Not yet. There aren't many people researching it now. Some think we should research it more. Some think we should stop. Some think we shouldn't focus on the hybrids at all, but the people who aren't hybrid. Find a way to save all the little children who die before they reach double digits."

All the recessive souls. The ones who hadn't been *lucky*, like me.

"Maybe it's better not knowing," I said. "Maybe all the intricacies of who survives and who doesn't . . . why some people are hybrids and some aren't . . . maybe it's just not something we're supposed to know."

Henri paused, watching me carefully. I struggled not to fidget. "Why do you say that?" he asked.

I thought about Eli and Cal. About Jaime with his broken sentences and lost half.

"Too much knowledge can do terrible things," I said.

For a long moment, Henri didn't reply. His eyes didn't leave our face. Our lips pressed together.

"People do terrible things," Henri murmured. "Knowledge is only knowledge." He hesitated. "What if they could find a *true* cure? Not just killing one of the souls, but . . . transferring it?"

<Transferring it?> Addie echoed.

I frowned. "You mean like taking me out of my body and just sticking me into another one? That's impossible. Where would you even get a—an empty body?"

"I'm only speculating," Henri said. "But bodies can be built."

"Built?"

"Yes. Cloned. It's been done with animals already. It makes sense that it would be possible with humans."

I could only stare and stare.

<They could build me another body> I echoed.

Addie didn't reply. Dimly, I was aware that she was shielding her emotions from me. But my own feelings—my own thoughts—were in too much disarray for me to focus on hers.

To build a body from nothing . . . could you do that? Could you create a fully functioning human being, minus whatever it was that sparked it? That thought, and felt, and dreamed?

And how could you transfer me? My thoughts? My memories? What if something got lost on the way over? Could I still be me if I were in another body? Would they make the second body just like my old one? Would I still have the scars on my hands from the coffee I'd spilled as a child?

Lyle with a new kidney was still Lyle. Lyle would be Lyle even if they had to replace *all* his organs—I felt that with unbreakable certainty.

But was this different? Would I still be me?

Would I still be *me* without Addie sharing my heart?

"You know this—this kind of thing is not possible now, right?" Henri said quickly. "It will not be possible in five years or ten or, I imagine, twenty or thirty years, either. I am not a scientist. But I only wonder. If there were the possibility of finding this kind of *cure*, would you wish them to do the research? Even with the harm some people might do with the knowledge?"

I just stared at him. I didn't know how to answer.

Addie was the one, in the end, who whispered <*It wouldn't be a cure, Eva. Nothing can be a cure to being hybrid, because being hybrid isn't a disease.*>

And she was, of course, right. These procedures Henri was talking about—they wouldn't *fix* us, wouldn't make us *right*. They would just make us *different* than we were now. They would change us.

Would I want that sort of change? I wasn't sure. Maybe I would. It would be nice, perhaps, to have the choice, even if Addie and I decided in the end that it wasn't for us. Even if we didn't want to change, perhaps some other hybrid would.

Henri forced a smile that wasn't really a smile, just a tightening of the lips. "Don't worry about it. This isn't what I meant to talk with you about, Eva, when I asked you to stay. I wanted you to tell me: Is something wrong?"

My mind still whirled with the idea of building bodies. From what? The dead? Or grown from cells? More and more, I realized just how little Addie and I knew. How little we'd been content with knowing.

We'd had no reason to doubt the truth of what our teachers taught us: that the Great Wars had swept across the rest of the world, bringing it to its knees. That the Americas were a haven of peace and prosperity. That this peace and prosperity was contingent on keeping the country hybrid-free.

Why would we have believed differently? These were the things written in our history books and our newspapers, the things our parents told us. It was what our classmates and our classmates' parents believed. It was what the president said, and he'd been in office for over two decades. His uncle had guided the country through the start of the Great Wars and the invasions that had occurred on American soil. He should know.

"What do you mean?" I said. "Nothing's wrong."

"They try to hide it, but I hear Lissa and Ryan arguing. About something bigger, I think, than the things they usually fight about."

<*Concentrate, Eva*> Addie said.

She was right. I could think about Henri's ideas later. "I don't know what they're arguing about."

Henri studied our expression. I turned away, letting our hair fall into our face, and stared at the other papers on the table. Buried beneath two of the legal pads was a world map identical to the one he'd given us.

I ran our fingers across the glossy surface. "Why don't they help us? They know about us, don't they? About the hybrids? How we're treated?"

Henri hesitated. "They have more pressing concerns. The Americas are large, but you are . . . what's the word? You keep to yourselves. And you are not as advanced with technology. You are not a threat. The world has already seen too much war these past decades. There is little to gain from provoking the Americas when so far they have been peaceful."

"They haven't been peaceful to *us*," I snapped. I took a

deep breath through our nose. "They trade, though. Dr. Lyanne told us. There are countries out there trading with the Americas, helping them hurt us."

When Henri spoke again, his voice was even quieter. Contained. "Almost everyone was hurt by the wars. Some countries more than others. Some are very desperate now. Some would try to trade with the Americas in hope they might receive aid from them, if war came again." His expression showed how unlikely he imagined that help would be. "Others trade because the Americas can provide supplies they are unable to produce themselves and cannot manage to obtain elsewhere."

In the end, though, whatever their reasoning, the important thing was easy to understand.

<*They won't be helping us*> I said.

<*No, they won't.*>

We'd have to help ourselves.

NINETEEN

Ryan woke up soon after, saving me from more of Henri's questions.

"Eva?" His voice was rough with sleep. I perched on the edge of the couch, smiling automatically as his eyes met mine. If I bent down, just a little, I could kiss away the last of his dreams, my hair curtaining us from the rest of the world. "You're here early."

I shrugged, conscious of Henri at the dining table behind me. "I wanted to talk."

Ryan nodded and pushed himself upright. He knew what I'd come to talk about. I guess it wasn't hard to figure out. "I'll get dressed."

I sat awkwardly in the living room while Ryan went to get ready. We couldn't really talk, of course, with Henri listening in, so as soon as Ryan reemerged, I mumbled something about not wanting to leave Kitty alone and pulled him out of the apartment.

But when we reached Emalia's door, I hesitated. "Let's keep going." I took a step back toward the stairwell. "Let's go outside. We do it all the time to go to the photography shop, and nothing's ever happened. Nothing's ever even come *close* to happening."

<*Eva . . .* > Addie said.

But Ryan smiled. "Where do you want to go?"

To the last place we'd felt, just for a moment, happy, unburdened, and full of hope.

"The beach," I said.

I'd sought out Ryan so we could talk about Sabine's plan, but as the two of us wandered through the congested city streets, I didn't bring it up. The warm, sunny morning filled me with a happiness I was in no hurry to destroy.

We had no money for the bus, let alone a taxi, so we ducked into a tiny grocery store to look at a map and write down directions, then set out on foot. Emalia didn't usually get home until evening; we had plenty of time.

It was miles before we finally reached the boardwalk. But the sight of it—all vibrant colors and chaotic noise—made us forget how far we'd walked. Boats rocked in the distance, just visible between the brightly colored buildings. School hadn't started up yet in Anchoit, and children ran around, screaming laughter. Their parents trailed after them.

A burst of wind made me wrap our jacket tighter around our body, made our hair fly around our face. But it also brought us the rich, salty smell of the ocean mixed with a whiff of greasy food.

Ryan and I didn't bother with the little stores or the

restaurants or the arcade games with their flashing lights. We headed straight for the beach, where I took off our shoes and socks and Ryan left his on. It was almost noon, the pale sand warm beneath our feet.

Far out in the water, a small boat cut through the waves. I squinted at it, hand up to shield our eyes from the sun. During the early years of the Great Wars, refugees from the rest of the world came to the Americas in ships, seeking shelter and safety. At first they'd been allowed in, but then the invasions happened, anti-hybrid sentiment spiked, and the ships were turned away. Many of the hybrids already in the country were rounded up and placed into camps. Some say they were murdered—or executed, anyway—for suspected treason. The institutions were supposed to be a kindness, after that. A place of containment and safety, not murder.

This cure Jenson talked about. It must sound like a kindness, too.

"I thought we'd have the whole summer," I said over our shoulder to Ryan. I could almost taste the salt water on our lips, feel the slick of the sea on our skin. Everything smelled heady and rough and untamed. "Last time we were here, I mean. I thought we'd have the whole summer to come here and swim and be outside."

Ryan led us farther down the beach, away from the crowded boardwalk. Here, we were all but alone. I twisted our hair off our neck, wanting to feel the sun heat our skin. I imagined it could warm us all the way through, chase away the shadows I felt lodged in our chest.

"It's not supposed to get that cold here, even in the fall," Ryan said. "Maybe soon, they'll let us out of lockdown."

It was mid-August, but no one had said anything about enrolling us in school. I didn't know whether or not to be relieved. School might be hell—having to keep up a front at all times, trying to make friends we knew would abandon us if they got a hint of who we really were. But if Peter and the others weren't planning on enrolling us here, in Anchoit, it might mean they didn't expect us to stay long enough for it to be worth it.

I was silent a moment, our shoes hanging from our fingertips. I'd kept so many secrets these past few weeks. From Emalia and Sophie, mostly. But I realized now that I'd kept one particular secret from Ryan and Hally, too.

"Peter's planning on sending us someplace else."

Ryan spun around to face me. "*What?* When did he say that?"

"A little while back." I looked away. "It's not just Addie and me. He wants all of us out of Anchoit—you, Hally, and Kitty, too. He doesn't think it's safe."

"Peter doesn't think anything's safe," Ryan said. The sudden bitterness in his voice made the day a little less warm.

Then, with a sigh, he sat on the sand and tugged us down with him. He rested his head against ours, and I tried to relax, because this should have been so easy, so simple. But it wasn't. Addie's rigidity bled into our muscles, injected tension into our limbs. She said nothing, but she didn't need to. I should have moved away. But I didn't want to. Instead, I took Ryan's arm and pulled him close as I lay down, snug in the heat of the sun and the sand and his skin.

The sky was almost cloudless. So blue it hurt to look at.

"What do you think of their plan?" Ryan's voice was low, right next to our ear.

After so much quiet contemplation, it felt strange to hear the question aloud. It felt even stranger to realize we'd only heard of Sabine's plan less than twenty-four hours before.

"I want to do it," I said to the sky, the sand, the sea.

<Eva> Addie said. It wasn't an argument. She hadn't argued against the plan since last night. But she said my name like a warning. Or, not a warning. A plea, maybe. A plea to wait just one more moment, to think this through just a little more.

But I didn't want to think it through anymore. I'd woken up this morning wanting to talk with Ryan so I could figure out my thoughts, but as it turned out, I didn't need to. My thoughts were straight enough as it was.

"I want to do it," I repeated. "I think . . . I think—"

"It's right?" Ryan said.

I shifted so I could meet his eyes. "If it means one less Nornand for somebody else out there, then yes. If it means people reconsider, just a little bit, what they're doing to us, then yes."

He nodded. Addie didn't say a word. Maybe if I'd tried a little harder, I'd have puzzled out the knot of her feelings.

But I was too preoccupied with this out-loud conversation, the weight of my words, the boy I was sharing them with, the warmth of his arm around me.

"The government—those officials and doctors . . . we owe them nothing," I said.

Ryan shook his head. He pushed himself up on his elbows, his gaze sweeping out to the waves. There was sand in his hair, sand nestled in the crinkles of his shirt.

He spoke quietly, but I caught every word.

"*This*," he said. "This plan. We owe them this."

TWENTY

When we reconvened in the attic the next day and Sabine asked for our decisions, everyone else answered first.

Jackson and Vince. That knifing smile. *Yes.*

Cordelia and Katy. A solemnity. A series of quick, fluttering blinks. *Yes.*

Sabine and Josie. Smiling. Gentle. Already turning to the next person in the room. *Yes.*

Christoph. A sharp nod. *Yes.*

Devon and Ryan. A long, long pause, in which their eyes focused on nothing. Then, voice low. *Yes.*

I could feel the others' quiet relief, read it in their shoulders. All eyes were on Addie and me now.

<*Addie?*> I said, but Addie said nothing.

So I thought of Jaime. I thought of Kitty and Nina and Cal and Eli and Bridget and the girl with the silver-blond hair and the boy with the face full of freckles and all the other children who'd sat with us wearing Nornand blue.

I thought of Mr. Conivent.

Of Jenson.

Of Lissa and Hally in the basement, twisting in the grip of a nurse while another prepped a syringe.

"Yes," I said. I didn't whisper. I didn't let our voice waver or tremble. "Yes, we're in."

The frequency of the meetings increased. Soon we spent at least an hour or two every day at the photography shop, sometimes on the ground floor, but mostly hidden up in the attic. At first, we snuck out earlier in the afternoon, keeping a wide buffer between getting back to the apartment and Emalia coming home from work. But Emalia hardly ever strayed from her schedule, and we grew bolder. Going to the photography shop in the late afternoon or early evening was better, anyway—it meant the others were off work and we could all speak together.

Now that we'd decided to go ahead with the plan, we actually had to work out the logistics. We talked about explosives we might use, comparing compositions and complexities and quantities needed. We weighed liquids against solids—and threw out ideas that required too much bulk. We needed to transport the thing, after all, and only Sabine owned a car.

Sabine had copious notes: lists of possible chemicals and combinations and where they might be found. I spent hours trying to read through them as she and Ryan discussed what he might build to encase different reactions and how he could connect it all to a timer to make sure the thing went off when we wanted it to. They'd mulled over attempting to detonate remotely, but Ryan was hesitant about wiring together something sophisticated enough to work long-range.

It was disconcerting, sometimes, to see Ryan and Sabine together, hear them speaking and only vaguely understand what they were going on about. Ryan was alive during these discussions like he rarely was other times. There was no inhibition, no hesitation, no awkwardness. There seemed, in fact, to be nothing in the world but his books, notes, and diagrams—and Sabine, of course, who navigated this world as easily as he did. The two of them seemed to communicate half in code.

More and more, Addie and I felt out of our depth. We'd always ranked as clever. Above average. We'd tested well enough to earn a scholarship to our private school, and classwork had rarely been difficult. It was one of the benefits of having two minds to everyone else's one. At the end of the day, though, we'd never bothered to study chemistry beyond what we were assigned, and this was definitely beyond our freshman syllabus.

Sabine had never officially completed middle school, let alone high school. Emalia and Sophie hadn't yet joined the Underground when Peter rescued Sabine and Christoph, so there hadn't been anyone to forge identification. For years, they'd lived as society's ghosts, undocumented, half-hidden. But Sabine read. Voraciously. And like Devon had told us, once she got old enough, she started sneaking into the lectures at the college downtown, soaking up whatever she could.

"Liquid oxygen and kerosene," Sabine said one afternoon. Cordelia was still downstairs, since the shop didn't close for another hour, but the rest of us lounged around the attic, buried in books and Sabine's notes. The muggy warmth had made me sleepy, but Sabine's words snapped me back to attention.

<Liquid oxygen . . . > Addie repeated. *<We read about that in her notes.>*

Liquid oxygen. LOX. Freezing point below –300 degrees Fahrenheit. There had been more, but I didn't remember it.

Jackson whistled low. "Isn't that—"

"Yeah, kind of like rocket fuel." Sabine leaned back against the sofa. The research and planning engrossed her as much as it did Ryan, but Sabine also had work during the day. It seemed to be taking a toll on her that the Lankster Square plan never had. She was as steady as ever, but sometimes looked a little faded. "We wouldn't need much. We *would* need supplies, though. A thermos for the liquid oxygen—"

"Forget the thermos." Jackson tried to flip the page in Sabine's book, and she brushed his hand away. "Where would we get the liquid oxygen?"

Sabine's voice strengthened as she settled into her explanation. "We take it from the hospital downtown."

"You want to steal it," Addie said. "From a hospital."

"That does seem to be what she's saying." Jackson grinned, but he was the only one. Christoph stared up at the ceiling. Ryan paged through Sabine's notes.

"They keep it stored in tanks out back. It gets converted to gas form before—you know." Sabine mimed an oxygen mask. "I went downtown yesterday and took a look at the tanks. If we approach at the right angle, we can avoid the security cameras, and there's no guard. At least not while I was there." She pulled a wry smile. "All we'd need to do is hop the fence around the tanks and tap the relief valve. Or just take a whole tank. Some of them aren't very big."

I hesitated. <*Stealing from a hospital* . . . >

It made me think of our little brother. Of how badly he needed everything the hospital was able to provide him.

"Addie?" Jackson waited for Addie to raise our head. He wasn't smiling anymore. His voice was gentler. "We wouldn't be taking much." He glanced at Sabine as if for confirmation, and she nodded.

"One tank. They've got dozens, and it's not like they can't get more."

Addie shrugged and looked away again. "It just feels weird. To steal from a hospital."

"Well." Jackson came around the couch and walked toward Addie and me. "It's not like you haven't done it before."

Addie frowned in confusion. Sabine rolled her eyes, but allowed herself a small smile. "He means you."

Addie and I still didn't understand. It must have come through on our face, because Jackson laughed. "You're hybrid, Addie. By law, you're practically hospital property. Escaping like you did . . ." He grinned. "Well, that was kind of like stealing yourself back from them, wasn't it?"

Christoph groaned. "You and your metaphors, Jackson."

"I don't think that counts as a metaphor," Sabine said, laughing.

But in a way, Jackson was right.

Having specifics put things in a different light. We could have talked about different kinds of explosives forever, could have joked with Jackson and Vince about dynamite permits forever, but now we had a plan, and bringing down the Powatt institution became that much more real.

<*We're really going to do this*> Addie said.

It wasn't quite a question, but it was far from a statement. We looked at Ryan, so engaged in his conversation with Sabine. Did he ask himself if we were doing the right thing? Did he doubt? What about Devon? He wasn't the sort who changed his mind easily. Did they argue about it constantly? It didn't seem like it. Ryan seemed focused, assured.

Maybe he just kept in mind all our reasons for doing this. The people we would save. The message we would send. The setback for the government this would be. Maybe he kept in mind the quiet words Jaime muttered to a soul who no longer existed, the long scar across his skull. Maybe he just thought about his sisters and how close we'd come to losing one or both of them.

<*We are*> I said.

"You're quiet," Jackson said.

Addie shrugged. "Guess I don't have much to contribute."

"Not everyone can be geniuses." Jackson tilted his head

toward Sabine and Ryan. They were too enthralled in their conversation to even hear us. "But don't count yourself out."

Our stomach twinged, but I felt a ghost of a smile, so faint it was hardly there. So faint no one would have caught it but me, because Addie's mouth was mine.

"I won't," Addie said.

Ryan was almost always the one in control when we were up in the attic. I wondered sometimes whether Devon bothered to be there at all, or whether he simply went under and let Ryan handle everything. Since his initial derision of Sabine's plan, he hadn't spoken up again. But he didn't bother pretending to be involved, either.

When Devon did appear, the others tried to draw him into their conversations. Sabine even brought in a cutaway lock when I jokingly mentioned Devon's interest in lock picking. He was willing enough to listen as she explained how it worked, and he seemed to get the hang of it pretty quickly, but it made him no more eager to join in the other discussions.

I didn't think too much about it, to be honest. I was too busy trying to keep up with Ryan and Sabine.

Then one night, Devon showed up at our bedroom door. Emalia must have let him in. I was too engrossed in Sabine's notebook, which I'd convinced her to let me borrow, to notice him until he was standing in the doorway.

"Brought Sabine's notes home?" he said. "You're getting more dedicated than she is."

It was a little unsettling to be on the receiving end of his stare, but I tried to smile. "I'm just looking. I don't have anything else to do."

"And Addie?" he said. I frowned. He didn't break eye contact, and neither did I. "Doesn't she have anything better to do, either? Or did she have a change of heart?"

His voice remained impassive until the last sentence. Even then, I felt more than heard the accusation. I bristled anyway. "Addie—"

Addie shoved herself into control of our body. "I have the right to."

Devon's only reaction to the shift was a slow blink and the upward twitch of an eyebrow. "What did it?" he asked. "Changed your mind."

With Addie in control, I was free to focus all my attention on Devon, this boy who shared Ryan's eyes and hands and mouth. What was Ryan thinking right now?

Our eyes focused on a point over Devon's shoulder. Our lips thinned. At first I thought Addie wasn't going to answer his question at all. But finally, she said, "I realized that what we went through at Nornand . . . that's just the cotton-candy version of what other people have gone through, isn't it?"

Devon gave no reply.

Addie sighed. "Jackson told us how he spent three years in one of those institutions, and . . . and just knowing that every single person in that attic has been through ten times worse than what we went through—I . . . Well . . . if there's anything we can do to help make sure another kid out there doesn't suffer that, we should do it."

"So, sad stories," Devon said. "That's what did it."

Addie frowned, closing Sabine's notebook and climbing to our feet. "If that's what you want to cheapen it to, then yes, sad stories. That's what changed my mind. Other people's sad stories."

"Everybody's got sad stories." Devon's voice was as ungiving as stone. "And everyone thinks they're so very special and broken because of them."

"What's that supposed to mean?"

He shrugged.

"You came back to the attic with us," Addie said. Our fingers tightened around the notebook, the cover biting into our skin. "You could have refused. You're the one who said you'd go."

"You were going to go." Devon wore the look he usually saved for other people. The one that said, *You're being very stupid, but I'll speak slowly in hopes you might understand.* Addie rolled our eyes. "You really believe Ryan would have allowed us to stay behind if you went?" He hesitated. Had we ever seen Devon hesitate? He always either spoke or he didn't—no vacillation. "Ryan cares about Eva. Which means he cares about you. Which makes you and Eva . . ."

"Makes us what?" Addie snapped.

"Makes you one of us."

"Us?"

The hesitation ebbed from Devon's body. He was all quiet, steady confidence again. He nodded.

"Who's the rest of *us*?"

"Hally," he said, "and Lissa."

"Oh," Addie said.

"We look out for one another." His eyes were bright and intent on ours. There was almost a dare in them. "No matter what happens."

Addie nodded. Something transpired between the two of them. Something I didn't understand. Without another word, Devon turned and headed back down the hall.

<*Wait*> I said. Addie grudgingly allowed me control, and I repeated the request aloud. Devon came back into view. "Can I . . . I'd like to speak with Ryan."

Devon frowned, and for a moment, I was afraid I'd offended him. Would I have been offended if someone had told me, *Step aside, I want to talk with Addie, not you?*

Probably.

Yes.

Sorry, I started to say, but I didn't get the chance.

"Ryan isn't here," Devon said.

I shut our mouth so quickly our teeth clicked against one another. It shouldn't have felt this strange, knowing Ryan was temporarily gone. I'd disappeared myself. I'd been with Ryan without Devon there. But watching those familiar eyes, that familiar face, and knowing Ryan wasn't looking back at me . . .

I thought Devon would just leave again, but he lingered a moment at the door.

"Look," he said. "Everyone's telling stories. Everyone has something they want. You can't trust them all."

"Who are we supposed to trust, then?" I said.

He studied me. Said, quietly, "I don't know."

This time, he left and didn't look back.

TWENTY-ONE

Emalia and Nina were huddled on the couch when I finally ventured from our bedroom, Emalia's arm around Nina's shoulders, both of them laughing at a television show. I'd just poured a cup of juice when Addie said <*I'm going under, Eva*> and was gone, just like that.

Left me in the middle of the kitchen, a glass of orange juice halfway to my lips, my feet cold against the tiles.

Nina called, "Can you pour me some?"

I gave her mine, since I didn't want it anymore. Somehow, it hadn't fully struck me until now how Addie could leave me when I didn't want her to go.

"Join us?" Emalia said. I shook my head.

The knock at the door came long after the show had ended. Nina was in the shower. I was milling about our room and only came out when I heard Emalia say, "Oh, hi, Lissa. How're you?"

"I'm fine." Lissa's voice was barely above a whisper, and she didn't speak again until she saw me in the hallway. She cradled a roll of clothes and a towel in her arms, a small denim bag slung over her shoulder. "I was wondering . . ." Her dark eyes shifted between Emalia and me. "Could I spend the night here?"

I didn't speak. I'd barely seen Lissa or Hally since the day they refused to go back to the attic. They'd stayed secreted away in Henri's apartment, burying themselves in books, I guessed. Or maybe just staring out the window, the way they used to.

"Of course, Lissa," Emalia said finally. "You can sleep over whenever you want."

Emalia didn't own a sleeping bag, and the twin beds were too narrow to share, so Lissa and I laid out blankets in the living room. Of course, Nina wanted to join us. She grabbed her blanket and declared ownership of the couch while Lissa and I were still carrying the coffee table out of the way.

We moved awkwardly, not meeting eyes.

Emalia, who had work the next day, went to bed. The rest of us watched late-night television with the volume barely loud enough to hear. Eventually, Nina drifted asleep. Lissa and I watched for a little longer after that, but soon most of the channels showed nothing but infomercials, and I switched off the television. The living room dipped into darkness and silence. Addie still hadn't returned. The warmth where she should have been was dark and silent.

Lissa lay curled away from me, so still I thought she'd fallen asleep, too. But then I heard a quiet "Eva?"

"Yeah?" I whispered.

She turned to face me. She'd removed her glasses, and her face looked different without them—more vulnerable. I braced myself for any number of questions: *What are you and the others up to now? Why are you doing this? Why haven't you talked with me? Why have you left me alone?*

The question she asked wasn't any I'd expected.

"You ever wonder why we're like this? Why people are hybrid? Why some of us are and some of us aren't?"

Lissa's eyes searched mine, and I nodded. Of course I had. How could I not?

And what do you think?

That was the natural next question, but she didn't ask it, and neither did I. It felt too private to ask. All hybrids must wonder why they were born to this fate. I'd wondered as a child alone on the playground. Lissa had been kept cloistered at home until second grade, seeing no one beyond her parents and her brother. Did that mean she'd started wondering later, or earlier?

"It's always been this way," Lissa murmured. "Since human beings first came to be. And I . . . I guess it doesn't matter, does it?" She shifted onto her back, her long hair tangled beneath her. "My father used to tell Hally and me stories, when we were really little. I don't think he knows we remember, but we do."

"What kind of stories?"

"Legends," Lissa said. "Of how the world began. Of how

the hybrids began. His grandma taught them to him, before she died. He had to translate them, since she didn't speak English. There were ones about Purusha, and ones about Brahma. And others, too. He used to tell us so many. We'd beg for them." She twisted a curl of hair around her fingers. "This was before we started pretending we'd settled. He never told us any more after that."

I'd never heard those stories, but I'd been taught others. At school, we'd learned what the ancient world believed—that their gods had created all people to be hybrid, so they'd never have to suffer the agony of loneliness. Then one man had committed some unpardonable sin and, as punishment, the gods tore out his second soul. He was cast from society and left all alone.

Finally the people took pity on him and brought him back into the fold, where he was allowed to stay as a second-class citizen, doing menial labor. Only menial labor, because who could trust higher-level jobs to a man with only one soul? One mind?

The first time Addie and I heard the legend, we were in third grade. The only unsettled child in our entire class.

What a cruel story, the teacher had said, *invented to justify the hybrids' even crueler treatment of our ancestors. Do you know what* ancestor *means?*

We'd lingered at the door at the end of the day, waiting for the teacher's attention to fall on us. We'd been comfortable with her. Eight years old and unsettled, we were unusual but not obscene, and she'd been kinder than our peers.

Who did he marry? I asked.

She gave us a confused smile. *I'm sorry?*

The man who wasn't hybrid. He must have married someone. So they had kids. Otherwise, there wouldn't be more single-souled people.

Addie, she said. Everyone called us Addie then, because it was mostly Addie in control. I didn't bother correcting her. *It's only a story. He didn't marry anyone. He didn't even exist. The hybrids just made it up so they could feel better about treating the non-hybrids so horribly. Do you understand?*

Yes, I'd said, though I didn't. How could the hybrids have felt better about themselves if their story didn't even make sense?

"How can you think Sabine's plan is a good idea, Eva?" Lissa's question pulled me back to the present. Her moods tended to be less extreme than Hally's, so maybe I ought to be grateful for that. But the quiet disappointment in her voice made my stomach squeeze, made a wrecking ball of my guilt. I needed Addie here for this. I didn't want to face Lissa's question alone.

"It's just a building," I said. "Think about how it'll strike a blow against the government."

"Strike a blow against the government?" She propped herself up on her elbows and stared right at me. "Come on, Eva. You didn't come up with that. You don't talk like that."

It was something Vince had said, actually, but I kept quiet.

"Have you talked to Ryan about this?" I said.

She sighed, flopping back down on the ground. "Yes, but he's Ryan. Give him a project, make him feel like he's needed, and he's set. He won't listen to us. We thought you would."

"The explosives—"

"The bomb, Eva," Lissa said. Her eyes narrowed. "It's a bomb."

"The bomb." The word felt heavy, bitter on our tongue. Like how *settling* had felt once, when Addie and I were small and confused and linked it to something we were doing wrong, something that was wrong with us.

I forgot what the rest of my sentence had been. *Bomb* filled my mind, pushing everything else away.

"Maybe you should tell Peter about it," Lissa said softly.

"Peter?" I said. "Peter wants to send us all away, and you think—"

"*What?*"

The word cut through the room. We both checked on Nina, but if she'd woken, she pretended otherwise. Still, I waited a moment before replying. I needed it to steady my breathing. "Ryan didn't tell you?"

"Tell me what?" Lissa tried to whisper, but her voice kept rising. "Peter wants to send us where? He told you that? When?"

"I don't know. A while ago. He—" I pressed my fist to my forehead. "It's not decided. I thought Ryan or Devon had told you. But Lissa, he's the last person we can go to, all right?"

A hundred emotions flashed across Lissa's face, each bleeding into the next. She took a shaky breath and shoved them all under control.

"Henri, then? Emalia?" There was something pleading in her expression. "*I* could tell them, Eva."

She wasn't really asking for permission. She could tell anyone—I couldn't stop her. But she wanted acceptance. My support, when everything came apart. Vince would be furious. They'd all be. God knew what Christoph might do.

"Ryan would probably hate me," Lissa said. And maybe I should have said, *No, he wouldn't. Of course not,* but I didn't. Because the unasked question growing between us was: *Would you?*

I didn't answer it. I said, instead, "Don't, okay?"

She didn't sigh. Hardly reacted at all. But I caught the dimming in her eyes.

"Please." I sat up, drawing my blanket against me, feeling it bunch beneath my fingers. "Tell Emalia or Henri, and they'll immediately go to Peter." I reached out hesitantly, and touched Lissa's arm. "Don't tell anyone. Just . . . just trust me, okay?"

"I *do* trust you. It's just—"

"It's going to be okay," I said. My mouth was so dry I could barely get the words out. "I'm going to make everything okay."

"How?" Lissa demanded.

"I don't know. Just—just give me some time, all right? I promise. I'll figure it out."

An eternity passed before Lissa replied. A hundred

thousand years separating our bodies in the dark.

"Okay," she said, and I hated the unease on her face. The knowledge that I'd put it there. But I didn't have a choice. She couldn't tell anyone. She just couldn't.

Lissa sighed and lay back down. I watched her stare at the ceiling fan until her eyes slid shut and her breathing grew shallow. I sat there for what seemed like hours more, my thoughts stumbling around in the darkness.

Entombed in the silence of my own mind, I waited for Addie to come back.

I fell asleep before she did.

TWENTY-TWO

The next couple weeks passed quickly. Sabine decided we should have a test run before the real thing, so Ryan had to make two containers, one much smaller than the other. The two of them calculated how much kerosene and liquid oxygen they'd need, and what dimensions the containers should be.

Ryan spent hours and hours in the attic, looking through his books, fiddling with his designs. Cordelia or Sabine came up occasionally during the day, but they had customers to deal with. The others visited during the afternoon. Most of the time, it was just Ryan and me. Really *just* Ryan and me.

Addie had developed a new fervor for practicing just how long and accurately we could go under. The two of us spent more and more time alone in our body.

<Two hours> she'd say, and I'd hold that time in my mind as tightly as I could while letting myself fall asleep. It wasn't easy. You could only go under by utterly letting yourself go. Latching on to the idea of *come back in two hours* was like holding on to a buoy and trying to dive.

But little by little, we managed it. Ten minutes. Twenty minutes. An hour. Three hours. I'd go under just after breakfast and wake up hungry for lunch. I'd disappear in our bedroom while still in our pajamas and wake up in open air, dressed in clothes I had no memory of putting on.

At first, Addie and I filled each other in on everything we'd done while the other was asleep. But soon, we stopped. Most of it wasn't important anyway, especially since the others could tell between Addie and me now and didn't expect one of us to know what the other had been up to.

For the first time in our lives, we had some modicum of privacy. I could be with Ryan alone. Without Addie's emotions fogging up the back of my mind. Without the taste of her disapproval in my throat.

<Is it weird for you?> I asked her one day. I didn't want to. But I had to. *<Not . . . not knowing what we do when you're gone?>*

She took a long time to answer. But finally, she said *<It's your body, too. And I trust you, Eva. I trust you to tell me what I need to know.>*

Trust was all we had to get us through this. Nothing in our lives had ever prepared us for it. No one had ever taught us how to handle it.

Months ago, during that first night in Anchoit, Ryan and I kissed, floundering, in the hallway of Peter's apartment. There was something to be said, certainly, about first kisses. But there was more to be said about the ones that came afterward. We kissed urgently at first—driven by a sense of secrecy, of stolen time. Then languidly, softly, knowing there wasn't any rush. We lived in the circle of fairy lights, hidden in an attic that seemed like its own world.

I told Ryan about our old apartment in the city. About the fire escape that had felt like our sanctuary. About the teachers at school only calling Addie's name, even when mine had also been on the roster, because otherwise the class was simply too hard to quiet down again.

One morning, Addie asked *<Are you telling him everything, Eva?>*

She didn't preface the question with a name or any sort of explanation at all, and it took me a moment to realize who she was referring to.

<We just talk> I said.

We were eating breakfast, and she was quiet a long moment. *<All right. I'm not saying stop. But Eva—just remember, they're my stories, too.>*

And I did keep that in mind, from then on.

Two weeks passed. Then three. October approached. Back home in Lupside, the leaves would be changing colors, drifting like embers from their branches. There were no trees on the walk between our apartment building and the photography shop, but the odd holiday decorations started popping up on the store windows: miniature pumpkins, black witch hats, frightened-looking cats.

Insulated by the attic's sloping walls, there didn't seem to be any need to think about time.

At first, Ryan's ideas only existed on paper: words and diagrams. One day, I found him staring at his notes and laughing quietly to himself.

"What?" I shifted closer and tried to read his handwriting.

He lifted his head. I reached over and smoothed down his hair as he spoke. "I'm going to need tools. And supplies. Possibly a welder. Where am I going to get a welder, Eva?"

My hand stilled. I stared at him until the absurdity of it got the better of me and I had to laugh. I laughed more now than I'd ever laughed in my life. I laughed as often as I could, savoring it.

"Ask Jackson," I said through the giggles. "He probably knows someone who knows someone with power tools who owes him a favor."

Turned out Jackson did. Addie was hesitant about sneaking out late at night. We didn't need to go. But if Ryan was going to chance being caught, then I was going to risk it with him, and Addie eventually came around.

We broke curfew to spend late nights secreted in a garage downtown, surrounded by power tools Jackson admitted we didn't *technically* have permission to use, so hurry up and get it done. I woke once in the semidarkness of the garage, hearing Ryan working in the background. Jackson was laughing. I—Addie—was laughing, too. She quieted a little once she felt my presence, but didn't lose her smile.

Twice, we were almost caught leaving the garage. But

both times, we got away, safe and triumphant and filled with a breathless sort of glee.

Then came the morning I walked up the attic stairs, still yawning, and Ryan turned to me.

He said, before I could speak: "I think it's finished."

It had been a while since the atmosphere in the attic was like this. Tense. Stretched. Vince lounged on the green couch, Sabine next to him. Christoph and Cordelia took up the other sofa. Ryan stood; he'd just finished explaining the workings of the contraption sitting in the middle of the rug. Addie and I leaned against the wall.

"It'll do the job," Ryan said into the silence.

"Not doubting it," Vince said. The two shared a tense but genuine smile.

"We'll test it next week," Sabine said. "We'll drive way out to Frandmill. There's a lot of deserted land around there. We'll get the liquid oxygen tomorrow night, after dark but before curfew. Not all of us."

"I'll go with you," Vince said, and she nodded.

"I'll go, too." I wasn't sure whether to be gratified or insulted by the startled silence that followed my words.

<Eva> Addie said quietly. *<I don't think that's a good idea. If we get caught—>*

<We won't get caught> I said. I was being stubborn, but I couldn't help it. Not after the look that had followed my volunteering. I needed to help out in some way. That was

why Sabine had invited me to join her group in the first place, wasn't it? To help?

"If we're going to go before midnight, Emalia might not be asleep yet," Sabine said.

I shrugged. "We'll just say we're going up to Henri's for a bit. We got out fine to work in the garage. She never checks."

It was yet another risk, but to be honest, I was no longer particularly worried about Emalia or Sophie finding out about our trips outdoors. They seemed happily oblivious that we'd even think about sneaking out.

Ryan glanced at me. "If four isn't too many . . ."

"Three is enough," Sabine said. "We only need two to carry the tank, and then one more to stand guard."

"But two standing guard is better than one," Ryan said.

Sabine's lips pressed into a smile that quickly faded. She hesitated, then took a deep breath. "It'll be worst for you if we're caught."

He shrugged. "It'll be night. I won't attract more attention than any of you."

Which was only true as long as we weren't seen. But Sabine didn't argue further, just nodded. "Tomorrow night, then. If that turns out badly, we'll try again Friday."

And just like that, another chunk of the plan fell into place.

TWENTY-THREE

A birthday cake on a polka-dotted tablecloth
With white frosting
And sliced strawberries
And five candles weeping wax, burning
Five candles
And two breaths
Before they all went out.

Addie's old black sketchbook
Spine cracked
Pages lolling out
Bloated with paint and wrinkled
Sketches of our stuffed animals
Of Lyle. Of Nathaniel.
Of Mom napping on the sofa
Hair in her face
Exhaustion, Addie says when her art teacher asks:
What will you name it?

Laughter.
Beach, sun, waves
The feeling like a seesaw
Like a rope swing
Like rising and falling and rising again—

Like falling against Ryan in the hallway
In that morning
With the curtains pulled tight
In the darkness
And suddenly, his mouth—
And—

I woke to the taste of someone else's mouth.

I woke to an arm curled around my waist. Fingers I didn't recognize tangled in my hair. The warmth of some stranger's body.

I tore away. I stumbled in the semidarkness.

<Eva, don't scream—>

I clamped my—*our*—mouth shut. A strangled cry ground through our teeth.

"Addie?" the stranger said. But it wasn't a stranger. It was Jackson. Jackson with his hair mussed. Jackson with his hands, and his mouth, that had been touching mine—

<Eva. Eva, calm down—>

I struggled for breath, and Jackson—Jackson *laughed.* He tugged at his shirt, setting it straight on his shoulders. It was too dark to read the expression on his face—I was too muddled—

"Eva?" he said. He reached for me. I shoved his hand away.

"Where—where am I?"

He laughed again, but I'd recovered enough to hear how forced it sounded. "Welcome to my room. Just got in. Haven't, you know, gotten the chance to turn on the light and stuff." He'd been against the wall, but he circled around me—*us*—as he spoke, until he reached the opposite wall and the light switch. The brightness slashed across our retinas, made us squint.

Jackson's room was small. Messy. Decorated in shades of dark green and brown. That was all I could take in. My focus was limited to the boy. The boy who shifted on his feet, eyes never leaving ours. He kept a careful distance.

<Give it back!> Addie said. *<Eva, give me control back. Now.>*

She fought for it, and maybe I should have given it to her, but I couldn't. Everything in me screamed against it. I wrapped our arms around our body. He hung by the light switch, looking increasingly uncomfortable.

"Addie was telling me you guys were practicing going under more and more." He gave me a hesitant smile. "Obviously, you haven't quite got a handle on timing yet. You'll get it. Everybody goes through a sort of transition period. Once Katy came back right in the middle of Cordelia—"

"Stop," I said. Our voice was hoarse. He stopped. I finally managed to look away from him, toward the door.

<Eva!>

"I've got to go," I said.

"Right, okay." Jackson hesitated, as if he might say more, but finally just shut his mouth and gestured to the door as if I couldn't see it.

<Eva!> There was another, enormous wrench for control, so strong I froze midstep, trapped in Addie's screaming. *<Eva, let go!>*

<No> I said. *<No. No—>*

I shoved her aside. I hardly had to think about it—I *couldn't* think about it. All I knew was I had to get out. Had to get away from this room, this apartment, this building. This boy.

Our legs started moving again. I didn't look back, and

Jackson didn't speak again. Everything from his bedroom door to the building lobby was a blur.

<*Eva*> Addie said. My name had never been spoken so caustically. <*What the hell are you freaking out about?*>

<*What am I freaking out about?*> My voice squeaked. <*I'm sorry. Did I just misinterpret what was going on in there?*>

<*We were kissing*> she said. I flinched. <*You know, that thing involving mouths that people do with people they like—*>

<*People they like—*>

<*—which I happen to know you and Ryan aren't exactly unfamiliar with—*>

<*You don't even like him*> I shouted.

Her voice turned deathly cold. <*And how do you know, Eva?*>

I faltered. <*Because I would know. If you liked him. I—I would know.*>

I felt so many of Addie's other emotions, didn't I? I knew when she was angry or sad or happy or frustrated or frightened. I would know it if she loved or even just especially *liked* Jackson, and she didn't.

She didn't.

Addie laughed. <*Right. Because you've been paying so much attention to who and what I like, Eva.*>

<*I—*>

<*It's not like you haven't been too busy focusing on*

what you want.> Her voice had gone shrill. Her entire presence next to me was so tight and sharp and hard I didn't dare go anywhere near her. <*You want Ryan to love you. You want—you want Sabine and Cordelia and Christoph to think you're so amazing. You've been so wrapped up in trying to get what you want—*> She shuddered. <*And you know what? I've taken it. Because I felt bad. But what about me, Eva? You always wanted your freedom. What about mine?*>

<*You have your freedom*> I protested.

Somehow, I'd made it out onto the street. I could hardly remember how I'd gotten there. It was evening. Warm and darkening quickly. Cars zoomed past. Where was I? Right. Jackson's apartment. Where was that?

<*I have my freedom?*> Addie said. <*Because what just happened in there—that didn't feel like freedom.*>

In the very last second, I scrambled to reach out for her. I tried to grab on to her—

But she cut away from me. The nothingness dropped, sharp and sudden and painful as a guillotine.

I was left stumbling on the sidewalk, on a street I didn't recognize, in front of an apartment building I didn't remember entering, in a city that suddenly felt incredibly hostile and empty and vast.

TWENTY-FOUR

I had to ask for directions to get home. There was no way I was going back to Jackson, and it took several minutes to dredge up the nerve to approach someone else—several more to find the right words to say.

Finally, I picked a middle-aged woman with a kind face. My voice was surprisingly steady. I tried to smile when she finished explaining.

She'd moved on half a block before I realized I hadn't taken in a single word.

I picked another person, a young man. I managed to follow his instructions this time.

It didn't take very long to make it back to Emalia's apartment building. I lingered in the ground-floor lobby.

<*Addie?*> I whispered.

Of course, she didn't respond. She was gone, lost in dreams.

Was what she'd said right?

I took a sharp breath, pressed the heels of our—my—hands to my forehead. Had I been ignoring what Addie wanted? I hadn't.

Had I?

Maybe I had.

But she should have told me about Jackson. It was my body, too. I deserved to know. I had to know, or it wasn't right, was it? It was too confusing—and hurt too much—to think about. I kept feeling phantom hands on me. Kept tasting Jackson. Kept feeling—

The front door opened, ramming into me from behind. I cried out.

"Addie!" Dr. Lyanne said. Surprise bleached the usual dignity from her body. But the shock only lasted a few seconds. She shut the front door behind her. "What's wrong? What were you doing outside?"

Her eyes swept over me. I didn't even know what to hide—how to hide. I tried to school my expression into something blander, but I couldn't.

Addie. Addie, Addie.

"Come on." Dr. Lyanne grabbed my arm and swept me up the stairs. I didn't resist. I had Emalia's spare key in my pocket, but I let Dr. Lyanne knock on our door. Kitty answered with round eyes.

"I just went outside for a walk," I said before Dr. Lyanne could ask again. "I got tired of being inside and I went out. Nothing happened. The sun didn't explode."

"Just going outside wouldn't leave you a mess like this." Dr. Lyanne tried to steer me toward the dining-room table. Like how she'd steered me back at Nornand. But that girl in

Nornand's blue uniform felt like a different person. A child who could be directed and handled and frightened into obeying.

I was suddenly furious. Being angry was so much easier than being confused, or scared, or guilty. I let it fill me up, occupying the space where Addie should have been, shoving away everything I didn't want to think about, didn't want to feel.

"I'm a mess," I snapped, "because I can't remember where my own body was for the last few hours. I can't remember because I wasn't there. And now Addie's gone, and I think she hates me, and I have no idea when she's coming back, or what we'll do then. Have *you* ever been in a fight with someone in your own head?"

Dr. Lyanne was silent, but only for a second. When she spoke again, her voice was sharp, her words blunt. "Eva, tell me what's going on."

But I couldn't.

I spun around. Ran out the front door. I slammed it against Dr. Lyanne's voice, the call of my name. I ran for the stairs—not up, but down, toward the street. Up, and she could corner me. Down, I could be free, if only for a few more hours.

My feet slipped on the last flight of stairs—I grabbed for the railing but slammed onto my tailbone anyway, so hard I bit back a scream. I slid down the remaining stairs, coming to a painful stop at the bottom.

"Eva!" Vince shouted. He'd just entered the building. He darted toward me. "You all right?"

I nodded, brushing aside his hands as he tried to help me up. It had always been Addie who hated being touched. But right now, the disgust at the feel of someone else's skin was mine alone.

Vince was smiling. It contrasted so sharply with what *I* felt that I just stared at him, like my mind couldn't comprehend how we could feel such different emotions at the same time, in almost the same space. "I was coming to get you," he said. "It's now. It's happening now."

"What is? What's happening now?"

His voice dropped to a whisper. "We're going to the hospital. To get the liquid oxygen, remember? You said you wanted to come."

To the hospital to get the liquid oxygen. To steal the liquid oxygen.

"Ryan—" I said.

Vince's smile dimmed. He reached out again, and this time I didn't shy away. "Look, I know he said he wanted to go, and I get he wants to help. But it's going to be dangerous enough for the rest of us, let alone him. Think about what happens if he gets caught, Eva."

There were footsteps on the stairs above us. The click of heels. It might not be Dr. Lyanne, but I wasn't going to stay and find out.

Vince was right about it being worse for Ryan if he was seen. If we went and we were caught, I'd never forgive myself for having put him in danger. Not when I could have kept him safe.

"You ready?" Vince's expression was so open, his eyebrows raised.

Don't do this, a part of me whispered. *Don't go. Stop. Just stop. Go back upstairs.*

Next to me, Addie was a great black hole.

I straightened and tried to ignore the pain shooting up my spine.

"I'm ready," I said.

TWENTY-FIVE

Vince and I melted easily into the evening crowd. When Ryan and I walked through the streets, people tended to pay attention. People shot us looks—some covertly, some not. It was a lot better than it had been in Lupside, at least. Ryan always ignored them, and I'd grown used to doing the same. Walking with Vince, there was no need to pretend no one was staring, because no one was. Eventually, I even stopped checking over my shoulder for Dr. Lyanne.

"What?" I said, when I caught Vince watching me.

He gave a one-sided shrug. He was so much taller than me that it felt awkward to crane my neck up when we stood side by side. "Look, about what happened back at my place—"

I flinched and almost stopped walking. "You were there?"

"No, no, of course not. Jackson told me, though, after. Before he, you know, vanished." He grinned. "I think you freaked him out a bit with the screaming."

"I didn't scream." My eyes cut away from his, searching for something to feign interest in.

"Hey, I'm just kidding," Vince said. We stopped, waiting for the walk signal at an intersection, and he bent down a little, lowering his voice. "You're all right, though, aren't you?"

I met his gaze. He looked uncharacteristically serious, and I nodded.

"Good." The stoplight changed. He took hold of my arm and said, with cheeky aplomb, "Come on, then. Let's go commit a crime."

Josie met Vince and me at the photography shop. She'd gathered her hair up in a tight ponytail, emphasizing the blunt cut of her bangs. Her jacket was dark, almost black. She looked harsher than I'd ever seen her before.

I wished it were Sabine in control. Sabine's confidence meant a lot, I was coming to realize. It came through in the steadiness of her gaze, the grace of her walk. And it bled into everyone around her—made them confident, too.

Sunset came slow and late here, even in fall, but darkness cloaked the city by the time Josie pulled into a parking lot near Benoll Hospital.

We crossed the street, Josie whispering directions as we walked. "Vince, I need you over the fence with me. Stay close behind. We don't want to give the security camera any footage. Eva, stand watch for us."

On the far end of the hospital's back lot, encircled by a tall chain-link fence, loomed the dark shadows of the oxygen tanks: one big cylinder a couple feet in diameter and twice as tall, several smaller ones about waist height. Some kind of rack stood inside the fence, too, with what I guessed to be the smallest tanks. The area was thankfully unlit.

"I have a pretty good idea where the camera's blind spots are, but just in case one of us does get in its line of sight . . ." Josie pulled three makeshift masks from her bag. Ski masks, with eye and mouth holes cut out. Like the ones criminals wore in movies. Laughter gurgled, sickly sweet, in the back of my throat.

"Really?" I whispered.

"This way, at least they can't get a shot of your face." Josie tossed a mask at me, then pulled on hers. "Come on."

The wool was hot and itchy against my skin. I grimaced and pulled at it, trying to make it more comfortable. With their faces covered up, Josie and Vince were strange, dark figures. What did I look like? Purposeful, menacing, like them? Or just some stupid girl wearing a ski hat over her face?

Josie motioned for me to stop walking when we were a dozen or so yards from the fence. She shoved a tiny flashlight into my hands. "Stand here. If anything happens, flash this in our direction, okay?"

I nodded, gripping the flashlight.

The fence around the oxygen tanks was tall, but Josie and Vince wedged their shoes in the chain-link and climbed it easily. The fence clinked under their weight. I held my breath as Josie swung over and let go, Vince only a second behind. He turned on a flashlight as they neared the rack of tanks, shielding the beam with his hand.

The back lot was deserted but for us. There weren't even any parking spaces—just an expanse of bare, black pavement.

What would Addie think if she came back now?

No, I couldn't think about Addie. I couldn't afford to be distracted.

Josie grabbed one of the tanks and began sliding it free. Vince moved to help her. They'd managed to get the tank halfway out when Vince lost his grip on his flashlight. It cracked to the ground and rolled away, spilling yellow light.

Josie cursed and darted after the flashlight. Left Vince to bear the oxygen tank's weight.

I took a step toward them. "Are you okay?"

They were too far away or too preoccupied to hear.

I was about to ask again when the hospital's side door swung open.

A man stepped out.

Right between me and the others.

I froze. Mouth open. Words crashing into one another in my throat.

The man stood silhouetted in the doorway, his thin body encased by blue scrubs. His hands shook slightly as he tried to light a cigarette. I swiveled back toward Josie and Vince. The flashlight was still on the ground, its beam directed away from the oxygen tanks. A beacon in the darkness. If the man turned his head a few degrees to the right . . .

Come on, Josie. Come on, come on—

Why was she just squatting there? Hadn't she noticed the man in the doorway? Didn't she know—

Then I realized. The flashlight wasn't in the enclosure at all. It had spun outside the fence, and she couldn't reach it.

<What should I do?> I said to Addie. But Addie wasn't there.

The doctor's cigarette smoke wound up into the sky. If Josie climbed the chain-link fence, he would hear her. If she left the flashlight where it was, he would see it at any moment and go investigate.

I took a deep breath.

Then I slid my flashlight into my pocket as deep as it would go, ripped off my mask, and hurried toward the doctor.

"Excuse me? Hello?" I shouted, hoping Josie and Vince would take notice. I didn't dare check if they did.

The doctor was in his early thirties, maybe. Light haired. Pale-eyed. He looked somewhat embarrassed as I approached. "Yes? Do you need something?"

I didn't have time to come up with a proper story. The ski mask had left my hair wild with static electricity. It clung to my cheeks and forehead. Coupled with the flush I felt rising on my neck, it must have made me look half-feral—some freak girl spit out by the night. I stuttered.

Then the words came, almost unbidden: "I'm trying to see my brother."

As soon as the words left my tongue, Addie was back.

It only took her a second to take everything in: the doctor's tired, questioning eyes; the smell of his cigarette; the yellow light of the hospital hallway.

<What the hell is going on, Eva?>

The man said something—something about general visiting hours being over—but I couldn't concentrate with Addie's sudden fury next to me.

<Where are we?> she demanded. *<Who's he? What are you doing?>*

<Calm down> I managed to bite out. *<Calm down, or you're going to make everything worse!>*

She went silent, but her anger slashed at me, tattering my thoughts.

"Are you all right?" The doctor lowered his cigarette to his side, frowning. His voice was gentle. "Which ward is your brother in?"

"I—um," I said.

His concern was melting into confusion, and confusion was a precursor for suspicion. I had to cut him off.

"He's in PICU," I said. "He's only eight."

PICU. The Pediatric Intensive Care Unit. A collection of letters I'd never wanted to learn.

"Are your parents here?" the doctor asked.

I shook our head. Maybe it was my imagination, but I thought I heard the clinking of a chain-link fence. Josie was climbing. I had to keep talking.

"How old are you?"

Please, please let Josie move quickly. I couldn't drag this

conversation on much longer. He might ask for a name next, or take me to the front desk, and then they'd know I was lying.

"Thirteen," I murmured. Back home, siblings under fourteen didn't have visitation rights unless they had a parent with them. Addie and I had been thirteen when Lyle's kidneys first failed.

"Sorry?" the doctor said.

I swallowed and repeated, louder, "Thirteen."

<Thirteen> Addie said disdainfully.

Addie and I weren't particularly tall, but we could hardly be mistaken for thirteen, either. Hopefully, the darkness cloaked my lie.

The doctor didn't sound suspicious as he said, "I'm afraid they're probably not going to let you in unless you've got your mom or dad with you. I'm sorry about that. Do your parents know you're here?"

I was already backing away, keeping our body angled so his eyes stayed away from the oxygen tanks. The clinking sounds had stopped.

"Yeah," I said. "Yeah, they do."

He squinted after me. "Do you live nearby? Are you going to be okay getting home—"

"I'll be fine," I said. "I'll, um, come back tomorrow with my mom."

I walked all the way across the street, past Josie's car, and around the side of a building before I dared to look back toward the hospital. The doctor took a drag from his cigarette. Vince's flashlight was no longer shining.

<I can't believe this> Addie muttered.

<You knew we were going to do it, Addie.> Why didn't that doctor finish his cigarette and go back inside? Why was he even smoking to begin with? Shouldn't there be some rule that doctors couldn't smoke? *<You were there when we agreed to come—>*

<When you volunteered to come> Addie snapped. The drowsy confusion that accompanied waking up had burned completely away. She wielded her words like knives.

<You didn't argue—>

<I tried, Eva!>

Had she? I remembered her saying something, but—but she hadn't said much. Had she held back because she knew I wanted so badly to come?

Had I been too caught up in myself to notice?

Across the street, the doctor dropped his cigarette. It stayed lit, a fallen ember, until his foot ground it dark. He turned and headed back into the building.

A beat of stillness.

Then Josie—or some shadowed figure I guessed to be Josie—crept toward the fence. In a minute, she was back over and heading for the oxygen racks, helping Vince ease the tank all the way free and carry it to the fence. One of them climbed to the top first, then balanced there as the other passed the tank up.

The shadowy figures started toward us across the pavement,

keeping to the darker spaces. But soon, they crossed the street. They took off their masks, and the lamplight caught them, illuminated them, made them Vince and Josie again.

They both grinned as they set the oxygen tank down. Before I knew what was happening, Vince picked us up and swung us around. Our stomach lurched. Addie was an impenetrable mess beside me. But Vince laughed. "You really pulled that off, didn't you?" he said.

I made myself smile. "I guess I did."

There was one brief, kicking moment of anger from Addie. A flicker of disappointment.

Then she was gone again, as if she couldn't even stand to be around me any longer.

TWENTY-SIX

Josie and Vince talked excitedly all the way home, but I just sat in the backseat, cradling the oxygen tank, listening to the silence Addie left behind. I'd expected a rush of exhilaration now that the heist was done. But I could think of nothing but Addie. We'd fought all the time before I'd lost the power to move, and after, too. We'd go silent and not speak to each other for hours. We'd slam that wall between us and live huddled in our own minds, trying to keep each other out.

But we'd never left each other. We couldn't.

No matter how bad the fight, we had to stay together. And sooner or later, one of us would give in. The wall would crumble, and we'd forgive each other.

Now when we fought, we had somewhere to run to. And Addie had run.

"Eva?" Josie said. I looked up. Both Josie and Vince had turned in their seats to stare at me. We'd parked.

"You okay?" Vince asked.

"I'm fine." I moved to get out of the car, carefully shifting the oxygen tank so it lay flat on the floor. It was a little less than three feet long, maybe half a foot in diameter. Josie and Vince climbed out, too, our doors slamming shut in quick succession. It took me a moment to absorb our surroundings. Josie had practically driven me to my doorstep.

I didn't want to go back into that apartment building, where no doubt Emalia was waiting for me. Maybe Dr. Lyanne and Henri and Peter, too.

And Ryan. What would Ryan think?

The anger powering me before had drained away, leaving me a husk of guilt.

But I had to face them all sometime. I'd run as long as I could.

"Hi, Eva," Sophie said when I knocked. I wasn't sure who felt more uncomfortable, her or me. Kitty and Nina were nowhere to be seen, so either they were hiding in our room, or they'd gone up to stay with Henri.

I'd expected Sophie to be angry, though I'd never seen her that way. She wasn't smiling, but she didn't seem mad, either. The coffee machine beeped.

"It's decaf," Sophie said, seeing the look on my face. "You want some?"

Always, she'd asked, and always, Addie and I had said no.

"Okay," I said.

I didn't really know what to do with myself as Sophie poured the coffee. She asked if I took milk and sugar, and I nodded. She set the mugs down on the dining table.

She sat. I sat. The coffee steamed between us, heady and sweet. My heart thudded so hard I could feel it knocking against my ribs. Harder, it seemed, than it had back at Benoll, talking to the doctor.

Sophie brought her mug toward her lips, but set it down again without actually taking a sip. "I didn't know you were friends with Josie."

How much did she know? Only three people could have told her anything—Kitty, Hally, and Ryan.

Ryan knew where I was tonight, but no matter how angry he was at being left behind, he wouldn't reveal anything.

Hally and Lissa? I doubted it. Not after they'd promised. Which left Kitty and Nina. They'd promised silence, too, but they were only eleven, and probably frightened.

"I ran into her," I said. It wasn't all lie.

If Addie had been here, she and I could have spoken to each other, at least. Between the two of us, we'd have figured out how to act and what to say.

"Eva?" Sophie asked. I looked up. "Is Addie here right now?"

Dr. Lyanne must have told her about my outburst. Slowly, I shook my head.

She nodded. "I just wanted to say that Emalia and I *do* understand what it's like to fight with someone inside your own head. And we know what it's like, not always being in control of your own body. How discomforting it can be to wake up and not know where you are or what has been happening the last few hours. We should have made it more clear that if you ever need anyone to talk with, or want to ask anything, we're here for that. Okay?"

She kept trying to meet my eyes, but I could only manage it for a few seconds before looking away. I'd rather her be angry than hear her blame herself—or feel guilty, or whatever this was. This sounded like something a mother might say in a television show, only Sophie was far too young, too unfamiliar, too *different* to be my mother. Of course, my mother could never say what Sophie had just said, because my mother *didn't* know any of those things. She never would.

"Yeah, okay," I said.

Neither of us touched our drinks. *She doesn't know about the plan*, I thought. Sophie thought this was just a one-time thing, that Addie and I had fought and I ran off, and that was the end of the story.

But why would she think differently? How could she even imagine what we were planning, let alone that I was a part of it?

"I need to talk with Ryan," I said, "and it's getting late."

Immediately after saying it, I wished I hadn't. Even to my own ears, it sounded rude. I could never say what I wanted to say just the way I wanted to say it. And that was the problem, wasn't it? For so many years, I'd never had to wonder what I should and shouldn't say aloud. I'd fed words to Addie sometimes, and felt superior about knowing what to say when she was too flustered to speak.

But it was different actually being in control. I'd spent so long watching Addie live. What if watching hadn't been enough? What if I was doomed to be behind forever, stuck in some childhood I'd never actually gotten the chance to live? What else was I screwing up?

Maybe it was a deeper problem. Maybe I really had been meant to fade away. Maybe the universe simply hadn't been meant to contain one Eva Tamsyn. Not for so many years.

If Sophie was angered or hurt by my words, she hid it. "Okay."

I felt like I should say something more. Thank her, maybe, for what she'd said. For being kind, because she *had* been kind. Because she hadn't had to take us into her home, but she'd done it. She'd hidden us when even my own parents hadn't.

That wasn't fair to think. Everything felt so awkward, my tongue lying useless in my mouth.

"Sorry," I said instead.

I left it up to her what I was sorry for, and fled.

I'd spent my conversation with Sophie wishing for Addie's company. But now, as I stood outside Henri's door, I was infinitely glad she wasn't here. Some conversations were better undertaken alone.

I took a deep breath and knocked. One, two, three, four, five, six seconds passed.

"Hi," I said quietly when Ryan opened the door. He didn't

smile, like he usually did when he saw me. He didn't invite me inside. He came out instead, and shut the door behind him.

"Did you get it?" His voice was quiet.

I nodded. I tried to read his expression. But he must have learned well after sharing a lifetime with Devon. He betrayed nothing.

He was studying my face, too. Was I a more open book? "Everyone's okay?"

"Yeah, everyone's fine." My fingernails dug into my palm. "It happened really fast, Ryan. I came back and ran into Dr. Lyanne, and it—it got hectic."

"What were you doing outside?" His voice was controlled, but I could tell it was a question he'd been waiting to ask.

It was also one I wasn't entirely prepared to answer. It wasn't something I could think about without feeling phantom hands on my body, and the foreign warmth of another boy's skin. I'd felt his teeth graze my lip before I pulled away.

"I don't know." I took a deep breath. "I wasn't the one who left. Addie was. And now she's gone, and she won't talk to me, so—"

Ryan frowned. We'd both kept our voices to a whisper—we had to—but his raised a little now. "She let you wake up somewhere by yourself and then abandoned you? Where did you wake up?"

I took his arm, reminded him with a look that we couldn't be overheard. I thought, *No, I woke up kissing Jackson, and then she abandoned me.* But maybe I was the one who abandoned her first, because I was too selfish to think about what she wanted while I ran after my own goals.

No matter what I tried to tell myself, I was lonely without Addie. We'd taken our first breath in unison. The face in the mirror was hers as much as mine. The faint scars on our hands from the coffee we'd spilled at eight, the cuts from the windows we'd smashed at fifteen. They were ours.

"It's just something between Addie and me, okay?" I said quietly. Ryan hesitated, his eyes sweeping over me, before moving back to my face. But he nodded. He accepted it, because he was hybrid, too, and he understood. "Vince arrived, and with Dr. Lyanne and Henri upstairs, I couldn't . . . I couldn't come get you. And with Dr. Lyanne coming down behind me, we couldn't wait." I let out a frustrated sigh. "I was worried about you—what would happen if we got caught, and how much I didn't want you to be there if we did. And I don't know if how I reacted was normal or not, but that's how I felt. I don't know what normal *is* in a situation like this, Ryan."

All I know is that I care about you, and I want to protect you, and I never want to see you hurt.

Ryan wasn't looking at me anymore. Why couldn't he just be angry or upset or *something*? I had no idea what he wanted or needed to hear. Was this something I was supposed to know? Was this yet another bit of life I'd missed out on learning?

I just wanted to do the right thing. I just wished I knew what that was.

I died and died again in the silence that followed my words.

Then Ryan laughed. Quietly, but he laughed. "A couple months ago, a man in a suit came to take us away from our homes. We spent a week in a mental hospital, and now we're on the run from the government. I think we've officially left *normal* behind."

He had to whisper, because of course all this was completely secret, but somehow the whispering made everything seem that much more ridiculous. How had all this happened? How had Addie and I traded honors biology for Sabine's notes on bomb making? How had we gone from *high-school freshman* to *fugitive of the law*?

"Eva," Ryan said. "I get that you didn't want me with you in case you got caught. But trust me, if you'd gotten caught, the only place I'd want to be is next to you. Okay?"

"Yeah," I said softly. "It goes both ways."

He nodded. Smiled, just a little. "You threw everything into an uproar when you left. Dr. Lyanne kept demanding we tell her where you were, and we kept saying we had no idea."

"She believed you?" I said.

"Yeah. She did. Why not, right?"

"Why not," I echoed. I hesitated. "Ryan, do you think we should stop? With the plan?"

He frowned. "What?"

"Never mind. It was just . . . I just—never mind." I took a step toward him. I'd never felt uncomfortable around Ryan before. Especially not when Addie wasn't here. But now all I could think about was how she might react if she suddenly returned. "I should go back down. Sophie's probably waiting for me."

He knew there was something off. I could tell. But all he said was, "Okay."

There was a pause. Then he leaned down and kissed me, and it was right for a moment—it was eager and familiar and comforting. Until I remembered Jackson's kiss, and Addie, and without meaning to, I jerked away.

Ryan went very still. The hand that had rested on our shoulder hung in midair.

"Sorry," I said quickly, quietly. I looked over my shoulder. "I thought I heard something. I'm just still jumpy from tonight. You know."

After a second, he nodded and dropped his hand.

He tried to smile before giving up and going inside.

TWENTY-SEVEN

I sat in bed long after Sophie and Kitty had gone to sleep, my knees tight against my chest, thinking about what I should say when Addie came back.

It was right for us to have our privacy. Wasn't that the point of going under? To give each of us a taste of what it was like to be alone, to act and feel and *be* without thinking of the other.

But at the end of the day, my hands were still Addie's hands. Addie's mouth was my mouth. As children, back before I lost control, Addie had always been more capable in our body than I was. Almost always, she'd been able to overpower me when our wills clashed. But we were older now. Old enough, surely, to figure out how to share this body without hurting either of us.

Our nightstand drawer sat halfway open, Addie's sketchbook peeking out. I hesitated, then pulled it onto my lap. Between the moonlight and the streetlamps, I could just see the pages. I paused at the drawings of Hally. At the half-finished sketch of Kitty watching television, her face tilted away from us and almost complete, but the rest of her body still flat—dissolving into nothing but lines and the suggestion of form.

The sketch after that was one I'd never seen. A drawing of Jackson, the lean lines of his shoulders and back, the way his hair was just a little too long and fell into his eyes. He was looking at me. At her. I stared back, trying—knowing it was futile—to remember those moments Addie had spent capturing his image in graphite.

My hands had drawn this. My fingers had gripped the pencil, held the eraser. My eyes had traced over his body, studied the creases in his shirt and the lines of his hands. But I would never remember it. Addie hadn't sketched a background, only a faint outline of the chair Jackson sat in, so I didn't even know where the two of them had been when this happened. I didn't know what they'd talked about.

I replaced the sketchbook just as Addie eased into existence.

<Addie, listen.> I reached for her the way I had when we were children. My carefully planned sentences tangled together, my words tying themselves into knots. *<I'm sorry I got so caught up in everything that I forgot about you. That I was selfish.>*

It was a long moment before Addie replied.

<You weren't selfish.> She spoke carefully, her voice soft. *<You just . . . I'm sorry. I was really angry, Eva. I was worried about you—about what you'd think. How you'd react, and you—>*

I winced. <*Reacted really badly?*>

<*A bit. Yeah.*>

<*But you never told me, Addie*> I said. <*I just woke up, and—I had no idea what to think. What happened to trusting each other to tell what we needed to know?*>

She sighed. <*At first, I thought I didn't need to, that it was obvious enough for you to just know. You never had to explicitly tell me about Ryan. And when it became clear you didn't know, didn't even seem to suspect, I guess I was angry that you didn't. That you weren't paying attention.*> I almost interrupted. But Addie's words tumbled out, and I held mine back to make room for hers. <*Then I didn't tell you because having something that was mine—just mine . . . well, it made it feel normal, didn't it? Jackson makes me feel normal. He can get me to forget where we are. Why we're here. He can make it seem like the only important thing in the world is how I feel about what's on TV, or this new restaurant he's found.*> She was quiet a moment. <*He makes me think I might be able to do it, too, someday. Just be happy, in spite of everything. Does that make sense?*>

<*Yeah*> I said. <*It does.*>

We closed our eyes, closed ourself off from the world. We shut away everything but each other. Addie and Eva, Eva and Addie.

<*But this can't just be mine*> Addie said quietly. <*I know it can't. I thought . . . I thought I could make it so*

it was just mine, but . . . >

But that was impossible.

<*I should have told you, Eva*> she said. <*I'm sorry. I—I never should have let you wake up like that.*>

<*It's all right*> I said. The words felt too small to encompass my meaning. But they were all I had. So I gave them to her, along with my forgiveness, because I'd always forgiven Addie, and Addie had always forgiven me. For everything. <*Does anyone else know about you two?*>

<*No. I don't think so. Are you going to tell Ryan?*>

<*I should, I guess*> I said.

<*Do you want me to do it?*>

<*No, it's okay.*>

<*He'll get it*> Addie said. <*He has to. We're all hybrid. It's just the way things work.*>

<*Yeah*> I said, but I couldn't completely erase my unease, and Addie couldn't completely hide hers.

I hadn't needed anyone to teach me that jealousy was a strange emotion for hybrids, especially when it came to people you cared about. We shared bodies. We weren't always in control of our own limbs. Some things were muddled and confusing to begin with.

But still . . . It would have been different, perhaps, if we'd grown up somewhere else. Somewhere overseas, where we'd have known other hybrids all our lives, where we'd have learned another set of rules for what was *normal* and what wasn't.

I laughed wryly. *<It's complicated, isn't it?>*

<We'll figure it out.>

<I know> I said. I spoke with more conviction than I felt.

Funny, how I used to always be the one who comforted Addie, not the other way around. But it didn't matter. Addie was back, and speaking with me. Addie thought we would figure everything out, that everything would be all right.

If she believed it, then so did I.

TWENTY-EIGHT

The day for the test run arrived.

Ryan and I snuck downstairs just as the sun came up, hurrying to meet the others at the restaurant parking lot. I laughed at Cordelia's jokes, waved hello to Sabine, smiled when Christoph offered a gruff *good morning*. The unease lingering within me burned away as Sabine and the others reenveloped me in their energy.

<Stop it> Addie said when our eyes caught on Jackson.

<What?>

<Wondering> she said. *<Just stop looking at him before he sees you staring. It's embarrassing.>*

I laughed and looked away. Ryan smiled, raising his eyebrows questioningly as we ducked into Sabine's car. My amusement faded. I still hadn't told him about Addie and Jackson. The two of us hadn't had a moment alone since the night of the LOX heist.

But that was an excuse, and I knew it. I didn't know how to tell Ryan. I was afraid of how he'd react. Afraid to think what would happen to us if he reacted badly.

Ryan's hands were warmer than ours. I entwined our fingers with his, and he shifted so he could lean his head on our shoulder. I smiled. Pushed thoughts of Addie and Jackson out of my mind for the moment. "Aren't you a morning person?"

Ryan yawned. His hair tickled our cheek. "Couldn't sleep last night."

Jackson squeezed between us and the window, then slammed the door shut. With Cordelia sitting on Ryan's other side, the four of us barely fit in the backseat. The two-hour drive to Frandmill would be tough to handle for anyone, let alone Addie and me. I swore silently that I wouldn't say a word.

Ryan stared at the cardboard box at our feet. Inside, the miniature bomb lay carefully packed. Every line of his body spoke fatigue, but his eyes were still intent, calculating. I could almost see the gears turning in his brain, running over every part and connection again and again, making sure there hadn't been any mistakes.

"Stop it," I whispered, and pulled him closer against us. His eyes lifted to meet ours, at first questioningly, then crinkling in a smile. He nodded and rested his head against our shoulder again.

"Everybody good to go?" Sabine said, pulling on her seat belt and starting the engine. There were various mumbled noises of assent. "You want the window down, Eva?"

I looked at her, startled and warmed that she'd remembered

my aversion to cramped spaces. I nodded.

We pulled out of the parking lot in silence, and in a mist of rain.

By the time we reached the testing field, the rain had reduced to low, gray clouds and a faraway rumbling. The air was cool, but so thick with moisture it seemed to weigh down on our skin. When we left the road behind, our shoes sank a little into the mud beneath the sparse grass. Sabine had taken us far from the main road. I shivered. Addie's presence next to mine was as still and heavy as the storm clouds.

"If we're lucky," Christoph said, staring at the sky, "anyone who does hear the explosion will think it's just thunder."

"Nobody will hear," Sabine said. "We're in the middle of nowhere."

Ryan and Jackson lugged the cardboard box between them, walking carefully even though Ryan had assured us the explosives wouldn't detonate from a little jostling.

The land dipped here, forming an embankment that overlooked a valley. Ryan, Jackson, and Sabine headed for the lowest point. I automatically started to follow them, but Cordelia, as if on a sudden impulse, linked her arm in ours as she turned in the opposite direction, up the hill.

I looked at her in surprise. She gave a breathy little laugh and a shrug, but didn't release our arm. Maybe with Sabine and Jackson busy, she needed someone to hold on to. I understood the feeling. We walked, together, up the embankment.

Christoph went ahead of us, the pale sunlight making a red halo of his hair.

Eventually, I realized he didn't know how far we were supposed to go. He turned and looked to me, as if Addie or I might have an answer. I glanced down the hill. From this distance, Ryan and the others looked like toys. It had to be more than far enough. Ryan had given us an estimate of how large the explosion would be, and surely, he was right.

Surely.

I stopped. Cordelia, arm still linked through ours, stopped too. We watched as the miniature figures of Ryan and Jackson and Sabine huddled around the box. Watched as they finally straightened and headed toward us—not running, but moving with the stiff urgency of people wishing they could run but held back by fear.

Or in this case, I supposed, pride.

How strange a thing pride seemed compared to a bomb.

Hurry, I thought, a sickness in our stomach. *Forget pride and hurry.*

They didn't run, but they reached us while the air was silent. Ryan took our free hand. I squeezed his. Addie felt taut as a violin string. We stood—frozen and silent and waiting—staring at the bowels of the hill.

Then the explosion came.

The noise and flame and fire came. It swelled up. Set us vibrating with its power.

It was over so quickly. A tongue of red and yellow. A boom

that echoed through our bodies.

Then again, silence.

"It worked," Christoph said in a voice that was not quite joy and not quite fear.

Our ears rang. I turned, searching Ryan's face, and found it wasn't Ryan at all.

Devon. Devon with cold, black eyes staring down at the smoke.

He said nothing. He looked back toward me, his expression a mask I couldn't break.

TWENTY-NINE

The drive back to Anchoit was at once more relaxed and more tense. The others chatted, even laughed from time to time. Devon—it was still Devon in control—was silent. I kept our hands in our lap, our arms tight against our body.

We reached the city limits, then the same parking lot we'd left from that morning. No one seemed to want to leave the car. To be alone with the immensity of what we'd done. Finally, Cordelia suggested we all have lunch in the attic.

Food didn't make me feel any better. Sabine was unusually quiet, focused on the turnings of her own mind. Jackson and Cordelia supplied most of the conversation, but eventually, even their well of words ran dry. The attic fell into a lull of silence that wasn't entirely comfortable. Takeout boxes sat littered about the attic, some still full of fried fish and sweet rolls, others with nothing left but a slick of grease.

Devon spoke first. "When are we going to do it for real?" When no one replied, he looked around the room and repeated himself. "When are we going to blow up the institution?"

"We know what you mean," Jackson said, but he was smiling, and there was no real heat to the words. Still, he didn't give an answer.

Sabine hadn't looked up at the sound of Devon's voice, and she didn't look up now. She studied the fairy lights strung around the room like there were answers hidden in their knots.

"Next week," she said. "Next Friday night."

Exactly seven days from today.

"Why Friday?" Devon said.

Finally, Sabine met his eyes. "According to the schedules we got from Nalles, they haven't set up the surgical machinery yet. They'll be moving them in all next week. They'll be done by Friday."

"You're sure?" Devon said.

Sabine nodded. "Like I said, it's in the schedules."

"Next Friday night . . ." Cordelia moved over to sit beside Sabine, putting an arm around her. "Are you sure, Sabine? It's so soon."

Sabine nodded. Her gaze had drifted again, to the floor this time. "Why not? We know it works. We've got the bomb. Why wait longer than necessary?"

"*I'm* ready," Christoph said.

"And Friday's a good day of the week to do it," Sabine said. "If anything does go wrong—if the government responds in some dangerous, unexpected way—Jackson and Christoph don't need to be in at work, and it's not suspicious if they don't turn up. Everything's less regulated on the weekends."

Cordelia nodded, her pale head resting against Sabine's shoulder.

"Not everyone needs to actually go to Powatt, anyway," Christoph said.

"Really, only one person needs to go," Sabine said. "I could go alone. It would be safer."

"It wouldn't be safer for *you*," Jackson said.

Some of Sabine's usual strength came back to her voice. "Not having you there to mess things up would make it a lot safer for me."

They smiled, the smile of old friends who didn't need words to understand each other.

"Still, you shouldn't go alone." There was steel underlying Jackson's words, a stiffness coming from something I couldn't pin down. Fear? Not quite fear. His eyes flashed toward ours, then away again.

"He's right," Devon said. His voice was low. He looked at us, then Jackson, like he'd caught his glance. "I'd like to be there. See the thing come down."

<Remember how he was against this, in the beginning?> I asked Addie. It seemed like forever ago. Like we'd been different people then.

Addie said *<Eva, could you give me a few hours alone today?>*

Neither of us had gone under since the day of our fight, and her request made something twinge inside me. But I said *<Yeah. Of course.>*

I meant it. Of course Addie would still want time to herself, just like I did. She hadn't even spoken with Jackson since I fled his apartment, and she wouldn't want me around when she did.

I needed time, too, to digest what had just happened. I wanted, maybe, just a little time to be asleep and not have to feel anything. Dreams were preferable to this. When I woke, I could sort things out.

<*Thanks*> Addie said.

I took one last look at the attic around me, the dark wooden boards, the fairy lights gleaming on the walls.

Then I disappeared.

Fireworks
The first time I saw them
Independence Day

I feel the bloom
The crack
Of their noise
As if they too are trying
To shake me loose
Shake me from my limbs
Make me fade away
Like they do

Here
A burst of color
Then gone

I woke in the middle of dinner, fork tines against our tongue, our elbows on the dining table. Even after weeks of practice, it was still disorienting to be thrust into the real world after living in timeless, liquid dreams.

Addie's first words were simple. A caution: *<Peter's here.>*

My dreams snapped away. Our eyes focused on the other people seated around the table: Emalia, Nina, Peter. At the moment, no one was saying anything, busy with their food.

Addie swallowed. She lowered our fork, setting it carefully on the woven placemat, beside our plate. *<Jenson's in Anchoit.>*

<What?> I cried.

But Addie shushed me as she said, aloud, "Did you always know he was coming, Peter?"

Peter sat to our left, lost in his thoughts and the mechanical motions of eating. His eyes lifted at the sound of our voice. He nodded. "He leads the government review board, after all. But apparently, he's been in the city for a couple weeks already. No public announcement. Nothing. No one's supposed to know."

<How does Peter know?> I asked.

<Shh> Addie said, but she explained quickly anyway. *<He's got someone planted in government. An informant.>*

<Didn't he tell Sabine it was too dangerous to go anywhere near the government?>

<Shh, Eva. And yeah, maybe because it's dangerous and he didn't want her to get hurt.>

"Didn't he visit Nornand before the hybrid wing opened there?" Emalia asked.

The Powatt institution would never open. Hybrid children would never fill its beds, sleepwalk through its halls, whisper fearfully to one another after lights-out.

We were making sure of that.

"He did, but . . ." Peter hesitated. "I'm not sure what the man is doing here so early. He went to the Benoll Hospital downtown as part of some kind of criminal investigation." Our heart stilled, even before Peter's next words: "An oxygen tank was stolen, or something like that. It's a strange thing for a man like him to be looking into. But I suppose they've got good reason to be taking these things seriously. It's nearing two months since Lankster Square, and they haven't caught anyone, haven't found Jaime . . . the curfew doesn't seem to have an end in sight . . . people are getting frustrated."

Addie controlled our breathing, averting our eyes—and caught Nina staring right at us.

The little girl frowned. "Are you okay?"

This, of course, made Peter and Emalia turn to us, too.

"Yeah," Addie said quickly. She faked a cough. Looked everyone in the eye and smiled, holding it for a count of *one, two* before ducking our head and taking a bite of dinner. She was getting better at lying. Or maybe she'd always been good. She'd lied for three years to our parents, hadn't she? "I'm fine. Swallowed something the wrong way."

"You don't need to worry about Jenson, Addie." Peter's

voice was gentle. "He's just a man."

"I know," Addie said.

Peter was right, in a way. Jenson was just a man, just a human being of flesh and blood. But he was a man with power over our lives. Power made a person more than a person.

"Has he been director long?" Addie asked.

Peter set down his fork. Everyone had given up the pretense of eating, even Nina. "A few years. He used to oversee a single institution, a bit like Daniel Conivent." He glanced at Emalia, then back at us. "Emalia said you've become friends with Sabine."

Was he trying to change the subject? It wasn't like Peter to be so obvious, so clumsy with his words. But Addie just shrugged. I'd told her about our conversation with Sophie the night of the LOX heist. "Sort of."

Peter nodded. "Sabine and Christoph knew Jenson, back before he was made director. He was the head of their institution."

<That's right> I said. *<Sabine told us, remember? When we first met.>*

But Addie had gone still, like she hadn't remembered until now.

"I don't think Sabine's heard about Jenson being here," Peter said quietly. "There's no need to upset her with the news, all right?"

I knew he meant to be kind, and not patronizing, but I couldn't help being annoyed anyway.

"Yeah, all right," Addie mumbled. Her mind was elsewhere; I could tell. But she offered me no explanation.

A silence fell upon the table, thick and muffling. Peter picked up his fork again but only stared at his plate. Emalia's eyes flickered up to meet ours, then quickly moved away again. Nina pushed at her food, cutting it into smaller and smaller pieces. This was like a mockery of a family dinner, everything the opposite of what it ought to be. I was suddenly so homesick it was a physical pain.

I wanted my family back. I wanted the family I'd had before Mr. Conivent came to take us away.

No. I wanted the family I'd had before Addie and I turned ten years old. Before we'd turned six. Before our parents had started to worry. Before the tests and the hospital visits, the medication and the counselors.

I wanted a family I could barely remember, that was half dream.

"I found somewhere safe to develop your videos, by the way," Emalia said, too brightly. She smiled at Nina. "It'll be done in a few days."

Addie bent our head and went back to finishing our meal. I was left with the strangest feeling—like even after so many minutes, I was still stuck in the disoriented state of having just woken to an unfamiliar world.

Addie said it would only be fair for me to have the rest of the night to myself, since I'd let her have the afternoon. Honestly, at the moment, I didn't care. I didn't particularly want to be alone. But Addie disappeared, and I was left with my thoughts.

Jenson was in Anchoit.

The poster of Jaime was still hidden under our mattress. I drew it out, smoothing the crinkles from Jaime's face. Did Jenson know Jaime was here? Was that why he'd come early?

What would he think when we blew up the Powatt institution? Security was already high around the city. It was sure to tighten even more after the bombing. Were we placing Jaime in more danger by doing this?

That hadn't been the point. The point was to *save* people, not hurt them.

I folded up the poster of Jaime and slipped it back under the mattress. Emalia and Peter had left together after dinner, so it was just Nina and me in the apartment.

"I'm just going upstairs," I told her as I pulled on my shoes.

Lissa opened Henri's door when I knocked. I tried to slip inside as soon as she did, and it took me a second to realize she wasn't stepping aside. Instead, she put an arm out to block the doorway.

"Hey," she said. Her voice was hard. So were her eyes, dark behind her glasses.

I tried to smile. "Hey. Are you going to let me in?"

"No." She let me stare dumbly at her a minute before sighing and coming out into the hall, shutting the door behind her. She pulled me to the stairs, speaking just above a whisper. "If you come in, then Henri will ask where Devon is."

I blinked. "And where's Devon?"

"Officially, he's downstairs with you." Lissa and I were in the stairwell now, and she checked both the next flight up and the flight down before saying, "That's what I'm supposed to tell Henri."

"Ryan told you to say that?" I kept my voice as quiet as hers. Sound traveled in the stairwell, bouncing against the dirty concrete walls. But few people would be suspicious of two fifteen-year-old girls whispering on the landing. We could be talking about so many things. Complaints about our parents. Our brothers. School gossip. Who was dating whom and who had broken up already.

Lissa shook her head. "No. Devon did."

Devon with or without Ryan?

"And you don't know where he really is?"

"Do I ever know where either of you are anymore?" Lissa said. "No. No one tells me, and I'm just supposed to cover for you two. And okay, that's what we do, right? We look out for each other. We cover for each other. But this is getting ridiculous, Eva." She took a sharp breath and looked away. "You wanted me to trust you. You said you were going to make things okay. Well, *make* them okay, Eva, or I swear, I am going to go to Peter. I don't care if he separates us. I hardly see you anymore, anyway. And—and I'd rather have us separated than . . . than have you guys go through with your plan."

Did she know about the test run earlier today? Did she know about Sabine's plans for next Friday?

Most likely, she didn't.

Lissa stared at the scratches and graffiti on the walls. "You know, Eva . . . when Hally and I first suspected that you and Addie might—well, might be like us, I . . ." She hesitated. "I was so hopeful, you know? I just really wanted someone—someone other than my brother—who knew what it was like. Who would *get* me. Who would understand. And maybe that was selfish of me, to drag you into this because I—"

"Lissa," I said. "You didn't drag me into anything. You gave me a life I didn't even think was possible, okay? That's—I've never even said thanks for that."

Lissa looked back at me, then nodded. "Look, I get where you're coming from. I get why you'd want to—to do what you're planning to do. But you can't, Eva. You just can't do something like this." She squeezed my arm. "I trust you, all right? I trusted you and Addie when I first told you about us, and I trust you now."

I found myself nodding, too. I was helpless to do anything else.

THIRTY

I didn't get the chance to speak with Ryan until later the next day. Addie wanted to spend the morning with Jackson, so I spent it asleep, dreaming soft dreams of the ocean, home, and everything I used to have. Our regular sleep was plagued by nightmares. When going under, I never had nightmares. Mostly, it was memories—so real it was like reliving them, but each slipping away after it was done, dissolving as the real world took its place.

This time, I woke in the stairwell to gray, dirty walls. There were no windows here, and it was impossible to tell what time it was, or how long I'd been under. But Addie knew that, and she said, quietly *<It's a little after ten a.m.>*

I could feel her distraction, even if I couldn't know her thoughts.

<How was it?> I asked awkwardly.

<Hm?> Addie climbed the last flight of stairs, then left me in control of our limbs.

<You were with Jackson, right? How was your morning?>

<Oh, good> she said. *<Thanks.>*

Her mind was elsewhere, as if she were the one who'd just woken, and not me. Whatever had happened while I was asleep, it had disturbed her. But she didn't offer any explanation, and I didn't press. A few minutes later, she disappeared.

Ryan dropped by Emalia's apartment to see me. It was the first time we'd been truly alone in a while, and as perfect a moment as I was going to get to bring up Addie and Jackson. I hid a bitter smile. This was my perfect moment: a little precious time salvaged before blowing up a government building.

Nerves made me bring up Devon first. "Do you know where he's been going?" I asked.

Ryan shrugged. "Devon and I haven't really been talking much for a long time. He never got over the . . . well, us agreeing to this plan."

"But he said he wanted to go," I said. "He wanted to go with Sabine to Powatt."

"I don't know, Eva," Ryan said.

"Can't you ask him?"

He hesitated. "I have before. He says he just walks around. Scopes out the city. Devon is Devon. Now that we can have time alone, I'm not surprised he wants some."

I understood his reluctance to make Devon divulge his secrets. As hybrids, we'd had so little room for things that belonged to us and us alone. But when did a secret become too big to be kept? When did it stop belonging to just one person?

"That day I went to Benoll," I said in a rush, "to steal the oxygen . . ." Ryan caught the change in my tone and shifted so he could see my face. I didn't fight it. I wanted to see his expression, too. "Remember how I said there was something between Addie and me?"

He nodded. I could feel my heartbeat thrumming underneath my skin. *Stop it*, I told myself irritatedly. Having a body that reacted to my commands was wonderful, but sometimes, my body reacted to my emotions even when I didn't want it to.

"Well, it's not entirely just between Addie and me," I said. Ryan didn't prompt me to continue, just waited. I kind of wished he would, just for something to fill the silences between my sentences. "She was with Jackson. They're together. Apparently."

"With him," Ryan echoed. His arm was still slung around my waist. I could feel the sudden tension in his muscles. "With him how?"

I restrained myself from rolling my eyes at him. Did he really want me to spell it out? As if this weren't awkward enough already. Thinking about Addie being with somebody was like thinking about *Lyle* in a couple years being with somebody, only a hundred times worse. Then I realized what Ryan was really asking.

"*No*, Ryan. They were kissing, all right? That's it."

"How do you know?" he asked quietly.

"Because Addie would have told me otherwise," I snapped. "And beforehand, not after."

Because at the end of the day, we trusted each other. Because that trust was all we had to keep us sane.

Ryan and I were silent. We both kept our breathing carefully controlled.

"Look," I said finally. "Who do you really think this is weirder for, you or me?"

I cracked a smile, and after a moment Ryan looked away. When his eyes met mine again, he wore the barest hint of a smile, too. He shrugged, his arm tightening around me, and conceded, "Maybe you."

I laughed. "Only maybe? Imagine if it were Devon."

"I'm really trying not to," he said dryly.

This time, the silence between us was more comfortable.

"How do you feel about it?" I asked. "Addie and Jackson?"

"I'm not sure," he admitted. He pressed a kiss against my forehead. "I'll figure it out. It's fine." He was looking at me, but I couldn't be sure if the assurance was for me, or himself.

I sighed, fiddling with the edge of his shirt. "Hally and Lissa want us to stop with the plan. They don't know about Friday, do they?"

Ryan didn't comment on my swerve in topics, just shook his head.

"This is still worth it, right?" I whispered.

"Yeah," he said.

But he sounded no more sure than I felt.

* * *

Saturday and Sunday passed. Then Monday. Three days of endlessly thinking about what would happen if I tried to stop everything. What would happen if I didn't.

When Addie and I were awake at the same time, I could tell the passing days weighed heavily on her, too. She spoke little, hiding herself from me. I tried to shield my worry from her, too.

Less than a week now until the bombing.

Less than a week to stop them, if you want to, a part of me whispered. Automatically, I clamped the voice quiet. It was easier to not think about things like that. At this point, it would be so much easier to just carry on, do what the others wanted.

When had it become a case of my doing what the others wanted? *I'd* wanted this. In the beginning, sitting on that beach with Ryan, I'd made the decision to be part of this. It had seemed like the right thing to do. At the time.

But now?

I'd promised Lissa I would make everything okay. That I would figure things out. It had just been placating words at the time, spoken half in panic. But it was still a promise, one now lodged deep inside me. One I had to keep.

But what did it mean to make everything okay?

Blowing up the Powatt institution was supposed to be a step toward making things better. A drastic step, maybe. But like Christoph had said once, this wasn't a game. We weren't playing for poker chips. There were children's lives in the balance—those already lost and those currently in danger.

Maybe I was just second-guessing everything because I was scared. Because I wasn't strong enough to do the things that had to be done. Was that it? Was I just weak? Eva, the recessive soul, doomed to be lesser.

Finally, I couldn't stand it anymore. When Addie left me alone late Tuesday morning, I snuck out of the apartment and traced the now-familiar path through the streets to the photography shop.

Sabine stood at the counter, rustling through the drawers as if searching for something. She was so absorbed she didn't notice me until I had almost reached her. Then she startled, her head snapping up.

"Oh, hi." She straightened and tucked her hair behind her ears. Smiled. "I didn't expect you to come by."

I shrugged. Sabine nudged the drawer shut with her hip. She was still smiling, but I caught the distraction in her eyes. The rest of the small store was empty, not a single customer browsing the rack of postcards or studying the larger framed works on the walls.

"Is Cordelia gone today?" I asked.

"She's at a wedding shoot." Sabine came around the counter, reaching for her purse. "And I was just about to go home for lunch, actually. What's up?"

I'd never been completely alone with Sabine before. After all this time, it should have been comfortable, but it wasn't. Sabine was steady. Sabine could inspire confidence like no one else. But Sabine also often wore a weighing sort of look, like she could search inside a person and measure the quality of his soul. She had that look on now.

"I just wanted to talk," I said. "About Friday."

"Sure," Sabine said lightly. She waved me toward the door and flipped the sign to *Closed*. "Why don't you come back to the apartment with me?"

Sabine's apartment was only a few minutes' drive away. The building looked a lot like Emalia's, old and run-down. The stairwell smelled like grease, and Sabine warned me not to put my weight on the railing.

"Home sweet home, I guess," she said, unlocking one of the identical doors on her floor. The apartment was small, and like the photography shop, it was covered in pictures. But unlike those, these photographs were of people I recognized: Sabine laughing into the camera, Jackson and Cordelia at the boardwalk, even Peter as he turned, surprised by the flash.

I stared at a panorama of the darkened ocean. There was something troubling yet seductive about the blackened water, the slivers of moonlight at the crests of the waves. Out of the corner of my vision, I caught Sabine's eyes sweeping the apartment, her forehead creased. Still searching for something.

"Cordelia and Katy are obsessed with taking the perfect night shot of the ocean," Sabine said, noticing my attention and directing it back to the photo. "That picture there gets replaced every couple months. They're never satisfied."

The apartment was messier than I'd expected. I guess I'd always imagined Sabine would be neat. The attic was well kept. So was the rest of the shop. The apartment was clean, but cluttered with books, camera equipment, and loose paper. I stared at a strange contraption on the dining-room table for a few seconds before recognizing it as the cutaway lock Sabine had used to teach Devon how to lock-pick.

"You know what I think the perfect picture of the ocean would be?" Sabine asked. "A beach covered with snow. But it never snows here. As far as I've seen, it's never even flurried. Did it snow, where you came from?"

I nodded. "Not often, though. And never very much."

"Back home, it snowed several inches every year without fail." She laughed suddenly. "Funny, isn't it, how I still say 'back home'? I haven't been there in eight years, but somehow, it's still home."

Sabine traced a finger down the edge of the photo frame. "Someday, when this is over, I'll head back up there. I'll walk right to the front door and ring the bell. And when my parents answer, I'll ask them what they were thinking, letting Jenson take us." She turned away from the photo. "If they're still there, anyway."

"You haven't forgiven them?" I asked quietly. If in eight years, Sabine hadn't forgiven her parents, what did that predict for me?

"No." She smiled wistfully. "But I'd go back anyway."

She cleared some clothes from the couch and motioned for me to sit. "You and Ryan have been really amazing, Eva. You know that, right? I'm including Addie and Devon, too, of course. None of this would be possible without you guys."

I shrugged, more embarrassed than pleased by her praise. "I haven't really been doing much."

"You drew the pictures for the posters at Lankster Square," Sabine said.

"That was Addie."

"But you two work together," Sabine said. "You're a team, Eva."

"Okay," I said, "but since then? Neither Addie nor I have helped. Not really."

I wasn't sure why I was pressing the point, other than the fact that I was getting increasingly upset and needed to lash out—about my own apprehension, my own possible cowardice, my need for Sabine to reassure me, and her inability right now to do so.

Maybe Sabine saw that. When she spoke again, her tone had grown a little harder. Not like she was annoyed with me, but like she understood I wasn't a child to be placated by compliments.

"Eva, I know you're probably having second thoughts about the plan. That's normal. Just remember why we're doing this, okay?" She waited until I gave a slight nod. "And remember, you don't need to come on Friday. I think it would be better if you didn't."

I imagined Sabine setting the bomb, alone. Watching it explode, alone. I could hear the screech and groan of the building as it crumpled, the roar of the fire. I could almost see the look that would shine in Sabine's eyes: quiet, powerful satisfaction.

"Peter—" I said.

"Peter's great; he is," Sabine said, cutting me off. Sabine rarely cut people off. She was almost always patient, ready to hear others out. "But if we keep going at the rate Peter's going, God knows when we'll be able to stop running and hiding, and start gaining ground." There was a frenzy to her voice I'd never heard before. She tripped over her own words. "Eva, I've spent so much of my life afraid—so much of it just trying to get by. Just trying to survive. I can't keep going like this. I don't want to be thirty or forty or fifty years old and looking at my life, and it's still the same, and I'm still scared and hoping that other people will make things change. *I* want to make things change. Now."

She looked me in the eye. "Peter thinks we're all children, Eva. But at some point, you've got to grow up."

Her words punched the air from my gut. Because she was right. I did have to grow up. I had to stop doubting myself, stop being so wishy-washy about things. Stop being so scared all the time.

"It's okay, Eva," Sabine said. She took my hand. The look in her eyes told me she understood everything. Understood *me*. "In a couple days, it'll all be over, anyway."

THIRTY-ONE

A swish of white cloth
A doctor's coat, coarsely woven
In our six-year-old hands
Do you want to be a doctor when you grow up?
No answer.
One of us wouldn't
Grow up

Horror.

I woke to complete and utter horror. Horror that choked like fingers inside our throat.

It took me a second to realize Addie and I weren't being attacked. Weren't running for our lives. We were just sitting quietly in our room. But—

<Addie?> I cried. *<Addie, what's wrong?>*

She tried to say something. Started to say something.

Then she was gone. Leaving me in the echoes of her terror.

<Addie?> I scrambled off our bed.

Nothing.

<Addie!>

Something had happened. Something must have happened.

Confusion and fear shoved me into the hallway. Made me shout, without thinking, "Emalia!"

Emalia and Sophie's door was half-open; I heard her humming as she folded her laundry. Her head jerked up. "Addie? What's wrong?"

"What was I doing?" I demanded. "Right before? A minute before? Where was I?"

Emalia abandoned her laundry and hurried toward me. "Eva? Are you all right? Calm down. You look—"

I backed away, too riled up to let anyone touch me. "Please—just tell me where I was a moment ago."

"You were in your room," Emalia said. "I thought Addie was sketching. I didn't—"

The phone rang, shrill in my ears. Emalia didn't look away from me, but she backed up a few steps and answered the cordless on her nightstand. "Hello?"

A pause. She lowered the phone. Her eyes weren't searching my face now. They moved over my body, taking in the faded, yellow shirt I was wearing. The jean shorts. As if she hoped to find clues in my clothes. "It's for Addie," she said slowly. "It's Dr. Lyanne."

I reached out my hand, trying to look more relaxed. I shouldn't have let Emalia see how freaked out I was. She was suspicious now, but still handed me the phone.

"Hello?" I said.

Dr. Lyanne wasted no time on pleasantries. "What the hell are you and Devon doing, Addie?"

I didn't correct Dr. Lyanne. Since visiting Sabine the day before yesterday, I hadn't left the building. I'd barely left the apartment. As far as I knew, Addie had stayed in, too.

I looked at Emalia. She'd gone back to fiddling with her laundry, making a poor attempt at pretending not to listen to my conversation.

Quietly, I slipped out into the hall. "I'm not doing anything."

"Like hell you aren't." Dr. Lyanne spoke in a low hiss. "You know how much of a risk it is for that boy to come to my office? Then I turn around, and you're both gone. If he needed to use a computer, he could have asked instead of going behind my back."

Devon and Addie had gone to Dr. Lyanne's office? If Devon needed the computer—well, it would make sense he would search out Dr. Lyanne. Her clinic would have a computer, and knowing Dr. Lyanne might allow Devon access to it.

But access for what reason?

"Addie," Dr. Lyanne snapped. "Are you even listening?"

"I'm listening," I whispered.

"No, you're not. I asked you what Devon needed a computer for so badly."

If only I knew. Dr. Lyanne sighed. I bit back my next sentence, waiting for her to speak again. Finally, she said, "I'm going to ask one last time. What are you and Devon up to?"

"We're not up to anything," I said.

I could almost see Dr. Lyanne on the other end of the line, standing with the phone to her ear, her sharp shoulders rigid, her eyes burning a hole in the wall. "Don't do anything stupid, Addie. And don't let Devon."

My mind whirled with questions I couldn't ask.

"Okay," I said.

"No," Dr. Lyanne said. "Not *okay*, Addie. Promise me."

I hesitated. I was making so many promises, and this one wouldn't even be in my own name.

"Addie," Dr. Lyanne prompted.

"I promise," I said. I reached my room and shut the door behind me. "I won't. And I won't let Devon."

Dr. Lyanne was quiet a long time. "All right," she said and

hung up. She wasn't one for drawn-out good-byes. I sat down on my bed, still clutching the phone.

Addie had gone to visit Dr. Lyanne with Devon, and I had known nothing about it.

I was still trying to process this information when Nina dashed into our room. "Eva! Emalia's setting up the projector so we can watch my films."

I can't right now, I almost said, but Nina looked so excited, I couldn't manage it. Emalia obviously hadn't told her about my strange behavior. I hated now to destroy any scrap of normality Nina and Kitty managed to salvage. So I just nodded and followed Nina out into the living room.

Emalia gave me a measured look, but didn't ask any questions. I had a feeling that she wouldn't—at least not while Nina was there. She wouldn't call and ask Dr. Lyanne, either. The two had never been close, and Emalia wasn't suspicious enough. Just like how Dr. Lyanne wasn't suspicious enough to bring up Addie and Devon's visit with Peter, as long as I promised to behave. No one would expect our plans to be as crazy as they were. A few months ago, *I* wouldn't have expected it.

"I can't find my old screen," Emalia said as she carefully fed the film into the projector. "I think I gave it away after the camcorder broke. We'll have to project it on the wall."

The projector emitted a soft, feathery clicking as the film began to play. I sat beside Nina on the ground. Emalia hadn't chosen the tapes in order, and the first video to appear on the apartment wall was of Hally. She laughed at the camera, posing like she was destined for the front page of a fashion magazine. The image jumped from time to time, blackness flickering through Hally's smiling face, her bright eyes.

"There you are, in the background." Nina pointed over Hally's shoulder. And there, indeed, I was. It was the day Ryan and I had made pancakes in the kitchen. The day I'd told him about Sabine's invitation and our plans to sneak out to meet her.

Mom and Dad had taken pictures of us growing up, but never video. It was strange to have my body projected onto the wall. A captured memory of myself that everyone could see.

The next segment was of Emalia. She grinned and waved at the camera, chattering about some movie she and Nina had watched. Halfway through, Nina turned the camera around and spoke into it herself, her small face made large by the lens's proximity, her voice distorted in the microphone.

The next shot was of the streets below.

The next of the sky.

The next was Addie and me. We were sketching. We didn't notice the camera until it was nearly upon us, and then we turned and laughed and said, *Kitty, stop snooping. Go away.*

Except I had never said that. I had no memory of ever saying that, or ever hearing Addie say it.

I'm not snooping, Kitty said. *And you messed up his jacket. It's missing a button—see? Here?*

She pointed at Addie's drawing. There, still barely more than a sketch, was a picture I recognized. A picture of—

Well, she's not done yet, is she? Jackson said. The camera lens swung up to catch his grin, his blue eyes. He sat, portrait-like, on a chair. The same chair as in the sketch.

The sketch I'd seen, but didn't remember drawing. Because I hadn't been there then. I hadn't been awake. I'd been dreaming.

Which morning had this been? I had no idea at all.

Stop filming, Kitty. I'm serious, Addie said.

Each film didn't last long. We watched them one after another. There were more shots of Addie that I didn't recognize: Addie tossing through our drawer for clothes, Addie putting up our hair. Addie laughing. Addie staring off into space. There were shots, too, of me when I knew Addie hadn't been there.

If Addie had been watching this, would she feel the same way I was feeling? What was I feeling? I couldn't fix it into words. Not *sad*. *Sad* was too simple. This was sadness, and confusion, and longing, and more.

Something stirred in the quiet beside my mind.

< . . . *Addie?*> I whispered.

She grew a little stronger, a little more tangible, at the sound of her name. I felt her focus on the video, on the months of our lives projected onto Emalia's wall.

<*Addie*> I said. <*Dr. Lyanne called.*>

Nina was still entranced by her videos, Emalia smiling next to her. Neither could have guessed the silent conversation between Addie and me.

<She said . . . she said you and Devon went to her clinic. To use the computer.> I spoke as calmly as I could. *<What's going on, Addie?>*

Addie's will overpowered my own. I didn't fight it, just let her take control. Our hands tightened into fists.

<Addie, I—>

<Sabine's not telling us everything.> Addie paused. A hesitation? A hope I might encourage her onward?

I didn't speak. I barely let myself think. Something terrible was coming—I heard the rumblings of it in Addie's voice.

<Tomorrow night . . . > she said. *<The building isn't going to be empty. There's going to be a group of doctors and officials visiting. It's going to be a big event—they're . . . they're giving them a tour of the facility, showing them the new surgical equipment. Jenson's going to be there.>*

Her words washed over me, trying to knock me over, but I would not I would not *I would not* fall.

<Eva> Addie said. There was a plea in my name. A plea and a reminder. A hand reaching out. A held breath, waiting for me to respond. *<I think Sabine's planning to set off the bomb when everyone's inside.>*

THIRTY-TWO

I waited and waited for the weakness to pass. For the riptide to ease and let me go. It didn't.

<You have to believe me> Addie said.

I didn't answer. But she could taste my disbelief, and I knew it. I couldn't help it. I couldn't rein it back.

<Devon never liked this plan. And I—after seeing that bomb go off at Frandmill . . . He wanted me to look into things with him, and I agreed. And once Peter told us about Jenson—Devon broke into Sabine's apartment. Took the floppy disk—the one they saved Nalles's files on. He looked through them at Dr. Lyanne's clinic. He figured out all the programs going on at Powatt. Who would be visiting. When.> It was Addie's weariness that affected me more than anything. It killed my protests before I could form them into words.

For a moment, I was not angry. I was not scared.

I was just . . . disappointed.

I had thought, for once, that I was fighting for something.

Taking action for myself, for something I could hold on to and lift high.

But all I'd done was entangle myself in another set of lies.

<*Who else knows?*> I said quietly. <*Besides Sabine?*>

It was a moment before she replied. <*I'm not sure.*>

<*Jackson and Vince?*>

She hesitated. I felt the stab of her pain. <*I don't know, Eva. I honestly don't know.*>

Murder. That's what this would be, if the bomb went off when there were people inside the building. Murders, plural. I waited for some kind of visceral reaction, some gut-wrenching, heartbreaking, tear-inducing reaction, but none came. After the initial wave of nausea, I didn't seem able to feel anything at all.

Someone knocked. I shuddered back into the world beyond Addie and me and the closed circle of our minds. Emalia shut the projector off and went to answer the door.

It was Ryan. He opened his mouth, but shut it again when his eyes focused on Addie and me. He frowned.

Then he wasn't Ryan anymore.

I couldn't tell what Devon read from our eyes and lips. I stared back at him. Somehow, control of our body had shifted back to me. I didn't want it. I didn't know what to do with it.

"Devon?" Emalia said. It was hard to miss the sober intensity on his face. But she didn't comment other than to say, "Come in."

I stood like I'd been waiting for him. Wordlessly, he came to me.

"You guys go on watching," I told Emalia and Nina before following Devon down the hall.

"Addie filled you in," he said once I'd shut our bedroom door.

Ryan, I thought. *Ryan, do you know? Are you numb, like I am?*

By unspoken accord, Devon and I waited in silence until we heard the projector start up again, heard the quiet mumble of Emalia and Nina speaking. I could feel Addie beside me, quiet but stronger, somehow. Bolstered. She'd accused me of being self-absorbed when I'd missed her relationship with Jackson. But I'd missed her friendship with Devon, too.

I motioned to the spot on the bed next to us, and Devon moved to fill it. No hesitation. No extraneous motions. The mattress indented under his added weight.

"Ryan—" I kept my voice low.

"He knows. I just told him." Devon met our eyes. "We need to figure out how to confront the others."

I kept getting flashes of emotion at the oddest moments—numbness, then a sudden wave of nausea, like someone was shoving at our organs.

It happened now at the word *confront*.

I took a deep breath. "Maybe . . ."

Maybe it's a mistake.

<*There's no maybe*> Addie said.

"Maybe what?" Devon said. "Maybe we're wrong?" The lift of his eyebrow made it obvious how likely he found that to be. "Then we're wrong. No harm in—"

I gaped at him. "No harm in accusing someone of—of—"

Of murder?

His eyes were steady. "And if we don't, and Addie and I are right?"

I looked away. My mind felt so strange. So strange and adrift and wrong.

"This is going to happen tomorrow," Devon said. He reached out and took hold of our arm. Our eyes jerked to meet his. I didn't remember Devon ever touching us before. "We don't have time—"

"Okay." I pressed our fingers to our forehead and turned away. "Okay, I know. I know. I—"

"We'll meet with them tomorrow morning," Devon said, and I nodded, our face still turned toward the wall. "As soon as we can get in contact with everyone."'

I just kept nodding. I closed our eyes.

THIRTY-THREE

The next morning, everyone gathered in the attic, just as we'd requested. Sabine and Josie. Cordelia and Katy. Jackson and Vince. Christoph and the ever-silent Mason.

Us.

Devon stood a few feet from us, apart from the others. They were all sprawled around the couches, chatting.

Sabine glanced up. "So, what's going on, Addie?"

Addie looked toward Devon, who gazed back at us. Addie had insisted that they be the ones in control when confronting the group. Or she'd insisted she be in control, anyway, and Devon had just turned up as if that were the natural progression of things.

Everyone was watching and listening. Expectant.

"Devon and I came up with a theory," Addie said.

Our voice was weirdly tight, strangely formal. We sounded like we had during oral presentations at school, when we knew we hadn't prepared enough and if the teacher asked the right question, we'd have to admit we had no idea what we were talking about.

Could the others see us trembling? Addie shifted, trying to find a way to distribute our weight to stop the shaking, but it wouldn't go away.

Finally, she just clenched our muscles as tight as she could. Our hand slipped into our pocket, fingers closing around our chip—the one Ryan had given us before Nornand. We hadn't carried it in a long time, but I'd slipped it in our pocket that morning, needing whatever comfort I could get.

"Why did you choose tonight for the bombing, Sabine?" The question had to be squeezed up our throat, forced from our mouth.

Sabine lost her smile.

I did not want to be here for this.

<No> Addie shouted. *<No, Eva—don't you dare; don't you dare. Please.>*

<I won't> I whispered. But it was so hard to stay.

The floor creaked. But no one had moved. No, Devon had. He took his place at our side, not touching us, but there, and the trembling didn't stop, but Addie said, louder, stronger, "Why are you so insistent it *has* to be tonight?"

Sabine's mouth dropped open. "*You're* the one who stole it? The disk? You stole my disk?"

Everyone else, I realized, was watching Addie and me, too. A few threw glances at Sabine, but always, their gazes returned to us.

Realization brought with it a cold, trembling sweat.

They were all in this together.

Our eyes found Jackson's. Addie stared at him, and he

stared back, and he was the first to look away.

<Oh, God, Eva> Addie whispered. If she were anyone else, I would say *I can't imagine how you're feeling.* But she was Addie, and I didn't need to imagine. I felt it with her: disbelief first, because both Addie and I had always been good at denial; then anger, all-consuming; then horror—and pain. Pain most of all. I didn't bother speaking. Just held her together when I knew she might have trouble doing it herself.

I knew how to do it. I'd done it our entire lives.

"Addie," Sabine said quietly. It was the gentleness in her tone that set Addie off.

Our voice went shrill. "There are going to be *people* in there! There are going to be *people*—"

"Addie." Christoph looked as if he might rise from his seat. "Not so loud—"

"Not so *loud*?" she screamed.

<Addie.> I hugged her against me. *<Addie, Addie.>*

"You all knew." Addie blinked rapidly. "We'd thought—we'd thought maybe some of you didn't know, but you—you *all* knew. You're all—"

"Eva," Cordelia said.

Addie whirled to face her. Our face twisted. "*No!* No, you do *not* get to do this to her. You do *not* get to play with her feelings anymore. She *trusted* you."

Devon's hand closed around our wrist. He squeezed gently, briefly, then let go again.

"It's over," Addie said, quieter. "It's stopping."

Jackson had remained silent and frozen this entire time.

Now he shifted, not toward us but away, his shoulders spreading against the back of the couch. I couldn't see him breathe.

"What do you mean by that?" he said.

It hurt Addie to look at him. A quick knife to the gut as they made and held eye contact.

"I mean everything stops." She took a deep breath. "We get rid of that liquid oxygen. Safely. We dismantle the bomb—"

Christoph—Christoph in all his bitter-eyed glory—laughed. He looked at the others. He didn't say it, but it was etched in every inch of him: *Can you believe this?*

"I'll tell Peter," Addie said. I wanted to sink under into my swirls of dreams. But I couldn't leave her here alone. I couldn't let myself run away and hide.

"*Eva*," Christoph said, a barked command. "Is she even there, Addie? Are you—"

<Let me> I said. *<Let me speak.>*

She hesitated. *<Are you sure?>*

<Let me.>

So she did, moving aside, allowing our limbs, our tongue, to fall under my control.

"I'm here," I said softly.

Somehow, it was worse, knowing that now they were all looking at *me*, that those looks of betrayal and frustration and anger were directed at *me*.

"You didn't tell me," I said, and cursed the waver in our voice. "You didn't say—didn't say there were going to be people inside."

"Eva," Christoph said. "We didn't want you to have to know."

I tensed. "What's that supposed to mean?"

"Well," he said, "if you didn't know, then if—*if* something did go wrong, it would be that much easier for you to argue your innocence, right?" He turned to the others. Jackson was the only one with the grace to look uncomfortable at the blatant lie. At least I wasn't the only one who tried to fool herself.

"Christoph, I'm *hybrid*. You think saying *Oh, I didn't know* would—" I took a sharp breath and cut myself off. It wasn't even worth the argument.

"Did you target these people specifically?" Devon asked in that steady, weighted way of his. "Or were you going to kill them because it was the most convenient?"

Christoph leapt off the couch. I made myself stay rooted to the spot, but he wasn't coming for me; he came for Devon, who simply stared back at him as if the older boy wasn't nearly shaking with rage.

"We're going to kill them because they've got it coming."

"Christoph," Sabine said, but he ignored her.

"We're going to *kill* them because God only knows how many children *they've* killed—" He punctuated his words with his hands, making wild jabs in the air that came dangerously close to striking Devon in the face.

For all he reacted, Devon might have been watching an unamusing puppet show.

"Christoph," Sabine snapped.

He breathed hard through his nose, his chest rising and falling like a bellow. He turned to face me and spat, "Go ahead and tell Peter. What do you think is going to come of that? Really think he's going to do anything?" He pulled a mockingly shocked and pained expression. "Think he's going to scold us?"

"He might not go to the police," I said softly, "but I will."

The room shut down. We'd been running on tension and cold fury before, but now it was as if the gauntlet had been thrown, as if I'd drawn a line in the sand.

For the briefest of moments, the look in Christoph's eyes wasn't fury, but hurt.

He took a few steps backward. At the same time, I felt fingers enclose ours. I looked to the boy standing beside me. He squeezed our hand, his mouth in a tight line, his jaw clenched, and I almost uttered *Ryan* aloud in relief. It might be Devon's right to be here, but I wanted—needed—Ryan next to me.

Christoph spun toward Sabine. "We should never have gotten her involved. We never needed to." His eyes lighted on Ryan. "We could have convinced him without her."

Was he just saying that because he was angry? Or was it true? Had they never really wanted me or Addie? I hated myself for still caring, for how much the implications hurt.

Cordelia wore what could only be described as betrayal in her eyes. Sabine, who still sat cross-legged on the sofa, bore an expression of quiet disappointment. Not disappointment that her plans were falling apart, but disappointment in me.

"They don't even know," Christoph shouted. He was speaking to the rest of the group now, not Ryan and me. As if we were too far gone to talk to. As if we weren't worth the effort. "They don't even *know*." His voice turned low, hoarse. "They don't even get how badly they're screwing everything up. One day they'll look back and realize how utterly stupid and small-minded they were." He swung to face us. "And it'll be too late."

Each word was a rusty nail shot between our ribs.

"They weren't there, Christoph," Jackson said quietly. In defense of us? Or in dismissal?

It was true. We'd never been in an institution. We'd been in Nornand for six days.

It sounded pathetic in my mind—but it hadn't been. We might have been fed and properly housed and allowed, every few days, to go outside, but—

"Then they shouldn't," Christoph growled, "try to screw around with things they don't understand."

"I think," Ryan said quietly but firmly, "we understand murder just fine."

Christoph sneered. He paced back and forth, as if his rage burned too hot to allow him to keep still. Then, as if he couldn't even bear to look at us anymore, he stalked past us and stood, stiff-shouldered, by the window.

Sabine said, quietly, "It's not murder if it's war."

Jackson didn't speak. Jackson, who loved to hear the sound of his own voice. Jackson, who had smiled even when crushed in that dark closet with us at Nornand Clinic, yards away from a nurse, and whispered for us to *keep hope*.

I met his pale blue eyes, but they seemed to stare right through me.

"Call the plan off," Ryan said. "I'll take—"

I saw Jackson's eyes widen. Saw his mouth open. He shot upright.

Then I just saw the brightest flash of light and crumpled.

THIRTY-FOUR

I didn't have time to scream before our head hit the floor.

Our vision blackened. First around the edges. Then completely. Darkness, utter and stifling.

"Eva!" Ryan shouted.

The world returned in patches. Fairy lights. A few planks of floor. Sneakers, blurred.

The blow had come from behind. Someone had hit us with something—something much harder than just a fist.

I tried to push ourself off the floor but everything spun

spun

spun

spun spun—

Somebody crashed down onto the floor next to me. Christoph. Blood on his lip. I tried again to push off the ground—

Christoph was the only one who'd been standing behind us. Christoph had attacked us. Before the thought could even settle in my addled mind, he'd leapt back up.

Feet, everywhere. Ryan shouting, furious. Everyone shouting.

Our head rang, sound funneling into our ears as if through water.

Then there was someone crouched next to us. Sabine. She grabbed our arm.

Ryan, I tried to say, then managed to—"Ryan—"

Sabine dragged us toward her. There was something in her hands, dully silver. Duct tape. I tried to scramble away, but she said, "Hold her!" and more hands—Cordelia's hands—clamped us down. I screamed, thrashing.

"*God*," someone said in horror. Jackson.

A rag was crammed into our mouth. We choked on it, gagging, our back arching. Our hair covered our face, our eyes. Someone yanked our hands behind our back. We heard the *skriich* of duct tape, then felt it against our wrists, wrenching them together, binding them. Something rammed into us, and Sabine swore.

"*Christoph! Get ahold of him*."

Ryan.

Our legs jackknifed outward, catching Christoph in the knee. He went down, but fell toward us instead of away, and we screamed into our gag as his weight slammed across our legs.

Then Ryan was there, pulling him off. Cordelia left us to tackle him. Christoph staggered back onto his feet. The three of them stumbled toward the other end of the attic—

Where Jackson stood, alone. Frozen.

"*Jackson*," Sabine snapped. "Get over here and help me."

Our arms were pinned. We tried again to lash out with our legs, but they didn't move properly, and they *hurt*.

Sabine pressed us against the ground. We fought, but our bound hands threw us off balance. The initial blow had shot stars in our vision. Even now, we felt nauseated, like we might throw up. We couldn't get the hair out from our eyes. Couldn't see.

Then we felt the tape winding around our legs. We heard Sabine say, "Here, do him, too. Quickly."

For a long moment, all we could hear was the sound of tape being pulled, the sound of panted breaths, of someone fighting to yell through a gag.

Then, quiet. Our cheek stayed pressed against the wooden floor, our eyes open. We saw nothing but the bottom of the green couch and our disheveled hair.

Someone pulled us into a sitting position. With our legs and arms bound, we almost fell over again. Sabine brushed the hair from our face, her hands soft. Her thick hair was tangled, too, her eyes wide and bright, her lips parted as she struggled to regain her breath. There was a scratch on her cheek. From us?

I found I still cared.

And I hated it.

I searched desperately for Ryan and found him at the other end of the attic, similarly bound. He watched the room.

Watched me. His left sleeve had ripped at the seam. Like me, he breathed heavily. There was blood smeared across his temple.

That was when I stopped caring who I hurt.

"I'm sorry," Sabine said quietly, pulling my attention back to her.

The gag prevented Addie and me from speaking aloud. Pure fury kept us from even speaking to each other.

"Christoph"—she turned to face him, and for a second the stubborn calm on her features dropped to reveal the anger underneath—"shouldn't have done that."

Christoph stood by Ryan, his lip split, his eyes wild. He clenched his jaw and looked away. Ryan tried to say something, but the rag in his mouth garbled it beyond comprehension. It did nothing to hide his vehemence.

Sabine ignored him. "I know you're upset, Eva. You have every right to be upset. But you can't go to the police. You're too angry to realize that right now, so we have to make sure you won't do something stupid until you can control yourself."

I put every ounce of rage I could into my glare, every bit of pain.

"We're on the same side," Sabine said softly. "You have to understand that. We don't have anyone but each other. And you'll get that someday. Soon, I hope." She seemed about to reach out toward us, but the look in our face stayed her hand. "If you went to the police, you think they wouldn't take you away, too? What if they traced you back to Peter? And Henri?

And Emalia? You could bring the whole Underground crumbling down, and then who would help all the kids who need saving?"

And what about what you were planning? What if they traced *murder* back to you?

"This is us looking out for you, Eva," Sabine said. "I know it doesn't seem that way, but it is."

She turned to the others, and in that moment, shifted. Why? Because Josie wanted her moment to speak? Because Josie was better at planning kidnappings?

Or because, despite everything, Sabine couldn't face us any longer?

"We're going to need to keep them here until it's over," Josie said.

"Then what?" Christoph looked at Addie and me from across the room, his eyes somehow distant. "You can keep them here until it's done, but as soon as you let them go, they'll go straight to Peter."

"They won't," Josie said. "Not after it's too late." Her eyes locked on mine. "It wouldn't make sense. Tell Peter about it after the fact? And what's he going to do? He wouldn't—can't—turn us in. You'd only be torturing him."

"She'd go to the police," Christoph said.

"She won't," Josie said. "I know she won't. Because the building will already be down; those people will already be dead."

You're wrong, some part of me screamed. *You're wrong,*

you're wrong. I would tell. I'd turn you all in, whatever the consequences.

But another part of me, buried deep, thought she might be right.

After the fact, would we have the courage to tell anyone? It wouldn't bring the dead back. It might punish these people here, but—we were all hybrid. Who was to say how a police investigation might turn out? Who was to say what Cordelia or Jackson or Christoph might tell an officer under interrogation?

Kitty and Nina, Hally and Lissa. They'd done absolutely nothing wrong, but no one would care about that.

We'd all have to run again. Separately, maybe, this time.

We might be caught. Kitty and Hally might be caught.

Could I take that risk for a few lives that were already past helping?

I couldn't.

I couldn't.

Jackson's figure was blurred, but we saw him turn away. We angrily blinked our vision clear again.

"I'll call Emalia and Henri," Josie said. "Tell them I went by and picked Eva and Ryan up so they could stay the night with Cordelia and me. Sabine and I will come up with something. They won't suspect."

Of course they wouldn't. Who would ever dream of the scene in this attic right now? Ryan and me gagged and bound with duct tape?

I screamed into our gag, writhing and straining against our

bonds. It didn't last long. Soon, we were out of breath and dizzy from lack of oxygen, from pure panic.

Josie's look was gently pitying.

"Please don't," she said quietly. "You might hurt yourself. You're already bleeding. Head wounds always do, worse than usual."

The trickle down our neck. I'd thought it was sweat. Was it blood?

"Someone's going to need to be here at all times," Josie said. "We'll take turns. I'll start."

THIRTY-FIVE

Cordelia left first. Christoph was next, moving slower. His lip still bled, and he kept rubbing at it, smearing the blood across his chin.

"Go clean yourself up in the bathroom," Josie said as he made his way down the stairs. "And bring me up the first-aid kit."

He made no reply, but returned in a few minutes with his face clean and a small, white box in his hands. Josie nodded her thanks. He walked away without a word and this time did not come back.

Now it was just Josie and Jackson, who still stood across the room, staring toward the window. His arms were crossed. We tried not to look at him. It hurt every time we did.

<Addie?> I ventured, but all I got was a wordless response that felt like a suppressed scream.

Josie approached Ryan with the first-aid kit. He didn't seem to be bleeding anymore—not profusely, anyway. He stared at her but didn't recoil as she cleaned the blood from his face.

"Jackson," she said as she worked. She didn't look at him. He didn't notice, because he wasn't looking at her. "You can go. It will be all right."

He half turned. For a moment, I thought he might argue. His eyes swept through a point a little above our head, his lips parting. But then he just nodded.

More than Christoph or Cordelia or even Sabine, I was furious at *him*. Because Addie had trusted him, had been happy with him. And now that was gone.

He disappeared down the steps.

Josie crouched in front of me. "Will you hold still if I try to get that blood out of your hair?"

The gag pressed against our tongue, the sides of our mouth. I didn't reply. She dabbed at the back of our head with a damp cloth.

She didn't try to say anything more to either Ryan or us, and while she was busy tending to our head, I met Ryan's eyes. He held our gaze a moment, then began looking around the room. At first I thought he was following the string of fairy lights.

Then I realized he was looking at the nails.

They were old, long but not particularly thick.

<*Addie*> I whispered. She was still curled up tight, and I knew how hard it could be to let go once you got like that. But I knew, too, that sometimes it was better to. <*If we could get to one of those nails . . .*>

Addie's voice was the faintest of echoes. <*We'd have to*

stand up first, Eva. And it would take forever. She'd notice.>

<Then we wait. Until the right moment. Or we figure out some other plan. But Addie . . . > I reached for her with ghostly fingers, drew her free from her hiding corner in the back of our minds. *<We're getting out of here before nightfall. And we're stopping them.>*

This was much easier decided than accomplished. Josie stayed with us all through the day, leaving only briefly when Katy dropped by in the afternoon to ask if she wanted to go home for a bit. Josie didn't, but she left us with Katy to run and get food as well as call Emalia. She closed the trapdoor, so her voice was muffled by the ceiling and layers of insulation.

Katy stood uneasily by the hatch, not looking at Ryan and me. I tried to take the opportunity to scoot closer to Ryan, but my movement caught her eye.

"Don't," she said. The command was strong, despite the guilt wrought into her body. The usual cloudiness in her voice was gone, replaced by a pained sort of steel.

I stopped.

The bell downstairs tinkled faintly, signaling that Josie had left the store. We hadn't heard any customers enter or leave all day. Josie must have closed the shop.

<Do you think she'll feed us?> Addie said.

<I don't know. Does it matter? We're not hungry.>

It had been hours since we last ate, but our stomach was

clamped too tightly for food.

<She'll have to take this gag off if she does, though> Addie said.

<I don't know how much screaming would help.>

We'd screamed earlier, but no one had come.

<Maybe we can bite her> Addie said bitterly.

I didn't answer. Bitterness was better than pain, better than paralyzing fear. I'd allow Addie all the bitterness she wanted. She deserved it.

<Lyle would be impressed> I said softly. *<First breaking out of Nornand. Now held captive in a secret attic room. Very adventure-novel.>*

Addie was quiet, and I was afraid it might have been too much to bring up Lyle at a time like this. But when she finally spoke, she said *<It's only a proper story if we escape. Lyle would never stand for a story where the hero doesn't escape.>*

I tested our restraints. Our wrists were crossed behind our back, and it seemed like Sabine had wrapped the tape in both directions. I could hardly budge our hands at all.

<She's got to let us use the bathroom at some point> I said. *<She'll have to unbind us then.>*

The bell downstairs rang again. Josie was back. She and Katy exchanged a few quiet words by the trapdoor. Then Katy glanced in our direction one last time, her eyes deadened, and went down the stairs.

Sabine—it was Sabine now, with her quiet, steady eyes and

that particular dancelike way she moved—brought over the plastic bags of takeout. "If you scream when I ungag you, Eva, I'll just have to gag you again and then you won't be able to eat."

I nodded.

She undid the gag. I didn't scream. I breathed several times, quickly, through our mouth, and swallowed, trying to get the taste of cloth off our tongue.

"I brought sandwiches." Sabine turned back to her bags. "I'll have to—"

"I need to go to the bathroom." I'd planned on saying it as innocently as I could, but I realized two words in that I had no idea how *innocent* sounded after being attacked and tied up by people you thought were friends.

Sabine glanced at Ryan. He'd slumped against the wall, looking back at her unblinkingly.

"I don't know if I trust him up here by himself," Sabine said.

"Then stay up here with him and let me go to the bathroom."

She smiled crookedly. "No, I think I'll come down with you." She produced a pocketknife and pointed it at our binds. "Same deal as with the gag. You only get one chance. Struggle, and it's gone."

I could feel how difficult it was for Addie to keep from taking over our limbs, from striking out as soon as our arms were free. Our muscles felt strangely wobbly. Sabine pulled our hands in front of us and bound them again, but looser, with a length of enforced duct tape about five inches long between our wrists.

She was more hesitant about our legs. Finally, she cut those bonds, too—but not before crafting makeshift manacles around our ankles.

"You're good at this," I said quietly, to hurt her.

"This is what they did to us, sometimes, at the institution," she said, to hurt me.

<That makes no sense> Addie said. *<Duct tape? As if they wouldn't have something more—more professional.>*

I felt the hit in our gut anyway. I didn't say anything else as Sabine pulled us to our feet.

"Be back soon," she said to Ryan, as if we were just popping off to the bathroom in the middle of a party.

We headed down the stairs, step by careful step. Sabine showed me to the bathroom in the back room on the other side of the store. "Don't take long," she said before closing the door.

As soon as she did, I locked it and whipped around, searching for something—anything—to free our hands. There was just the toilet, a sink with a drawer and a cabinet, and a mop in the corner, next to a stack of toilet paper.

Toiler paper. I turned to the dispenser, but it wasn't the sort found in department stores, with jagged edges. There was no paper towel dispenser, only a box of tissues atop the toilet tank.

I flushed the toilet and turned on the sink so Sabine couldn't hear what we were doing. The door might be locked, but I didn't doubt she had a master key.

I bit at the binds around our wrists, the duct tape bitter in our mouth. It stretched under the force of our teeth, but didn't break.

<Check in the drawer> Addie said, but there was only some drain cleaner and old air freshener. I tried to no avail to break the length of duct tape using the edge of the sink—

<Eva> Addie said. *<Eva, our chip is blinking.>*

<Our what?>

<Our chip. It's blinking in our pocket, and it wasn't a moment before.>

I threw a glance toward the bathroom door, but the chip's weak light wouldn't make it all the way out there. It was scarcely visible through our pants pocket.

The chip was barely pulsing, a good three seconds between flashes.

<It can't be Ryan> Addie said. *<If it was Ryan, both of our chips would have been glowing upstairs.>*

<Then who—>

Addie and I came simultaneously to the same conclusion. I knew because her rush of hope and fear only compounded mine.

Hally. Lissa.

"Eva?" Sabine called through the door. "You've got one minute before—"

“Before *what*?” I snapped.

Hally and Lissa were out on the street somewhere. Close by. Looking for us—because why else would they have Ryan’s chip?

In our hand, the chip pulsed faster and faster. She was getting closer. Should we scream? Would Hally and Lissa hear us?

Then, almost at the exact same moment—the pulse of the chip’s light became a steady, red beam. And there came a quiet knock.

Not on the bathroom door. Farther away.

The front door.

“HALLY!” I screamed, then again and again. *“HALLY! HALLY!”*

There was a great scuffling outside the bathroom. Sabine rattled the doorknob, trying to get inside. The knocking on the front door became a pounding—

“HALLY!”

The pounding became the shattering of glass.

THIRTY-SIX

The rattling on our doorknob ceased, but I didn't stop screaming Hally's name until Addie shouted *<Eva! Eva, we can't hear what's going on.>*

My next scream caught in our chest, a hard, aching lump beside our heart. We no longer knew what Sabine and Josie might do. Hally and Lissa were in danger.

Our fingers fumbled, but I managed to unlock the door and shove it open. I flinched, half expecting Sabine to jump us. There was no one there. Then there was, but it wasn't Sabine or Josie. It wasn't even Hally.

It was Jackson.

The sight of him stunned us to stillness. But only for a second. We barrelled past him, struggling in our makeshift bonds. "Hally!"

Hally ran into view, her eyes huge. She grabbed for our hands. "Where are Ryan and Devon? Are they okay? Are you okay?"

"Upstairs," I managed to say. I tried to move in front of her, shielding her from Jackson. "Go. Run. Get—"

"It's okay," Hally said. "Jackson came to get me. I didn't believe him at first, but—"

Jackson went to get her?

He looked away. His voice was low, dulled. "Sabine ran out when we came in. She knows when to cut her losses. She'll be headed for her apartment to get the bomb, then to the institution."

Hally grabbed a large shard of broken glass and sawed at the tape between our wrists.

"You shattered the window," I said hoarsely. Our eyes kept returning to Jackson, but each time, I forced them away again.

A shadow of a grin touched Hally's lips. "Yeah, well, a rescue for a rescue, right? Don't think you get all the window-breaking fun. I didn't even have a nightstand handy."

Hysterical laughter winnowed through us. At Nornand, we'd smashed a window to get to Hally's room. Then, to escape the security guards, we'd run up to the roof. Somehow, that escape seemed simpler. The bad guys were just bad guys. We hadn't spent weeks with them. Months with them. We hadn't eaten and laughed with them.

"I'll go upstairs," Jackson muttered. "Make sure Ryan's all right."

He never made it upstairs. He met Ryan on the way out of the storage room—Ryan, who grabbed him and slammed him against the wall. No warning. No words.

The picture frames jumped. One clattered to the ground,

smashing into pieces. More glass. More fragments.

"*Ryan,*" I shouted. I started for him and fell, our legs still hobbled. It was Hally who reached them first, who grabbed her brother from behind, saying *Ryan, Ryan, stop. Stop.*

He must have sawed his hands free against a nail. He'd also sawed up quite a bit of his skin. His hands were covered in blood. It soaked into Jackson's shirt, left smudges of red in the white fabric.

Jackson didn't speak. He hadn't even shouted out when Ryan attacked him. The two of them stared at each other now, Ryan's hands bunched around Jackson's collar.

Slowly, Ryan let go. Backed away. His eyes focused on me and Addie.

Then his arms were around us. He was whispering, "Are you okay?" into our hair. I nodded.

Hally demanded to know what had happened, so Ryan and I told her. Everything. All at once and stumbling over our words and interrupting each other. Jackson leaned against the wall. He didn't contribute to our story. He didn't speak at all.

Addie didn't speak, either.

I didn't know what to say to either of them.

"We have to get to Peter," Hally said.

I shook our head. "We have to get to the institution."

Ryan's hands were still bleeding. He'd pressed them against his stomach, staining his shirt with blood. The cut across his temple had opened up again, too. It wasn't bleeding much, but it looked painful.

"Whatever you guys decide, we have to get out of here," Jackson said. "Hally's smashed the display window. If somebody hasn't already called the police, they're going to do it soon."

Ryan caught my look and moved his hands away from his bloody shirtfront. "No one will notice."

"Ryan, go check if Peter's home." I cut him off before he could argue. "You're going to attract way too much attention running around the city bloodied up like that. Tell him what's going on and get a new shirt from him or something."

"I'm not going to attract any less attention going to Peter's," Ryan said.

"It's closer." I turned to Hally and kept our voice hard. "I need you to go and see if Sabine's car is still parked in its usual spot. There's a pay phone on that corner. Call Peter's place and let him know if the car's there or not."

"Are you going with her?" Ryan said.

I shook our head. "I'm going back to Emalia's apartment. I'll call her work number, tell her what's going on, and get her to come back home. If we can't get in touch with Peter, we're going to need some other way to get to the institution. Emalia's got a car."

"What about him?" Ryan nodded toward Jackson, who glanced at him, then at me. "What's he going to do?"

"I don't know," I said. "I don't care."

Jackson looked away again. Part of me was glad he didn't meet our eyes. Part of me was furious he wouldn't. Addie hadn't said a word since he arrived.

The four of us made it out onto the street, hurrying to the other side of the road just in time to see an officer round the corner. I averted our eyes. None of us spoke until there was a good two blocks between us and the store.

Then I said softly, "Meet back at Peter's."

"Twenty minutes," Ryan said, looking between us and his sister. "That's it."

I nodded. I reached up and kissed him. No one commented—not Hally, not Jackson, not even Addie in my mind.

Ryan tasted like blood. It only made me more sure that I was doing the right thing.

"Twenty minutes," I repeated, and, because I knew no one else would make a move until I did, I broke away from the others and headed down the street. I didn't look back until I'd counted to a hundred. By then, Ryan and Hally were gone.

<They'd only have gotten in the way> Addie said, which was her way of saying what I was telling myself: that they'd get hurt. Ryan was already hurt. Worse than he was letting on. And Hally—Hally and Lissa should never have gotten involved in the first place. This wasn't their mess to clean up.

Slowly, Addie and I walked back in the direction we'd come. Jackson was still standing where we'd left him. He seemed, if anything, a bit lost.

But he watched as we approached, and now, finally, he met our eyes. "You never meant to go to Emalia's apartment."

"I need to get to the Powatt institution," I said.

Even if we'd had the money, no taxi would take us all the way there. Any driver I asked would probably kick us out, think we were pranking him. But I needed to go, and we couldn't exactly walk. I could have waited for Peter, but God knows what Peter would have done. Peter with his careful plans and his details. I didn't have time for Peter.

Henri didn't have a car. Emalia wouldn't get home fast enough. Even if she did, she would agree to nothing before calling Peter, and that would take time we didn't have.

I could call the cops. Would they take me seriously? Would they act quickly enough to stop Sabine?

Was it worth the risk to all the other hybrids in Anchoit who were connected to us?

Addie and I could still stop this. We could still do it on our own.

"Do you know someone we can borrow a car from?" I said.

Jackson hesitated, then nodded. "But we're never going to make it in time."

I shrugged.

"Keep hope," I said.

THIRTY-SEVEN

Our car careened down the road, going so fast I feared each turn might send us flying into the air. Nearly half an hour had passed since we'd left Anchoit, and it had taken Jackson a while to contact someone who would lend him his car on such short notice. I tried not to think about Ryan and Hally, waiting for me to reach Peter's apartment, getting more worried by the minute.

I tried not to think about getting to the Powatt institution too late.

"We won't get there before Sabine does," Jackson said. "Not with her head start."

"Then we'll have to make sure no one enters the building." I stared out the window, keeping a sharp eye out for police. The last thing we needed was to get stopped for speeding. The scraggly landscape flew past, a blur of brown.

"How are we going to do that?" Jackson asked. "Stand outside the door and shout *bomb* at anyone who gets near?"

"If it keeps them away."

"It'll keep them away," Jackson said. "It'll also get us both arrested."

I said nothing.

"Eva." Jackson kept his eyes on the road ahead of us. "What Christoph said, about not wanting to let you know so you could argue your innocence—it's not entirely untrue. And what he said about how we never needed you—well, that was a lie." I still didn't speak. "Look, what happened back there—"

"What happened back there is that your friends attacked us and tied us up."

"They're your friends, too."

I laughed low. "They are?"

"*Yes*, they are. And I—" His fingers clutched the steering wheel, his knuckles bright. "Can I speak with Addie?"

<*No*> Addie said.

I shook our head. "She says no. Just drive."

For a while, he obeyed, and we sat in silence. But his eyes flickered toward us.

"I'm sorry, all right?" Jackson sounded as exhausted as I felt. "I'm sorry. You were never meant to get hurt."

Jackson parked by the side of the road, out of sight of the institution. The land here was as hilly as it had been in Frandmill. The sun was just starting to go down. I almost wished it were already dark. It might make me feel better. It would help us hide, maybe.

"This road loops around to the institution." Jackson turned

and looked out our window with us. "But you can walk up the hill and look down, see everything."

I opened our car door. Jackson reached to extinguish the engine, but I stopped him. "No, stay. I'll go check if there are any other cars. If not, we'll drive until we find Sabine."

I slammed the door shut before he could argue, and hurried up the hill. Our feet kept slipping against the steep, rocky ground.

<Think she's already here?> Addie asked. We hadn't passed any parked cars on the road.

<Maybe she's closer to the building. Maybe they're around the bend.>

<That would be too close> Addie said. *<They'd be seen by the officials.>*

<Maybe not.>

I glanced over our shoulder. Jackson was barely visible inside the car. Hopefully, he could see us more clearly than we could see him.

<Are we really going to let them take us, Eva?>

A rock turned under our foot, and we almost slipped. I lurched forward, regaining our balance at the last moment. I could already feel phantom hands grabbing our arms. I could see officers shoving us into a police car, forcing our head down. Would they cuff our hands behind our back?

Would our parents be told? Would they look up from dinner, food turning to ash in their mouths, at the sound of our names on the television, the sight of our familiar face?

Addie answered her own question. *<We're really going*

to let them take us.> She didn't sound angry or sad or accusatory. Just calm and a little numb. *<To save people who don't care about us anyway. Who would kill us given the chance.>*

<It doesn't matter.> I took a deep breath. A few steps more, and we were at the top of the hill. Jackson was a speck in the distance. *<I mean—it does. But . . . We're not going to murder them, Addie. I don't care who they are. I don't care how they would treat us. This is not how we're going to treat them.>*

We looked down at the institution.

<Maybe we'll run, and they won't catch us> I whispered. *<Maybe—maybe it'll be okay.>*

The Powatt institution was not Nornand. There was no green lawn, no bright panes of glass catching the sun. The main building sat cradled in a valley, maybe five stories high, rectangular, enormous. We were looking at its back. The walls were white. That much was the same. White walls and a dark roof and an asphalt parking lot baking in the slowly sinking sun.

There was a second, smaller building blocking most of the parking lot from view. I turned to the road where Jackson waited for us, and motioned that I was going to go down a bit to get a better look.

We saw eleven cars, none of which was Sabine's. There were twelve people standing around talking outside the building, a security guard among them. As we watched, another woman emerged from her car. We were too far away to see more than the rough shape and colors of her clothes.

I walked farther around to see the front of the building, where there were another two guards posted by the main entrance.

<*Addie . . .* > I fought down a sickening surge of hope. <*What if Sabine couldn't get in? What if—*>

A hand clamped over our mouth.

"*Shhh*, Eva," Sabine whispered in our ear. "*Shhh*. If you're quiet, it'll all be okay."

I struggled to wrench free, but Sabine was bigger than we were, and she had Christoph's help. He was grim-faced, almost mechanical. It was somehow more frightening than his usual explosive anger. The Christoph whose temper blew up at the slightest provocation was also the Christoph whose face softened when he smiled. This Christoph—eyes glassy, mouth hard—I almost didn't recognize.

"*Shh*," Sabine whispered again. "We don't want to hurt you, Eva."

I lashed out with our foot. It connected—with Sabine? With Christoph? Both cried out as one of them went down and dragged the rest of us with them. Sabine's hand still covered our mouth.

"It's too late," she said, breathing hard. "The bomb's set up. It's done, Eva."

It wasn't too late. It couldn't be.

"Eva," Christoph growled. He helped Sabine pin our

arms to our sides. "Keep *still.*"

I ignored him, twisting and turning until we were almost on our knees, almost upright.

"Eva?" Jackson called quietly. We could barely hear him. How far up the hill was he? How far away? "Eva, where are you? Answer me."

Sabine spun toward the sound of his voice. Her hand over our mouth loosened a little, and I jerked free.

"*Jackson!*" I cried.

Sabine slapped her hand over our mouth again. She kept looking between me and the crown of the hill, where Jackson might appear at any moment. "Eva, what can you do? Run down there? The building is going to explode. You'd die." Her eyes met mine. "I care about you, Eva, despite everything. You and Addie. You're one of us. We take care of our own."

I slammed our head back, catching Christoph in the chin. Our elbow jabbed into his gut. I let ourself drop, ducking just in time to avoid Sabine's hands. There was dust in our mouth and a ringing in our head and the sound of Christoph shouting as I rolled out of the way. I scrambled back to our feet, panting. Christoph lunged for us. I ran. Downhill.

"*Eva,*" Sabine shouted. Not a full-throated shout. She was still afraid of being heard. "Eva, *don't.*"

I could see the edge of the parking lot. The people were gone—they must have entered the building while I was struggling with Christoph and Sabine. Only the cars remained, glinting in the dimming sun.

I looked over our shoulder. Christoph had stopped

following us. His lip had split again. I could see the blood. Sabine stood a few feet behind him.

"How long do I have?" I demanded. "How long until the bomb goes off, Sabine?"

"Any second," Sabine said.

I shook our head. "You wouldn't have come this close if that were true."

"I came to stop you," she said. "I came to save you."

"And I'm going in there." I jerked our chin toward the institution. "How much time do I have to get out, Sabine?"

She took a step toward us. She clamped her voice back to its usual calm. "You don't have any time, Eva. Just come back—"

"I'm going in." I matched her calm. "I'm not going to let them die, Sabine. I can't. I won't live with that. I'm not going to let Ryan live with that." I stared at her. Whispered. "I'm not going to let *you* live with that, Sabine. Now, you can tell me how much time I have to come out, or I can just take my chances with guessing."

<She won't tell you> Addie said. *<She doesn't care, Eva.>*

Sabine just stared at us.

I turned and started for the institution.

"Thirteen minutes," Sabine said. "Thirteen minutes. That's it."

THIRTY-EIGHT

There was a guard at the back door. He startled when he saw me running toward him, then stepped forward, his arms spread out, his hands held high. "Hey—hey! What're you doing here? This—"

"They have to get out," I shouted. He grabbed at me, and I darted backward, out of the way. "You have to get them out!" Our heart pounded so loud I could barely hear myself speak, so hard each beat exploded in our chest. "There's a bomb. There's a bomb inside. You have to get them *out*."

The guard just frowned. He didn't believe me. Dear God, *he didn't believe me.*

I shoved past him, ignoring his shouts. It was cold inside the institution. My shoes squeaked against the tile, the sound reverberating off the white walls. There wasn't another soul in sight.

In seconds, Addie and I were across the lobby and darting up the stairs. What if they were on the topmost floor? On the other end of the building?

I looked at our watch. A little over eleven minutes left.

We reached the second floor.

"Hello?" I shouted.

Our voice echoed back, but nothing else. I ran down the hall, still shouting, peering into rooms, glancing through windows. We caught glimpses of narrow metal beds, sheets already tucked in tight. We saw flashes of spartan, locker room–style bathrooms, porcelain surfaces gleaming. But no people.

Then we were back in the stairwell, on the other side of the building. The stairs here were narrow and long—two flights for every floor. The running and shouting left us breathless.

It was with a weak shout that we crashed into the third floor hallway. *"Anybody th—"*

They turned as one. The entire group of them. We froze, our mouth still open, our throat still trying to squeeze out the end of our question.

Thirteen of them, a few more men than women, formally dressed.

The closest to Addie and me was Jenson.

He stared at us, same as the others. But unlike them, recognition bloomed in his eyes. His proximity almost made me stumble. I shook my head clear.

"You've all got to leave," I said. "You have to get out."

Nobody moved. A woman turned to Jenson. His eyes had not left our face. "What's going on, Mark?"

A glance down at our watch—eight minutes. They had

eight minutes. *We* had eight minutes.

<Just tell *them, for God's sake, Eva—>*

"There's a bomb in the building," I said. "You've got eight minutes to get out." Our voice didn't want to work right. It kept giving out. It wouldn't go loud, as I needed it to.

But everyone was listening now. Everyone was listening, but no one was *moving*.

"A *bomb*," I screamed. I seemed only capable of a trembling whisper or a full-on scream, nothing in between. One of the women cried out in response, a startled bird noise. I dove back the way I'd come, looking over our shoulder, hoping my movement would incite them to follow.

Something flashed across Jenson's face. A bolt of understanding, like he'd just put together the last pieces in a complicated puzzle.

I didn't have time to ponder it.

The man farthest away from the staircase was the first to move. He threw himself forward, nearly knocking over the man directly in front of him. For a second, he and the falling, flailing man were the only ones in motion.

Then suddenly, everyone surged toward us. An unbroken wave of terror. The people behind us shoved us into the stairwell. Elbows and limbs lashed out. Then it was down, down, down the steps, the walls echoing with the thunderous noise of our escape.

How much time left? Enough to make it down the stairs, across the lobby, and up the hill?

<Don't think about it> I whispered, to myself as much as Addie.

Don't think about the seconds clicking down.

Don't think about the nauseating crush of bodies all around us.

Don't think about Jenson, God only knew how far behind.

None of that could be helped by thinking.

Just keep moving. Keep moving.

We were just past the second floor when the man beside us stumbled. Knocked into us.

Made us slip.

We tangled with someone, our limbs knotting with his, his momentum kicking us forward. We screamed as his weight came down on us. He gripped the railing. We grabbed for it but missed—

Everything was chaos as we fell. People dove aside to avoid being pulled down themselves. I only knew the moment of impact by the searing pain in our leg.

For a moment, we couldn't see clearly. Couldn't hear clearly. When everything came into focus again, we saw some of the officials hesitate. A few almost stopped. One actually did. Our ankle burned, shooting pain up our shin.

"Keep going," Jenson said. There weren't many people left behind us now. Most had pushed on. "There isn't time. I'll get her."

There was no arguing against that voice, especially when there was so little motivation to do so. They fled.

And despite his words, Jenson went with them.

We tried to stand, but the pain in our ankle only got worse with pressure. Our watch had smashed during our tumble down the stairs.

How many minutes did we have left?

<*He said he'd get us*> I told Addie.

<*He'll come back for us*> she told me.

Neither of us believed it.

Gritting our teeth against the pain, we managed to shift onto our knees. Crawling was bearable, at least for short distances. But we still had an entire flight of stairs and the length of the lobby between us and safety.

There wasn't any choice but to try anyway.

We're going to die, I thought, dragging ourself to the final flight of stairs.

We're going to die, I thought, setting our palm on the first step down, trying to shift our weight so the rest of our body could follow. Our ankle and leg lit afire with pain.

Oh, God, please don't let us die. Please. Please.

How many minutes did we have left? How many heartbeats?

The door to the stairwell opened again.

Jenson stared up at us. We stared down at him. Swiftly, he climbed the stairs and leaned toward us. "Arms around my neck."

We obeyed without question. He picked us up. Our hands fisted around the back of his collar, crumpling it.

Please, God, don't let us die.

He didn't speak again, just ran back down the stairs as quickly as he could with us in his arms. Every jolt made us bite our lips to keep back a cry of pain.

He shoved the stairwell door open with his shoulder.

Please, God, don't let us die.

We were halfway across the lobby when the bomb detonated.

THIRTY-NINE

We were blind and deaf and weightless.

<*Eva?*> Addie said, or maybe I only imagined it.

Gravity returned first. I couldn't tell which way we were being crushed, only that we were. We tried to move and couldn't. There was something covering our face. We couldn't breathe.

No. No, we could. We could. We just had to keep calm.

We were alive.

<*Addie?*>

Everything had gone dark and silent.

<*Y-yeah?*>

<*We have to get out*> I said. But we didn't move. We didn't try to. We perched at the edge of hysteria, and as long as we didn't try to move, and fail, we could stay on this side of it, could stay calm, safe.

We were pinned under something. Nothing hurt. Was

that good? Or did that mean something was terribly, terribly wrong?

Focus, I told myself fiercely. *Focus. Focus.*

<*Addie?*> I said again, more to hear her voice than anything. Her wordless shaking frightened me. Her silent, compressed fear. This was the sum of all our worst nightmares. All the terrors we had of dark, enclosed spaces. This was the trunk in the attic when we were seven, and the mobs of Bessimir and Lankster Square, and—

<*We can't move*> Addie whispered. <*If we shift something wrong—*>

We might be crushed. Properly. Permanently.

We swallowed. Our eyes still saw nothing but darkness. Our ears heard nothing but silence.

<*Call for help*> Addie said.

The enormous pressure on our chest made it difficult to breathe, let alone shout, but I tried anyway. Our lips and tongue were leaden. Our voice sounded strange—muffled and far away.

Would anyone dare step foot into the crumpled building? Was there even a building left at all?

<*Addie?*> I said again. <*Addie, we're going to be okay.*>

<*Distract me*> she whispered, as she had at Nornand, when we'd been forced to lie inside that box of a machine for testing. Her trembling had escalated. It threatened to shatter both of us. <*Tell me a memory, Eva.*>

So I did. Memories from before Anchoit, before Nornand. Memories of home. Of Mom and Dad and Lyle and even Nathaniel. Of our little house with the dark roof and the strawberry-patterned kitchen curtains. Our heartbeat didn't slow, but the chaos in our head receded, just a little.

<Are we ever going to get back home?> Addie said softly. *<Are we ever going to see them again?>*

<Yes> I said.

<Eva—>

<Yes> I insisted. *<Yes, we are. We just have to get out of here first, okay?>*

There was a great groaning noise. Then something fell, slamming into the ground so hard it shook beneath us. There was a blast of heat.

Fire.

A strangled scream ripped from our throat.

<We have to get out, Addie> I cried. *<Now!>*

This time, she didn't argue.

Our arm didn't move. Our hand didn't move. But our fingers twitched. I tried our other arm, our left arm—

The pain came. Knives from our shoulder to our elbow and shooting down our back. We gasped and choked, coughing. More pain, in our ribs now. Our legs seemed freer than the rest of us. They felt hotter, too, as if flames ate the rubble next to them. I prayed I wouldn't accidentally burn ourself.

I tried, through brute strength of will, to force our head and torso up. But our spread arms gave no support at all. I shifted our left leg over our right and shoved upward with our hip and shoulder. Our chest left the ground an inch or two, but our arm was still pinned, and everything *hurt, hurt so badly.* I screamed, and it came out a whimper.

But the blunt force upward had caused something to shift. When I tried moving our right hand again, it was almost free. If only we were faceup, I could shove—

A great weight lifted from our body. I gasped, lungs expanding, chest aching. I coughed. Sputtered. Choked on ash.

Jackson? Had Jackson come to dig us out? We were still facedown. I saw nothing but blackness and stars of pain.

Something clattered to the ground. The pressure on our back lessened further. I didn't know which way to slide, but somehow, I figured it out. Then we were free. We weren't blind. We collapsed against a fallen bit of wall.

I looked up, eyes squinted, to see who had saved us.

Jenson.

The smoke-filled air obscured his expression. Or maybe that was the soot on his skin, or the blur in our vision.

He stumbled, and I flinched as he lurched toward us. His hand slammed the wall just above our head. He fell to the side, rolling at the last minute so his body didn't crush ours.

Then we were both sitting there, backs against the wall, as the Powatt institution snapped and burned around us.

We looked around at the devastation. The building was still standing; we saw no sky. But there was so much smoke and dust. Blown-apart bits of walls and ceiling and floor. We heard a fire crackling, saw licks of orange and yellow.

We coughed and whimpered when our ribs felt like they were cracking with each breath. I was too exhausted to move. There was blood on Jenson's face. On his shirt, which had been white but was now stained by soot and dark-red blotches.

"I knew I would find you." His voice was a hoarse, mangled version of its usual steel. He stared at Addie and me, as if all his attention was for us, even in the face of total destruction. Whatever strength had powered him in helping us from the rubble had seeped away. "The fireworks in Lankster. The police dashboard video. I saw you."

<*What's he talking about?*> Addie whispered. Her horror was a hard, black thing. Jenson spoke like a man gone mad.

Then I realized. There had been a police car at Lankster. The one that had hit Cordelia right in front of us. The policeman had met our eyes.

Police cars had dashboard cameras.

"The oxygen." Jenson groaned. His words dissolved into a gasp for breath. "The doctor—I spoke to him, and I knew. It was you. I said I would find you."

The doctor smoking in the doorway of Benoll, the end of his cigarette an ember in the darkness.

"*Where's the boy?*" Jenson grabbed our shoulder. His fingers were talons through our thin shirt. I gasped at the pain, trying to pull away. "They took him with you from Nornand. Where is he?"

"You can't have him," I whispered.

"Where *is* he? *Where is Jaime Cortae?*"

I shook our head.

"Eva!"

The shout came from far away. Both Jenson and I looked up, searching.

"Eva!"

Closer now. Louder. Clearer. A boy.

Ryan.

His name came to our lips but got no farther.

"Where are you?" Ryan shouted. Frustration ripped at his words, made his voice raw. There was too much smoke and debris to see more than a few yards away.

"Found her!" came a voice through the rubble. But it wasn't Ryan's.

Dr. Lyanne emerged from the smoke like an apparition. A ghost wearing an A-line skirt and unsensible heels, hair pulled back severely from her face. We were so dazed we just stared, watching her come toward us, looking so casual with her purse hanging from one shoulder.

She tensed at the sight of Jenson, then knelt in front of Addie and me. I tried to speak and started coughing again. We felt her hand slide up our shirt, feeling gently at our ribs. I hissed in pain.

"My ankle," I managed to say.

She moved to our legs. "Which one?"

"The . . . the right. *Don't,*" I gasped when she touched it. She reached into her purse and drew out a small first-aid kit before gently removing our shoe and sock. Our ankle had already started to swell.

Jenson spoke, his eyes on Dr. Lyanne as she rummaged around the kit for scissors and a roll of bandages. "What made you do it? Steal the boy? Betray all you ever worked for?"

"Can you move your toes?" Dr. Lyanne asked me. "Point your foot?"

I tried and managed to twitch a few toes. Pointing was harder. "Is it broken?"

"Hard to say for sure," she said. "Your other leg's all right?"

"I—I think so."

She nodded and I tried to stay still as she carefully bound our ankle. Everything hurt. Dr. Lyanne had a number of pill packets in her kit, along with a few small, packaged syringes. I was about to ask if any of them were painkillers when she reached for our hand. "Come on. I'll help you stand, see if you can put any weight on it. The security guard up front has already called the police. They'll be swarming the place soon."

Ryan crashed onto the scene before either of us could move. Jackson was only a step behind him. Both stared at me, then at Jenson, then back to me.

"God, Eva," Ryan said, and didn't seem able to say any more. He joined Dr. Lyanne by our side, reaching hesitantly for our face.

Dr. Lyanne climbed to her feet. "She'll be fine. Help me get her up."

It took a few tries, but with Jackson and Ryan helping, I

managed to stand, balancing on our good leg. Our body felt so heavy, our head most of all. I thought we might throw up.

Now, finally, Dr. Lyanne turned to Jenson. The two of them examined each other.

"You two get her out of here," Dr. Lyanne said to Ryan and Jackson. "Go the same way we came in. Don't let the guard catch you." She pressed a packet of pills into our hand. "Take these. Two every four hours. It'll help with the pain."

"What about you?" Ryan said.

Dr. Lyanne nodded at Jenson. "Somebody's got to get him out."

Jenson was silent. He had saved Addie and me, in the end. He'd come back for us in the stairwell, at great risk to himself. He'd unburied us from the rubble when he could barely stand. Perhaps he'd done it in pursuit of his own goals—his own obsessions—but he had saved us.

"Why are you helping him?" Jackson demanded.

"I'm a doctor," Dr. Lyanne said. "It's what I do."

The sky was purple and orange when we finally left the building behind. How long had we been unconscious? I looked at the wreckage. Half the building was nearly gone, collapsed like a child's toy in smoldering ruins. The other half—the half where we and Jenson had been—was still standing. It all burned.

By the time we reached Jackson's car, Addie and I were shaking, our muscles jelly. Ryan helped us into the backseat.

We collapsed in a heap, taking shallow breaths because our ribs hurt too badly for deep ones. I'd dry-swallowed the pills Dr. Lyanne had given us, but so far, they didn't seem to be working.

"I thought you were going to Peter's place," I whispered.

Ryan's eyes met ours. "I thought you were going back to Emalia's apartment. What happened to understanding that if you get into trouble, the only place I want to be is right there with you?"

I looked away.

"I did go to Peter's apartment," Ryan said. "He wasn't there. I waited until Hally showed up. Then she stayed there while I went to call Dr. Lyanne. She was the only other person I could think of who could drive us out here." He pulled the door shut behind us as Jackson threw the car into drive. His voice was edged. "I should have come with you, Eva."

"If you weren't here, you could argue your innocence," I said softly. Jackson's eyes met ours in the rearview mirror. I realized he'd claimed the same thing about keeping Sabine's real plans secret from Addie and me. But this wasn't the same. It wasn't the same at all. "Sabine and Christoph?"

Jackson explained how he'd run into Sabine and Christoph while searching for us. How they'd prevented him from going into the building after us—the guard I'd pushed past had run in after me, but another had replaced him at the door.

Those guards had, in a way, saved our lives. Unable to actually enter the building, Sabine and Christoph had set up the bomb outside, which was why only half the institution had collapsed.

If we'd taken the flight of stairs on the other side of the building . . .

"Everyone else," I said. "The officials, the other doctors . . . they all got away?"

Jackson nodded. "A crowd ran out right before the explosion. They left with some of the security guards. What happened in there, Eva?"

I told them about Jenson. What he'd said. How he'd been watching us, in a way, this entire time. We drove and drove and drove under a darkening sky. Everything was a too-sharp dream.

I lay our head against Ryan's shoulder and closed our eyes as the silence of the road became the night noise of the city. I tried at first not to think about Dr. Lyanne, because it hurt too much, and then I did think about her, because it felt wrong not to. I whispered quiet prayers that she would make it out.

We didn't open our eyes when Ryan said quietly, "We're almost there."

We didn't open our eyes when Jackson first whispered, "This isn't right."

We didn't open our eyes until the police sirens.

And then we did.

And the last piece of hope inside us crumpled.

FORTY

There was a roadblock all around Emalia's apartment building. Officers and police cars crowded the otherwise deserted streets.

<*Kitty*> I said. <*Nina*—>

Emalia and Sophie and Henri—

I didn't realize I was moving until Ryan's arms closed around our shoulders, forcing me to stop. Jackson parked on the side of the road, a few blocks from our apartment.

Darkness had descended upon the city, punctuated by streetlights and headlights. A tap on the car almost made us scream. Then a shadowed face appeared on the other side of the window.

Lissa.

I unlocked the door. Lissa eased it open and slipped inside, hissing *shh* when Ryan and I started to speak at once. She kept her head low and motioned for the rest of us to crouch down, too, so we were harder to see. Her eyes moved over us, taking in the bruises, the cuts, the blood with growing alarm.

"It's better than it looks," I said, which probably wasn't true, but that wasn't what was important right now.

"What's going on?" Ryan demanded.

Lissa spoke in a rush, like she'd been running the words through her head, just waiting for someone to take them from her. "I waited until Peter came home. I told him what was happening—I told him everything. Then Sabine and Christoph came back. But they were followed."

If they'd been followed, then someone must have connected them with the bombing. Was it because they'd left too late? Was it because they'd lingered, trying to stop Addie and me?

Addie must have felt my guilt. *<It's not our fault, Eva. We didn't make them do anything.>*

<I know> I said. *<I know.>*

But still.

Lissa had gotten caught up in staring at Addie and me again, her face twisting in worry. But a tap on the hand from Ryan prompted her to swallow and keep speaking. "They didn't know they were tailed, not for sure, but Sabine must have been prepared for this sort of thing. She parked a few blocks away—"

"So they're okay?" Jackson asked. Everyone turned to look at him, and he faltered a moment, but didn't qualify his question. Just stared back, wearing a touch of defiance.

"I don't know," Lissa said. "They came to Peter's, and everybody—everybody was furious. They left. Maybe they got away.

That was right before the police started arresting people—" Lissa hesitated at the horror on our face. She shrugged helplessly and wrung her hands. "For questioning, maybe. I don't think most of them are even really suspects—just . . . people around here got scared, you know? They started to fight back. Some of them got violent with the police."

Under the restrictions, the curfews, tensions had been brewing for weeks. I closed our eyes and willed ourself calm.

"Why Emalia's building?" Jackson asked.

Lissa bit her lip. Looked toward Ryan, then down at the carseat. "I don't know. Maybe people knew Ryan and I lived there . . . and Henri . . ."

"Where's Henri now?" I said. "And Kitty, and Emalia—"

"They're in Peter's apartment," Lissa said. "Peter called them over once he—once I told him what was going on."

"Why aren't *you* at Peter's apartment?" Ryan said.

"I snuck out when I saw the first few police cars drive by," Lissa said. "I couldn't just sit there. If anything's been proved, it's that nothing good happens when I just sit there and let you and Eva go off on your own!"

Peter's apartment was only a couple blocks away from Emalia's. The police garrison didn't extend quite that far, but it was a close thing. I scanned through the dark streets until I found the main entrance to his building. A few officers had stationed themselves nearby. Were they planning on entering? Were they already inside? If Peter and the others tried to leave, would they let them?

Jackson looked out the window, too. "We should get as far away from here as we can."

"We can't *leave*," Lissa said. "What about the others?"

"You think I want to leave them behind—?" Jackson cut off, his jaw hard. "Unless you have a plan, we should go before there aren't any more hybrids left at all."

Addie and I were still staring at Peter's apartment. So we were the first ones to see the small, black shape emerging from the tenth-story window. It crawled out slowly, too far away to be more than the faintest of shifting shadows. But we saw it, and our breath caught as we realized whose window it was. We'd spent enough time ducking through that window ourself, when we'd still lived in Peter's apartment.

<*Kitty?*> Addie whispered hopefully, but it was impossible to be sure. By this time, the others had caught us staring. They raised their eyes, too, squinting in the darkness.

Another three shadows emerged through Peter's window, all much taller than the first. I grabbed the back of the driver's seat, trying to pull myself forward and get a better view. My muscles screamed in protest. "It's them. It's Kitty and—"

Who were the other three? Emalia, Henri, and Peter? It made sense, didn't it?

"Are you sure?" Lissa clambered into the front seat so she could see more clearly. "They're too far away, Eva. I can't—"

"It's them," I said. "I know it."

"You can't know it," Jackson said. "They're too far, and it's too dark."

"It's them." I reached for the car door, but Ryan pulled us back. Our ankle bumped against the seat. I winced at the burst of pain. "It's them, Ryan. We have to—"

"Have to what?" Jackson interrupted. "Eva, you can't even walk. Look, we've got the keys. Let's get out of here."

"No," I said. "Not without the others."

The four figures on the fire escape descended slowly. Soon, they'd be too close to the ground to see very far. To see us.

But someone else had seen us.

I shifted our eyes from Peter's apartment building just in time to catch the flashing red-and-blue lights of a police car. Now it was Ryan reaching for the car door. "Everyone out!" he hissed, throwing it open.

I took one last look at the fire escape. The four people were on the move again, faster now. We had to tell them where we were before they disappeared into the darkness.

Ryan took hold of our arm. "Come on, Eva."

I scrambled out, leaning on him for support. Jackson threw our other arm over his shoulder. Together, the two of them rushed us from the car, Lissa just a few steps ahead.

We made it to the shadow of a nearby building just as the police car cruised up, lights flashing. We held our breath until our head swam. The police car slowed as it passed our car, then disappeared down the road.

We slumped against the side of the building, breathing ragged.

<*Morse code*> Addie said.

<What?>

Addie took control of our limbs, shaking off Ryan's hand and lurching back toward the front of the car. Dr. Lyanne's pain medication had finally kicked in a bit, but I could still hardly put pressure on our right ankle.

"Wait—" Lissa said. "What're you—"

<We taught Nina her name in Morse code.> The key was still in the ignition. Addie started the car. The lights on the dashboard lit up. So did the headlights.

"Addie?" Jackson said.

"Shut up and give me a moment," Addie said and switched off the headlights. Then on again. And off again.

N

I

N

A

We could no longer see anyone on the fire escape. Had they caught our signal? There were so many police lights already flashing.

We didn't dare do it again. With Jackson's help, Addie crawled out of the car.

"Are they coming?" Lissa called quietly.

"They're coming." Addie stared Jackson in the eye until he swallowed down his argument.

Ryan was still looking down the street. "I don't think we're going to be able to drive out of here. There're only police cars on this road, and on the one intersecting over there. I think they've shut these roads down."

Addie straightened. Jackson still had a hand under our elbow, helping us to remain standing, and she grabbed his shoulder for support as she hopped a few steps away from the car. She pointed. "I see them! There!"

The four figures were still about a block away, moving in bursts as police cars passed by, staying to the shadows. A relieved breath strained through our lungs.

"Yeah, I see them," Jackson said grimly. "I see the police filing in, too." He extracted himself from our grip, letting us rest against the car instead of him. "You guys stay here. They'll never find us in the dark at this rate."

And before anyone could say another word, he rushed off in the direction of Peter's apartment.

"*Jackson*," Addie hissed.

"*Shh*," Lissa said suddenly. She grabbed our hand and pulled us away from the car, deeper into the shadows, Ryan hurrying to keep us from falling over. Addie bit back a cry of surprise and pain as our foot knocked against the ground.

We pressed against the wall as another police car passed, going in the direction of Peter and Emalia's apartments. The same car as before? It parked a little ways up ahead. Two officers climbed out, bearing flashlights.

<Where are they?> Addie whispered, searching the darkness for Jackson and the others.

Lissa's fingernails bit into our palm. But the police officers weren't heading in our direction. They moved down the road, the glow of their flashlights growing dimmer in the darkness.

Ryan let out a sigh of relief.

Then, out the corner of our eye, I saw five figures hurtling toward us. *<There! There, see them?>*

Addie waved wildly, ignoring the pain in our arm. With every step, they became a little more human, a little less shadow. Soon, we could pick out the pale moon of Kitty's face, the curve of Jackson's jaw. The glint of a streetlight in Henri's eyes. The swing of Emalia's hair. And Peter, Peter hustling them forward.

"Come on," Ryan said as they drew up beside us. "Come on, let's go—"

Emalia's eyes swept over us. "Thank God," she murmured.

"Where's Rebecca?" Peter's gaze locked on ours. "Where's my sister?"

"I—I don't know," Addie said.

There was a flash of something in Peter's eyes, but he shook it away. "Let's go. We've got to get past the barricade. Then find a car."

"We're not going to get past the barricade," Henri said quietly. "Not now."

<The photography shop> I said. *<We can hole up in the attic. If it's inside the blockade, we can make it on foot. The police won't check there.>*

<But the window . . . It was all smashed, and—>

<They'll have checked that ages ago. You think they'll be worried about one smashed store window in

the midst of all this?>

<All right, all right> Addie said. She repeated my suggestion aloud. Nobody argued.

We set off in the darkness, ducking into the shadows whenever a police car passed. Addie and I gasped air through our mouth, our ribs aching. Our arms and ankle burned. Ryan and Jackson helped us along, but it was an uneven, jolting journey.

"Wait!" Kitty said suddenly. Peter rushed to shush her, but she twisted away from him, fumbling for the bag she wore across her chest. Her camera bag, I realized. "It's gone," she said. Her voice was high, panicked. "My video camera—"

"Forget about your video camera," Jackson said.

"It's *important*!" She looked desperately toward Emalia. "Tell them, Emalia—"

Emalia hesitated. "She filmed everything," she said softly. "The police dragging people out of the building. The initial chaos. But . . ."

"But it's not worth getting caught over," Lissa said. She took Kitty's shoulder and ushered her forward. "You—"

"But it's *there*," Kitty said, pointing. We could just see something glimmering on the ground under a streetlight, a block away. "I see it—it's just—"

Kitty ripped free. Darted back in the direction we'd come. Jackson ducked from under our arm and chased after her.

"*No*," Addie gasped. "No. *No*."

But we couldn't even stand without Ryan's help, let alone run after them, and by the time the thought seemed to cross anyone else's mind, they were too far away to easily reach. Peter swore.

Kitty was unbelievably fast, but Jackson gained on her. The darkness swallowed them, then spit them out again as they neared the streetlight.

We watched them reach the camera. Watched Kitty bend down and scoop it up. Jackson reached her a second after. Grabbed her. Shoved her back toward us—back toward the darkness. She disappeared.

I didn't see the officer until he shouted for Jackson to stop.

Jackson did stop. The officer's flashlight beam swung into view. The light struck him across the face.

Then Jackson ran.

But he didn't run toward us.

The officer yelled again for him to stop, and now there were two flashlight beams and two officers and Jackson was still running, still running *away* from us, heading across the street.

The officers pounded after him, flashlight beams crisscrossing the ground, the air, the empty cars. Jackson was fast, but so were they.

Kitty slammed into us, gasping. Addie clutched her against our side, tried to hide her face, but Kitty wouldn't let her.

<*Eva*> Addie screamed in our mind. Pure sound. <*Eva! Eva!*>

They're going to shoot him, I thought numbly. *What if they shoot him?*

What if they catch him?

Jackson had almost reached the intersection. If he managed to—

Another police car careened around the corner and screeched to a stop. Two more officers leapt out.

Jackson froze. Turned. He was more than a block away now, but I saw it like I was there beside him—the officers approaching, their skin mottled by the red-and-blue light, the first two breathing heavily, their faces red. We could feel his chest rising and falling. Feel his eyes searching for a way out. Any way out.

We felt the ground biting into our cheek when they knocked him down.

"We've got to go," Peter said. We could barely hear him. We were still with Jackson on the ground, in the middle of that ring of police officers. Peter shook our shoulder. "We've got to go. Now. Before they start checking this street for more people."

"No," Addie said hoarsely. "No, we—"

"We can't take this road anymore," he said. "We'll have to find another way to reach the shop."

An officer pulled Jackson from the ground. Shoved him toward the police car. We watched just long enough to see Jackson disappear inside.

Then Peter bent down, took us from Ryan. Picked us up like we were nothing but a shattered child's doll.

"We have to go," he said.

FORTY-ONE

We stayed in the attic the whole night. Peter, Emalia, and Henri sat on the couches. Gingerly. Like they thought the frames might not hold their weight. Lissa sat cross-legged in the corner by the usual pile of empty soda bottles, staring at the floor. Kitty curled up against her.

Ryan sat by the window, his back against the wall, our head against his chest, his arms around our shoulders, our fingers fisted in his shirt. For a little while, Addie cried. Almost silently, but not quite.

Police cars passed outside, throwing red-and-blue lights through the curtain into the otherwise dark attic. Ryan whispered *it's all right, it's all right* in our ear, sounding almost as if he believed it.

Addie's tears dried up, leaving a cracked riverbed of weariness in their place. She pulled herself together. Shifted out of Ryan's arms so we were holding up our own weight. There wasn't time, now, to fall apart.

"Are you hungry?" Addie asked when Kitty came up to us.

Our voice was hoarse, but didn't break. "They keep food up here—"

Kitty shook her head and looked away. "We ate. Emalia and me. Before they came."

I could have, should have stopped this. I could have, should have kept her safe.

"Kitty—" Addie said.

"Sorry," she mumbled. Her eyes were bright. But she didn't cry. I realized we'd never seen Kitty or Nina cry. No matter what happened. "For—for making him go back. For getting him caught."

"Kitty," Addie said, "it wasn't your fault. None of this was your fault."

Kitty hesitated, then shrugged. She knelt and set the camcorder in our lap. It felt heavier than it should have.

"It was on," she whispered. "I didn't mean to—but it was on."

For a moment, I didn't understand.

Then I did.

Our fingers shook as Addie pried the back of the camcorder open. Took out the cartridge with its bright yellow label. Ryan's fingers closed around ours.

"I wasn't pointing it." Kitty's voice grew high again. "I didn't mean—maybe it got nothing."

"I want it," Addie whispered. "Ryan, let go. I want it."

Slowly, Ryan released our hand.

We left the attic after dawn. The streets were nearly empty. Saturday. *Everything's less regulated on the weekends,* Sabine had said. Her excuse for bombing on a Friday. Now the Saturday-morning stillness was a strike against us—made us more conspicuous.

But we made it to Peter's van. We made it through the grid of streets. And finally, when the sun was high and blinding, we made it to a small house at the edge of the city, with a scraggly, unkempt lawn and a dark red door.

I was in control then. Ryan and I were the first to walk up the porch steps, so I was the one who rang the doorbell. I leaned back against Ryan, and waited. I was patient. I knew it might take a while. That walking was hard for him, sometimes.

He opened the door slowly.

"Hi, Eva," he said.

Jaime Cortae. Thirteen. Brown hair. Brown eyes. Lover of peanut butter. Sometime angel, sometime mischief maker. Always Jaime.

I threw our arms around him.

Everyone filed in. Jaime asked for Dr. Lyanne. There was a quiet moment. I'd been hoping against hope that she would be here. That she would just appear in the foyer, like she'd appeared in the smoke back at Powatt. Like she'd appeared at our door that last night at Nornand to set us free. Dr. Lyanne had, in so many ways, always appeared when I needed her most.

She wasn't here now.

Because of me.

Peter started making calls. Everyone else just sat around until Henri drafted Lissa to the kitchen to help him prepare some sort of meal. None of us had eaten since . . . I couldn't even remember when.

"You all right?" Ryan said, and I nodded. We sat on the couch, curled against each other. His fingers tightened around ours. "I still can't believe you ran *into* a building with a bomb in it."

"I had thirteen minutes," I whispered. "Sabine told me."

"What if they didn't believe you and kept you from leaving? What if Sabine had been lying? What if the bomb had gone off early by accident?"

"I knew it wouldn't," I said. "You made it."

He laughed hollowly.

Where was Sabine now? Had she and Christoph gotten away, in the end? What about Cordelia?

"I can't believe I let it get that far," I said softly, our head in the crook of Ryan's arm. I looked at Jaime, who sat at the dining table, staring at the whorls in the wood. Guilt was acid in our veins. It corroded everything. Our heart. Our lungs. Our throat.

"Don't," Ryan said. "Eva, don't. If we're going to lay blame, I've got a hell of a lot more of it than you. I made the thing."

Lissa emerged from the kitchen and saw us on the couch. She hesitated, then came over and sat down. Ryan pulled her close, brought her into our circle. Her hair whispered against our cheek. "We made food," she said quietly.

We had to rearrange the meager furniture, pulling the table to the couches, so everyone could have a seat. Henri brought in a pot of something that piped steam into the air. We all sat. All except Peter, who didn't join us until bowls had been rustled up, soup had been served.

It was then that we heard the car pulling into the driveway.

The room froze. A picture of fear. Peter, the only one standing, was the first to move again. He gestured for everyone to head toward the bedroom, where we'd be hidden from view. Silently, we obeyed. Ryan lingered back to help me walk, but I was the last to enter the hallway.

So I heard when Peter opened the door.

I saw who was standing on the front porch, face pale, eyes weary, lips pressed in a thin line.

"I've snapped one of my heels," Dr. Lyanne said, holding out the offending shoe.

Peter shook his head and laughed. The sound was so foreign, so shocking, so strange. I couldn't imagine laughing. Now, or ever again. Dr. Lyanne's eyes met ours. But she didn't say anything, and neither did I.

Later, when we were all seated again, she explained how she'd gotten away in the chaos. How she'd sedated Jenson once they were almost out of the building, so he couldn't alert security as to who she was. In the confusion, they'd believed her when she said she was one of the officials who'd come to investigate Powatt. They'd taken her to a hospital, where she checked in under a false name. Eventually, she was able to sneak away. Hide. Then come back to us.

It seemed like Dr. Lyanne always came back to us, in the end.

She told us Jenson would live. Would make a full recovery, most likely. But she didn't know what he would tell the police when he woke. She didn't know who, if any, real hybrids had been rounded up in the raid following the bombing. Through his phone calls, Peter had ascertained that many of the ones living in the area were safe at home, still anonymous and hidden. But there were a number who hadn't answered the phone. Who remained unaccounted for.

Sabine, Cordelia, and Christoph were among them.

Addie and I had run out of pain medication, and after eating, Dr. Lyanne ushered us into her bedroom so she could properly check us over. I sat as she examined our ankle again, then some of our deeper cuts. There was a dark bloom of bruises across our ribs, to say nothing of our legs.

"All in all, you're extremely lucky," she said. "I wish I could get that ankle x-rayed, but—"

"It feels better," I lied dully. We were both seated on her bed, a bottle of disinfectant and a box of bandages between us.

"Eva," Dr. Lyanne said. "Look at me." When I didn't, she put her fingers under our chin, tilted it upward. Her voice was low, raspy. "Months ago, I watched them cut into a healthy little boy. I watched them kill one soul and permanently injure the other. I see Jaime every day and I know—I know that I had a hand in it."

"You didn't do it," I said quietly. "Maybe you couldn't have stopped them."

Her mouth twisted. "That's not what you said back at Nornand. Sometimes we make mistakes, Eva. Sometimes we make mistakes and they're so terrible the word *mistake* doesn't seem big enough to encompass it. But it happens. And the only way to ever make up for it is by cleaning up the mess."

Addie and I were silent. Dr. Lyanne's eyes never left ours.

"I think we've ruined everything," I whispered.

"You haven't," she said. "I won't lie—you've caused an impressive amount of trouble for someone who's barely old enough to drive. But you haven't ruined everything. You think Peter and the others didn't have plans for something like this? Well, not *this, exactly*," she said, taking in the look on our face, "but similar situations. You know how Peter likes to be prepared."

Somehow, I managed a wan smile. It didn't feel right to smile. But I suppose it didn't hurt anyone, either.

"Thank you," I said.

She shrugged and stood, gathering the disinfectant and the bandages. "For what?" But she lingered at the bedroom door. "I'm serious, Eva, Addie—both of you—forget all this *I ruined everything*. Focus on cleaning up your mess."

We nodded.

"Promise me," she said.

"Promise," we said.

And we meant it.

Dr. Lyanne came back with a wheelchair. Jaime didn't need one, but it was easier, sometimes—especially on his bad days—to have one on reserve.

"I'll see if I can get some crutches later," she said as she helped Addie and me into the seat. "But in the meantime, keep weight off that ankle." She shook her head. "You have no sense of self-preservation, you know that?"

<You know> Addie said quietly. *<I thought that made us brave.>*

Was it bravery? Or stupidity? Or both?

"I just wanted things to change," I said, running our fingers along the wheelchair's padded armrests.

Dr. Lyanne gave a dry, humorless laugh. "Funny. I decided to be a doctor—to specialize in hybridity, to work at Nornand, because I wanted the same thing."

Peter, Sophie, and Henri were gathered in the living room. Dr. Lyanne went to join them. Addie and I wheeled our way to the dining table. There, Jaime and Kitty sat alone, paging through a comic book. I could hear Devon and Hally murmuring in the kitchen, but their voices were just barely audible over the sound of running water and the clink of dishes.

"Hey, Jaime," I said. He looked up, taking in the wheelchair. He grinned. "I know, I know. I'm just borrowing it for a little while."

He made a face. "You . . . you c-can . . . *keep it.*"

"Do I get to push you around?" Kitty asked.

I rolled our eyes but couldn't help a small smile. "We'll see. Do me a favor first. Run and get me a pencil and a sheet of paper?"

"Why?" Kitty asked. "Is Addie going to draw something?"

<Addie?>

<Yeah> she said softly. *<I'd like that.>*

Kitty scrambled from her chair. In a few moments, she came back bearing a legal notepad and a pencil. She handed them to us, then leaned over our shoulder.

"Me?" Jaime said as we turned to face him.

Addie was the one who nodded. She touched the pencil point against the paper. Made the first light mark to capture Jaime's face; his short, curly hair; his smile.

We were so absorbed, we didn't notice Hally and Devon watching us until Hally asked, several minutes later, "Another Addie masterpiece in the making?"

Addie looked up. "I just realized I've never drawn him before. I—oh, Devon, don't—Jaime, if you *move,* then I can't—"

Devon had sat down next to Jaime, nodding questioningly at the younger boy's comic book. Jaime, ever eager, turned to show him the cover.

Addie rolled our eyes. Jaime muffled a laugh. Devon—Devon, for the briefest second—wore a small, smug smile. Then it was gone. He looked over at Peter and the others congregated on the sofas. They were too far away, and spoke too quietly, to hear.

"Planning again," he said. "We're going to need our own plans."

Addie glanced down at her incomplete sketch. "Or we could work with them."

"You think they'd listen to us?" Hally asked.

"We have to try."

Because in the end, we all wanted the same thing. To be safe. To be free. To stop the pain, and the suffering, and the fear.

To *keep hope*, not just for our own sakes, but for those who relied on us to help them when they could not help themselves.

"Come on." Addie set the legal pad on the table. "I'll finish it later. There's a meeting going on."

We all moved to the living room, even Kitty. Peter was the one speaking. He paused when he saw us approaching. His eyes met ours. I didn't look away.

Finally, he nodded.

"All right," he said. "Here's what needs to be done."

ACKNOWLEDGMENTS

I want to say an enormous thank you to all the book bloggers and reviewers who have taken the time to read and promote *What's Left of Me*. You guys do so much. Every happy email, "Waiting on Wednesday," "cover love," or even just plain tweet of excitement really makes an author's day. I never knew about this enormous community before entering the book-blogging world myself as an aspiring author, and I'm so glad to have discovered it.

Again, I have to shout out to the fabulous ladies of Pub(lishing) Crawl. All of you are incredibly dear to me. A great big thank you, too, to the creative writing department at Vanderbilt University. I had the best four years I could hope for learning under you guys.

A few special notes for the people who critiqued drafts of *Once We Were*: Savannah Foley, you've always been there for me, and I appreciate that so very much. Jodi Meadows, thank you for cute ferret pictures and for calming me down when the publishing craziness takes over my brain. Amie Kaufman, your notes make me feel like I'm a better writer than I actually am, and I love you for it. Cindy Wang, I can count on you to tell it like it is, and writing is no different—thank heavens for that! Biljana Likic, you are my three a.m. Skype buddy, my snarker-in-arms, and I swear your life *is* a YA novel sometimes, so that's always cool. ;)

Kari Sutherland, editor extraordinaire, much of the time I spent writing and revising *Once We Were* was spent in a state of terror that this book was too big for me—that I was tackling something beyond my abilities. You helped me take the enormity of the story in my mind and get it pinned down on paper. Endless thanks.

Emmanuelle Morgen, I'm obviously not your only client, but you often make me feel like I am. I'm trying to come up with some metaphor about publishing being like a river and you being like my skipper, but I think that would make me a boat, so let's not go in that direction. Thank you for being such a champion of the Hybrid Chronicles!

Huge thanks to everyone at HarperTeen who helped *Once We Were* make it onto shelves. Also to the Epic Reads girls—who are even more epic than their names might suggest: my publicist, Alison Lisnow, Whitney Lee, and all my other foreign agents.

Dechan, this book is dedicated to you. Thank you for fifteen years of friendship and many of the best parts of my childhood. You once referenced *Anne of Green Gables* to describe us, even though neither of us have actually read *Anne of Green*

Gables (we need to get on that!). I looked up the quote. Here it is: "A bosom friend—an intimate friend, you know—a really kindred spirit to whom I can confide my inmost soul." I think that nails it, don't you?

And finally, hi, Mom and Dad. There isn't much I can say in words. Thank you. Love you!

EXTRAS

ONCE
WE
WERE
THE HYBRID CHRONICLES

An Interview with Kat Zhang

Two Bonus Scenes from the Hybrid world:

Sailing
(From Addie's Perspective)

Things We Overhear as Children
(From Lissa's Perspective)

Ten Writing Tips from Kat Zhang

A Look at *Echoes of Us*,
the Final Book in the Hybrid Chronicles

An Interview with Kat Zhang

You've often talked about the source of your inspiration for *What's Left of Me*—wondering what it would be like if that voice in the back of your head were a real person trapped inside you. The idea of hybrids—two souls in one body, with one disappearing over time, could have gone in a much darker direction—with one soul having to actively push out/silence the other to survive. What influenced you to make the connections between the hybrid souls more positive?

It did cross my mind, before I'd even started writing, that the relationship between hybrid souls could be very antagonistic and competitive. But I was more interested in exploring a very close, almost codependent, bond instead. The friction between Eva and Addie and all other hybrids seemed like something that would come about naturally as a result of their situation, and I wanted that relationship complicated by how much they do love and care for each other. In the end, though, once I started writing, the characters' views of each other quickly became clear.

At the core of the story are some beautifully rich and complex sibling relationships and yet you don't have any siblings of your own—did you grow up wanting one? How did you create such incredibly realistic relationships (with all the annoyance, humor, selfishness, envy, pride in each other, compassion, and love)?

Apparently, when I was little, I did! I think as an only child, you're automatically curious about what it's like to have siblings (I don't know if people with siblings wonder what it's like to be an only child). I've been lucky to have very close friends who've grown up with me, though, so I suppose that's my closest approximation. Otherwise, I guess it's all imagination. ☺

You wrote the trilogy while also finishing college, including a hefty premed program. How did those premed classes impact your writing?

They balanced me out really well, actually. There's a part of me, obviously, that loves the messiness of creating a story. But there's also a part of me that enjoys equations and facts and how math problems (at least at the level I do them) always have a correct answer at the end of the day. My premed classes always seemed to recharge me for diving back into a story, and vice versa.

You were a teaching assistant in a class that was assigned to read your book! What was that like?

It was pretty cool! I was a teaching assistant for a seminar on the psychology of young adult fiction, and the professor put *What's Left of Me* on the reading list. The class spent a few periods discussing it, and it was really interesting to hear *What's Left of Me* interpreted by them.

You've been writing from a young age, but *Once We Were* was the first sequel you've ever tackled. Did your writing process change from *What's Left of Me* to *Once We Were*? What was the most challenging part of writing a series?

Yes, it definitely did. Part of it was that *Once We Were* was a sequel, so a lot of things were already set from book 1, like the characters and the basics of the world. Part of it was that

Once We Were was the first book I'd ever written completely on contract—and thus, at the time, the quickest I'd ever drafted a book. And part of it was simply the fact that *What's Left of Me* was only the second book I'd ever completed, so my writing process is still changing as I figure out how to best do this thing!

I think the hardest part of writing a series is that with each consecutive book you have to stay within the parameters you set up with the previous books, but hopefully, make the book even more exciting, with even bigger stakes, and so on. Also, I'm the sort of writer who is constantly discovering things about her characters and world as she writes, which is fine if you're writing a stand-alone and can edit in new information, but more disappointing when you can't do the same for a series since the previous books are already out.

Hybrid romances are tricky! In *Once We Were,* Eva and Ryan's connection deepens even as Addie gets a love interest of her own. Did either of the romances surprise you as you were writing them? Which guy would be more your type?

I think Jackson and Addie surprised me more, in that I didn't originally plan for them to get together, but it made sense to me once they did. I think it sometimes works out better that way. Characters have chemistry or don't the same way real people have chemistry or don't, and sometimes you'll plan for two characters to get together only to realize that on the page, they don't spark at all.

I don't know which one would be more my type! Ryan and Jackson fit Eva and Addie well, and I've always found it difficult to say whether I identify more with one of the girls over the other, so maybe that's why I can't pick.

At the end of *Once We Were,* Eva and Addie's friends turn on them in a pretty shocking scene. Have you ever been betrayed by a friend?

Never like that, thankfully! Thinking about it now, I can't really remember any instance where I've felt horribly betrayed by a friend. I suppose I'm lucky in that. I think everyone's felt disappointed by people before, though—when they don't quite turn out to be the sort of person you imagined or hoped.

Eva and Addie get to experience a lot of things for the first time over the course of the series—first kiss, first time in the ocean, etc. In *What's Left of Me,* Eva re-experiences a lot of firsts since it's been years since she has spoken aloud, taken a step, or made a friend. What are some of your favorite first moments?

One of the great parts of writing YA is taking your characters through a lot of firsts. When I started college, I started performing with the Spoken Word group at my university. Prior to that, the only theater experiences I'd ever had was a part as a bat in a play about the environment in second grade and a part as Random Townsperson in my eighth grade chorus's rendition of *The Music Man.* Spoken Word pretty much cemented a love of being on stage. I'd never really expected that of myself, so it was great to find out.

Did you always have the end of the series planned out? Or did it take shape as you were writing?

I'd had an idea of where I wanted the series to end by the time we sold the series, but the journey the characters took to get there definitely solidified as I wrote the books.

Now for some lighter, rapid-fire questions! What's your favorite type of place (i.e. ocean, desert, lake, mountain, bookstore)?

Those big old-fashioned libraries like in *Beauty and the Beast.* ☺

What city or country would you most like to visit (or revisit)?

I'd really like to return to Spain. I was there for seven weeks for a study abroad program, and didn't nearly get enough of it! As for countries I've never been to before, though, I'd like to visit Australia.

What's the highest number of times you've rewritten a sentence?

I'm a big rewriter, and I'm picky about my sentences, so a lot! Sometimes, though, if a sentence really isn't working no matter how many times I edit it, it probably means it needs to be cut.

What TV show or film would you like to live in?

I'm going to have to be stereotypical and say the Harry Potter movies. Magic, please. Especially that quill thing that writes for me. Could I get that functionality magicked onto a laptop?

Great! Thanks so much for letting us pick your brain, Kat! ☺

Sailing

Eva had gone under for nearly an hour when I met Jackson at the dock. The sun was powerful, the breeze off the water blustering at my hair and clothes. I had to squint to see him as he hurried toward me. Once he'd reached my side, I barely had time to smile before he kissed me, like he couldn't even wait to say anything first—or ask if Eva was still there.

He should have asked, probably. But it was nice, the selfish part of me thought, that he didn't. That I could pretend, when I was with him, that I was the only girl who inhabited my skin.

The wind was so loud he had to talk right into my ear. His arms were still wrapped around me, cocooning us against the rest of the world. "The boat's just a little way down the pier."

We ran along the boardwalk. With Jackson, it seemed like I was always running, always in a sprint to get somewhere. It should have been too much—I'd never liked it when Eva rushed into things. But it wasn't. It was nice. It was thoughtless, and careless, and everything I didn't usually associate with myself.

The boat we stopped in front of was smaller than I'd expected, but its mast stretched to the sky. Jackson clambered on, setting the boat rocking even harder than before. He held out his hand, and I gripped it for balance as I stepped on after him, the boat shifting beneath my feet. I'd only ever been on rowboats before, on the relative serenity of mountain lakes and ponds. This water felt like a turbulent, living thing. Like our staying afloat depended on its pleasure.

For a few minutes, Jackson hurried about, getting things ready for launch. Or whatever it was called when a sailboat started moving. "Watch out for the boom!" he called.

"The what?" I managed to say before a long, thick pole came swinging in my direction. I ducked just in time.

"You all right?" Jackson sounded concerned, but he was laughing, too.

I rolled my eyes at him and didn't reply. When it came time to raise the sail, it struggled against the wind, flapping like a frantic animal tied to the mast. For a moment, it snapped and flailed. Then with a suddenness that made my breath catch, the sails billowed out taut.

We glided out onto the water. Free.

The day was windy, and we made good speed through the waves. Jackson made adjustments to this and pulled on that, but I was content to just sit and stare at the gleaming water, enjoying the sun. Lately, Eva and I had split our days between Emalia's apartment and Sabine's photography shop attic. Maybe it was the small quarters—or maybe it was my growing doubts about everything we were supposedly working toward—but I couldn't shake the feeling of something looming. Something bad.

Eva didn't share my worries. I didn't have to ask to know. She'd always worried less than I did. Part of me found it a little exasperating. A lot of me was jealous.

I couldn't completely relax, even now.

"We're not going too far, are we?" I called to Jackson. "Because Eva could come back—"

"You said she was planning to be under for hours," he said, and I shrugged uncomfortably.

"Yeah. But you never know."

He looked at me, his hand up to block the sun. And maybe, also, to shield his expression a little. His voice was unusually neutral, careful. "Why don't you just tell her? Don't you think she's going to find out one day, anyway?"

Was he asking if I thought the two of us were going to last long enough for Eva to find out? Was that what he really cared about? Or was he just worried about how Eva would react if she suddenly woke during the middle of a kiss?

My stomach squeezed at the thought. God knew I didn't want that for her.

There had never been boys, before, in our lives. Never been anything close to dating. Eva and I had been far too caught up in dealing with each other and our secret for there to be room for much else. I felt ridiculously behind.

But I wasn't going to let Jackson know that.

"I'm going to tell her," I said. "Soon. She has . . . she has a lot of stuff on her mind right now."

Like Sabine and her crazy plans. Only those plans were Jackson's plans, too, so I couldn't say that.

The boat rocked with every lapping wave. Jackson nodded and looked toward the horizon, where the water glistened so bright it was hard to see. "We could sail this thing right across the ocean and land in Europe," he said. He laughed at my doubtful expression. "But today, we'll just stick with the bay. Here, want to learn how to steer?"

He led me toward the rear of the boat and showed me how to use the tiller. I could feel the resistance of the water, the way the boat veered as I moved the tiller right or left. Jackson kept his hand on top of mine at first—just to make sure I didn't accidentally capsize the boat, he said.

"We're going pretty fast, so you don't need to turn the tiller so much, even if you're trying to make a really big turn. Just keep it steady and wait. The boat'll turn." He grinned at me, his hair wild in the wind, and I was lost in the way the sunlight caught the edges of his face, outlined his nose, highlighted his hair, glinted in his pale eyes. Watercolor, I thought, because my mind was completely scattered by the way he looked right now, by the way his fingers were brushing up my wrist. I'd capture him best in watercolor. Anything else would be too heavy.

"Just have faith in it, Addie," he said.

"I do," I protested. For a moment, I couldn't say anything more. Then my thoughts coalesced again. "I'm more patient with it than you are, probably."

He just kept grinning. The boat made a slow arc across the bay.

"Did you always know how to sail?" I asked. "I mean, did you know how to sail before . . ."

"Before I was institutionalized? Sort of. My dad used to take me out on his boat, but I was still pretty young then, and I forgot a lot in the three years I was locked up."

"You guys had a boat?"

Jackson nodded. "We didn't live so far from the ocean, and my dad was a bit of an amateur enthusiast."

"But . . ." I threw glances at the other boats dotting the water, as if one of them might reveal a man with Jackson's eyes. "Not near here, right? I mean, you didn't live here? Before?"

His smile was soft-edged and a little dull. "I lived about a three-hour drive north. No idea if my parents are still there now." He shrugged. "Maybe they moved."

"You haven't found out?" I said. Too sharply. But there was no one to feel my embarrassment but me. "I mean—"

Jackson was Jackson, and he didn't seem offended. "I try

not to think too much about it."

There was a moment of uncomfortable silence, which he broke with a laugh. "It's better not caring, Addie. Better not knowing where they are, if they still think about you, what their phone number is . . ."

He still had to strain to be heard clearly, and after a moment, he motioned for me to wait as he reduced the sails and dropped the anchor. The wind felt a lot calmer once we stopped moving.

Jackson settled down next to me again. "You can't tell anyone I told you this. But Sabine and Josie—their family's still in the same house as before they were taken. Same phone number and everything. Know what Sabine does every month? She thinks we don't know, but we've all caught her at the pay phones around her apartment."

"She calls them," I said quietly, not waiting for Jackson to tell me. I already knew. Eva and I had been dying to do the same the day of Lyle's birthday.

Jackson nodded. "They can't really talk to them, of course, or tell them who they are. So sometimes they pretend to be one of those telemarketers, and sometimes they pretend they called the wrong number, and sometimes I think they just stand there and say nothing at all."

We were both quiet.

"So," Jackson said finally. "It's better not to know. Because it's not like we can do anything about it."

Was that the best way of going about things, in the end? Was it better not to know things, so it didn't hurt? To not think too hard about some things, because of the trouble it might bring?

Jackson stood and pulled me up with him. He said, "Want

to?" as he tugged me closer to the edge of the boat, and I waited for myself to resist, to shake my head and dig in my heels—to protest that we didn't even have towels, and were both going to freeze with the wind we'd encounter on the way back to the dock.

But I was tired of worrying. Of being scared and thinking about consequences when it seemed like no one else was.

For this moment, for this little thing, I wasn't going to let myself worry about anything at all.

I pulled off my shoes. I smiled and said, "Yes," and squeezed his hand as we both jumped overboard.

The water was cold out here, far from shore. I tasted salt on my lips as my head broke through the surface of the waves. I thought, reflexively, of Eva. Only Eva wasn't there.

"Addie?" Jackson said, reaching for me. He was treading water, looking halfway between amused and sheepish. "I didn't think this through. We're going to need to figure out how to get back onto the boat."

I laughed, swallowing salt water in the process.

"Don't worry. We'll manage it," Jackson said.

I nodded. I trusted us. We'd find a way.

And I was going to tell Eva everything. Soon.

Things We Overhear as Children

When they were very young, it was just the four of them—Hally and Lissa, Devon and Ryan. And their parents, of course, but they hardly counted. Their world consisted of the old, big house and the fields beyond. They weren't allowed to leave the property by themselves, so they invented elaborate games to pass the time. They fought wars hidden in the tall yellow grass around the porch, crawling on their stomachs to avoid detection, hiding under the porch only to shoot out and tackle the other to the ground and crow victory. Well, Hally would crow victory.

They dressed up in Halloween costumes in the middle of summer so they could reenact scenes from their books. They pulled the blankets from their beds and snuck them outdoors to hang over tree branches and make tents. Their father tried to keep them indoors, telling them they had to do schoolwork, but as soon as he turned away, they'd be gone again. Up in the attic, digging through dusty boxes. Out in the fields, watching cars pass in the distance.

"If you do it right, you can use your glasses to start a fire," Ryan told Lissa, and Lissa didn't believe him at first. But he showed her the book that said it was true, and they tried it the next day on the very edge of the field, squatting down and tilting her glasses this way and that until a tendril of smoke rose from the dry grass.

Stop it, some small part of Lissa had said. Stop it. It's dangerous.

But she didn't speak it aloud—didn't even say it for Hally to hear. She just watched, mesmerized, as the smoke grew thicker, and then seemingly out of nowhere, the flame bloomed.

Ryan stomped it out, and she was disappointed.

Sometimes, she'd catch their parents talking about them, when they thought she wasn't paying attention. It was so silly, how grown-ups never thought kids were paying attention. Lissa was always paying attention. She had to be, to keep up with a twin soul like Hally and brothers like Ryan and Devon.

"They're just running around," Mom said. "Are you even following the books? I never see them doing any of the work—"

"They know what they need to know," Dad said. He and Mom were in the kitchen, while Lissa sat in the study. She couldn't see them, and they couldn't see her, but she could hear them loud and clear. "More than what they need to know, I think. They all read so much. Devon was telling me about—"

Mom sighed. "Reading is all well and good, but what about—what about math and science and history and—"

"They're reading about that, too," Dad said, his voice getting tighter. Lissa felt Hally fidgeting beside her and tried to soothe her without breaking her concentration on her parents' conversation. "They're all brilliant at math."

Neither Mom nor Dad said anything for a long while. Then Mom sighed again.

"How long do you think we're going to be able to keep them sequestered like this? Devon and Ryan are eight years old. And all day, every day, they're stuck here seeing nobody but us and their sisters. What about when they get to be ten? Twelve? Fourteen?"

<What's sequestered mean?> Hally said.

<Dunno> Lissa said. She filed it away, to be looked up later.

"Nobody ever said this was going to be long term, Sarah," Dad said.

"It's been two years!" Mom said. "Isn't that long term enough already?"

"Isn't it better that they're safe?" Now Dad was the one who sighed. "Look—maybe things with Devon and Ryan will . . . settle out soon. Then it'll be a lot better. Safer. And Lissa and Hally—"

"Lissa," a voice said quietly, and Lissa jumped. She'd been so intent on her parents she hadn't noticed her brother approach.

It was Devon, and she whispered, "They're talking about us again."

"I know." He held out his hand to her. "Come on."

She hesitated, then climbed down from the desk where she'd been sitting. "Where're we going?"

"To battle," he said in his soldier voice.

She smiled and tried to hide it, tried to be a soldier, too, grim and steadfast. Devon seemed to do it so easily.

"We'll defeat you," she said, as fiercely as she could. She'd used to say we'll *beat* you, but Ryan had told her defeat sounded more soldierlike.

He took her hand and began pulling her out of the study. Their parents were still talking, but she no longer paid them any mind.

"Not today," Devon said. "Today, we're gonna be on the same side."

Ten Writing Tips from Kat Zhang

1. Keep writing. This might seem like a strange "tip" on a list of writing tips, but writers are notoriously good at not-writing. Whether you want to publish or are just looking to improve your skills, writing sits at the core of everything. Write another poem, another short story, another book.
2. Look for inspiration not only within your discipline, but in all kinds of art. If you're a novel writer, study some poetry. If you're a poet, see if you can learn something from the novelists. Check out what kind of techniques the screenwriters are using. In fact, don't even limit yourself to the written word. Go study some visual art, or watch a dance, or see an opera. It's all storytelling, in the end.
3. Don't worry too much about writing the "right" way, but try everything at least once. For example, if you've tried outlining, and you're terrible at it, don't fret. But if someone suggests a new technique, give it a go. Who knows? It might turn out to be the best thing you've ever done. Don't be afraid to retry things, either.
4. Read critically. When you find a book you love, figure out what it is that you love so much about it. Is the pacing really great? Do the characters feel completely real? Is it the writing style itself? Could you learn something from that? Likewise, if you read a book and don't enjoy it, figure out what turned you off. Are you doing the same thing in your writing?
5. Find writing buddies. Writing might often be an independent kind of thing, but having similarly minded friends and a support group makes everything better. If you're more of an in-person sort, see if there's a local writing group in

your area. Otherwise, there are lots of writing communities online you can check out.

6. Treat your characters like real people. This doesn't mean you should start introducing them to your friends! But when you're writing, your characters ought to be making organic, natural decisions. Your characters should drive your plot, not the other way around. Stories are about people.
7. Don't be afraid to make a mess. There might some people who write perfect first drafts, but I've never heard of them. Everyone else writes varying levels of bad drafts, then revises (and revises, and revises) them into something better. If you're too focused on making everything perfect the first go-around (or even the second, or third), it's very possible you're not allowing yourself the freedom to come up with some of your best ideas.
8. Write the parts that are important, and only the parts that are important. Or, you can write everything you like, but at the end of the day, cut everything but the parts that are important. This goes for everything: unimportant characters, unimportant scenes, unimportant sentences. Of course, sometimes it can be difficult to tell if something is important or not, which leads us to . . .
9. Give yourself time away from your work, if at all possible. Even a week away from a story can give you perspective you didn't have before. A month's break can make you realize that scenes you thought were absolutely essential actually aren't.
10. Finally, try not to stress too much about the whole thing. Writing is supposed to be a little (or a lot!) magical. Enjoy it. The story will probably come out better that way, anyhow.

A Look at *Echoes of Us*, the Final Book in THE HYBRID CHRONICLES

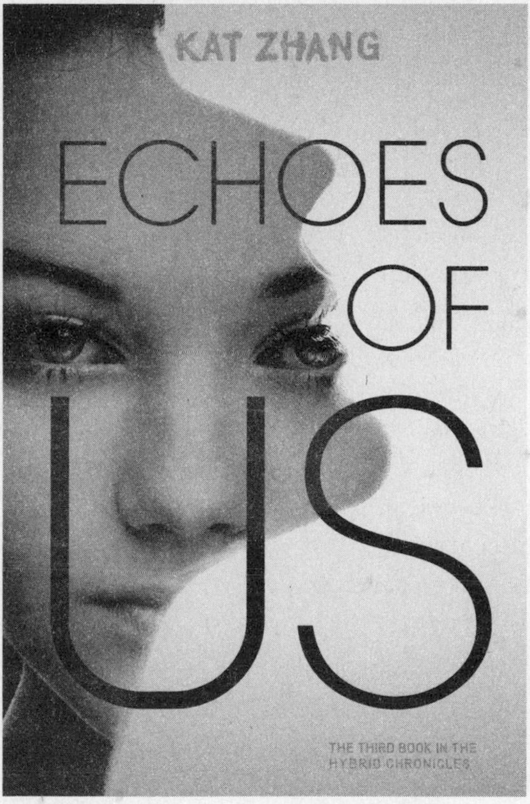

ONE

On the day Henri was supposed to leave us, Addie and I woke to a news anchor's quiet murmuring. We crept past Kitty and Hally, both still asleep, and slipped from our shared bedroom.

Devon sat downstairs in the semidarkness of just-before-dawn, his eyes fixated on the tiny television. The screen cast strange, flickering shadows in the living room. There was no one else in sight.

"They haven't left yet, have they?" Addie whispered as she joined Devon on the lumpy couch. He didn't take his eyes from the television, but shook his head.

<*Where are they?*> I asked, and Addie was about to repeat my question aloud when Henri's bedroom door opened. That was answer enough.

Henri smiled at us, his teeth a flash of white against the darkness of his skin. "I thought we said our good-byes last night so you wouldn't have to get up this early."

He carried only a small suitcase with him. Most of his

things had been abandoned when we fled Anchoit. I imagined the police stumbling onto them, rifling through his notes and half-written articles. They'd know to be on the lookout for him now. A foreign reporter living in the Americas was in a lot of danger, and Henri had finally given in to pressure from friends and family overseas to fly home while he still could.

He leaned over the back of the couch to get a better look at the television. "Jenson again?"

Devon nodded. It was an old clip. Mark Jenson had given so many speeches and interviews over the past few weeks. About hybrids. About Powatt. About the safety of the country at large.

It was hard to reconcile the presence he broadcasted to the world—calm, sleek confidence—with the man who'd tried to carry Addie and me from Powatt after we sprained our ankle. The man who'd dug us from the wreckage after the explosion, his eyes frenzied, his shirt bloodied.

Every time I saw him, I felt a phantom pain in our shoulder—his nails digging into the bruised skin. *Where's the boy?* he'd shouted at us. *Where is Jaime Cortae?*

"He's trying to take control of the situation." To someone who didn't know him, Devon might have seemed bored by the whole thing. But I caught the sharp way his eyes followed Jenson's movements. Devon was often the most perceptive of us, for all he acted like the world was only a vaguely interesting shadow play.

"Doesn't seem like it would be Jenson's job to control

things. But I guess he is supposed to be an expert on the hybrid issue." Henri straightened, and Devon finally looked away from the television. His face held its usual lake-water placidity, but something rippled through it as Henri said, "Well, I guess it's time to go."

Devon and Ryan were early wakers, but four a.m. was a bit extreme to just get up on a whim.

"Here—" Henri reached into his pocket and took out his satellite phone. He handed it to Devon. "You remember how to use it, right?"

Devon was already turning the phone around in his hands, checking the nearly palm-size screen, the miniature keyboard, the port where it could connect to a computer. He nodded as he fiddled with the antennae, then looked back up at Henri. "You won't need it?"

Henri shrugged. "It shouldn't take me more than a few days to get home. I've let my people know to expect no calls until I arrive. Besides, I need a way to stay in contact with all of you." He smiled a little. "Be careful, though. These things aren't impossible to track, if the government starts getting suspicious. Limit call times. And don't let Ryan take it apart. He might not be able to put it back together."

Devon—*Devon*—almost grinned. "I could put it back together."

I laughed silently in the corner of my mind and wondered what Ryan had said to that.

The back door opened, revealing Emalia and Peter. Emalia

didn't seem surprised to see Addie and me up, though Peter raised his eyebrows.

"Are we ready to go?" Emalia said, pulling her jacket tighter around her. She and her twin soul, Sophie, had volunteered to drive Henri to his contact in the next state, arguing that they were the best choice since the news broadcasts lacked their face. Only Kitty and Nina had likewise escaped exposure.

Jaime's information, of course, had been circulating in the media for months. Out of all of us, he was the one Jenson most desperately sought—the one child to survive the operation when Nornand's doctors stripped away his second soul.

But Jenson had also seen Ryan and Dr. Lyanne at Powatt, when they came to rescue Addie and me after we'd tried to stop the explosion. He must have intuited that Hally would be with her brother, and the police raids would have found enough incriminating information about Henri and Peter to label them as suspects.

It pained me to have them all share blame for the bombing.

"Be careful on the road," Peter said. He and Dr. Lyanne would stay here at the safe house with us in case anything went wrong. That was the phrase hanging over every second of our lives now: *in case anything goes wrong.*

Henri looked at us and Devon one last time, like he wanted to memorize our faces.

"Stay safe," he said, finally, and joined Emalia at the door.

They left, leaving the rest of us watching after them.

* * *

"I can't believe you didn't wake me up," Hally said hours later. She sat next to Addie and me on the indoor balcony, overlooking the living room and the foyer. Our legs swung over the edge.

Ryan, on our other side, reached through the balcony rungs to steal half of Hally's peanut butter sandwich. She snatched her hand away a second too late and settled for looking aggrieved.

"It was four in the morning." Ryan offered me a bite of the sandwich. Peanut butter oozed onto his finger, and he put it in his mouth, muffling his next words. "You don't like to get up before ten."

"I would have gotten up if the rest of you were up," she complained.

I could hardly believe that once, Addie and I had passed Devon or Ryan in the hall at school and barely noticed. That we'd gone out of our way to avoid Hally, because we feared her foreign looks might bring us more trouble.

Now, they counted among the most important people in my life.

Ryan's eyebrow quirked up when I stared at him just a little too long, his mouth softening into a smile. *What?* it said, and I shook our head with a smile of my own.

We'd gotten good at communicating through glances—through a touch, and the slant of the mouth. Small gestures were all we had. The safe houses were rarely large. Even if both of us weren't sharing bodies, we'd have trouble finding time and space to be alone together.

Sometimes, Addie would offer to temporarily disappear. But guilt usually made me turn her down. Addie's thoughts were filled with a boy, too. One who wasn't even there to steal kisses with her at the end of darkened hallways, laughing and ignoring the knowing way Emalia looked at us when she passed.

Hally finished off her sandwich and stood, brushing crumbs from her blouse. "Well, if—"

The doorbell rang.

Hally's mouth snapped shut. Addie whispered *<But no one—>*

No one rang the doorbell. This house was a little less remote than the first two we'd lived in, but it was still almost an hour from the nearest major town. People didn't just stumble onto our doorstep.

Dr. Lyanne emerged from her downstairs room, her hair damp and braided after her shower. There was something naked about her expression as she looked up and motioned for us to be quiet.

Peter joined his sister in the foyer. The windows were all curtained. Our remaining van was in the driveway, so we couldn't pretend the house was abandoned, but we could pretend there was nobody home.

For a long moment, no one spoke. No one made to open the door.

The doorbell rang again.

Then the knocking started. Sharp raps against the door.

A woman's voice rang out.

"Excuse me," she said. "My name is Marion Prytt, and I would like to speak with Addie Tamsyn."